Head Over Heels

© Sara Downing 2011

The right of Sara Downing to be identified as the author of this work has been asserted in accordance with the Copyright, Designs and Patents Act 1988.

This book is a work of fiction and any resemblance to actual persons, living or dead, is purely coincidental.

© Cover Design: Gemma Lewis 2015

SARA DOWNING

Head Over Heels

For my husband

One

'Give me that bloody gas! Arghhhh… FUCK!... OWWW!... You are NEVER coming near me EVER AGAIN!' I yell at him. 'There is no way am EVER EVER going through this again! Arghhhhhhh!'

My face contorts with pain and I am struck dumb (for the time being – a rare event) as another contraction hits and the gentle, Irish midwife, who under any other circumstances I would probably adore, tells me to push again. She's wearing nice shoes, I notice, despite my agony, as I bend double, trying to find a position against the wall in which I can get some relief. Although you can't see much of them under those awful, blue, stretchy plastic things the medical staff have to wear in the delivery suite, for some silly hygiene or health and safety reason or other. Still, reassuring to know at least one member of my delivery team has some taste in my moment of agony. And it gives me something to focus on whilst I'm screaming.

If I had the time and energy between screams to reply to her, I would tell that lovely midwife, who really does only have mine and my babies' welfare at heart, exactly what I think of her, and where she could stick her pushing. I might even manage to do her an injury with one of the pieces of equipment which are provided – supposedly – to ease my discomfort. God, I could certainly do some damage with a gas cylinder and epidural needle, the way I feel right now.

But for the time being, I have to be content with (and I am FAR from content – can you tell?) lots of swearing and loads of shouting, something which is a bit of a departure for me. Labour has turned me into a monster. I am incapable of coherent thought and have turned into a blaspheming, fist-waving, fish-wife with murderous tendencies.

'No one told me it would hurt this much,' I wail with despair, sounding like a banshee on anti-depressants and alternating between tears and anger. Well, it bloody does. More than anything I could ever have possibly imagined, and it's far from over.

And I am going to make sure every damn person in this hospital knows it. All the female ones of child-bearing age, at least. I am now single-handedly responsible for preventing any more women going through what I am experiencing right now. The human species will die out in a few years if I get my way.

Watch out you young lovers and newly-weds wandering the corridors, contemplating a family of your own. Once you hear my ear-splitting screams and cries of pain, none of you will be stupid enough to get yourselves pregnant, you'll see. I'll be the world's most effective contraceptive device. Labour just isn't human; in fact it's totally barbaric, prehistoric and I am amazed no one has found a cure for it. Apart from having a caesarean, I suppose, but even then you have to practically have your lower body sliced off to get the damn thing out and can't stand up straight for six weeks. Your girly bits might remain intact and pseudo-virginal but you have a lovely abdominal scar to show for it and no amount of crunches will get rid of that saggy tum. What a major design fault we women have; the one key thing we were (originally) put on earth for, the most natural thing in the world, is a near physical impossibility because someone forgot to make the hole big enough. If it were the men having babies, they would have invented a special zip that could be installed once they hit child bearing age, or maybe some of those nice little poppers that you find all over babygros.

'BASTARDS,' I yell, bending double again, my predicament being the fault of all men. Right now, I hate the opposite sex *en masse*. My children will be the spawn of the devil, I am sure of it, and HE is Satan himself.

'Push,' the midwife urges impatiently. Does she not understand what I'm going through here? She probably hasn't even got children of her own.

'SOD OFF!!!!!!' I yell at top volume, then regret it. Maybe that was a bit coarse. Although this time I do as I'm told. I have to get these babies out somehow and they aren't going to do it without my help. I'm aware of a cringing male presence beside me; his hands go to the sides of his head and he winces as I let rip on another string of expletives. He must be mortified. But it helps, so I have to do it. It doesn't make the pain go away, but there is something therapeutic about swearing like a builder when normally the strongest word I can muster is a 'blimey'. In my job I have to watch my language, so I hardly ever swear. How liberating to be given full reign today. And all in the name of pain relief.

Several long hours later and calm reigns. No more swearing, pain long since forgotten. On either side of my bed in my little private room (yes, on the NHS – amazing how having twins makes them lay out the red carpet for you) is one of those delightful Perspex cribs so beloved by our health service. I gaze at each one in turn, trying to take it all in. One pink bundle, one blue bundle. I can't believe just how beautiful they are. PERFECT. And asleep too; they look like a pair of *putti*, perfectly crafted cherubs on a Renaissance ceiling. I am exhausted but a wonderful sense of tranquillity has enveloped me. I feel beautiful (surely impossible after fourteen hours of labour, sweaty hair plastered to my scalp, face red and blotchy) and serene and I am floating on that clichéd Cloud Number Nine (which is of course nothing to do with the quantity of drugs I have imbibed over the past few hours). No one had told me how much it would hurt, but nor had they told me JUST HOW MUCH I WOULD LOVE THEM. Instantly. I would lay down my life for them, even though I barely know them yet and giving birth had felt like a near-death experience.

Here he is, back by my side now, after nipping home for some sleep and several tonnes of clean baby clothes. Holding my hand, gazing at his little angels and at me in amazement.

'My darling girl,' he whispers, eyes brimming with

emotion and kissing my forehead, 'you're so clever.'

The smile I give him pardons him for getting me into this situation in the first place – look what the end result is. I wouldn't change this for the world.

Two

About One Year Earlier

'Hey, birthday girl!' comes the chorus as Mark and I struggle to negotiate the narrow steps down to the little landing platform at the river's edge. We're hampered by the myriad of gorgeous shopping bags which are dangling from each of our arms, plus the fact that my heels keep snagging in the wooden slats. They'd seemed fine for a shopping trip but in retrospect probably aren't that suited to a life at sea, or rather on the river. A nice pair of sensible deck shoes would have been much more appropriate, but hey, sorry, I just don't do flatties.

The others appear to have been there a while; they look very comfortably ensconced at the little table on the covered decking area and haven't waited for us before getting stuck into the champagne. They've clearly brought this with them, complete with plastic goblets, as there is no bar in sight; instead they are surrounded by open cool boxes, spilling their contents onto the decking.

'Well, we didn't know how long you'd be,' Evie jokes,

seeing me clock the quantity of bubbly and nibbles they have come armed with. 'We all know what you're like once you get in the shopping zone. How's your head?' she asks.

She looks more than a little pasty herself, and sipping her (hopefully) first glass of fizz of the day, I notice a bit of a hung-over sheen to her forehead. Oh God, I hope I don't look that bad. I start to wonder how our stomachs are going to hold up to a four hour river trip – plus more alcohol. Apparently it's going to be quite a smart boat, so Mark tells me, some fancy barge they normally hire out for corporate do's, and we have it all to ourselves, complete with silver service staff. Someone he knows from work managed to help him pull it off. Sounds fun, and heaps better than sitting in some stuffy wine bar for the afternoon.

My head *does* feel a bit fuzzy, but I'll cope. It's just such a luxury having my birthday on a Saturday this year. No work today, bliss. The downside (or is it upside?) being the temptation to make a weekend of it, which is what I seem to be doing. After all, I'm not too old to party, am I? Evie and Alex had taken me into town last night, we'd done the usual bar crawl; we'd tottered from one drinking hole to the next in our very high heels, looking like an ageing set of hen-nighters only without the fluffy deeley boppers and just married signs. We'd chatted up blokes young enough to be at high school, just for fun, because we could, and because after that much booze we considered ourselves still gorgeous enough. We'd had one of those lovely, carefree, fun evenings that just happen if you relax and enjoy and take things as they come.

'It'll be better once I've had some of that,' I gesture to the open bottle, prompting James to reach for a couple of the very posh plastic picnic glasses and pour some of the delicious bubbles for Mark and me.

'Getting through it fast, you boozy lot,' I say. 'Let's hope they're well stocked on board.' I shake one arm free of some of my bags and we exchange air kisses, everyone wishing me many happy returns.

I've barely had a chance to get some bubbles on my lips when Mark calls out 'Transport's here!' I crane my neck around the side of the gazebo in search of our barge. What I see is at completely the opposite end of the style spectrum from what I'd envisaged; a long and sleek, shiny white motor yacht literally glides up to the landing stage, barely humming as the driver (or would he be a captain or a pilot?) adeptly parks (I'm sure there must be another name for that too, my nautical terminology isn't up to much). Anyway, whatever you call it, he pulls alongside, and when we have all picked our tongues and our shopping bags up from the ground, we traipse across the platform and onto this beautiful, gleaming beast. I have never seen anything like it. The interior is awash with highly polished chrome and acres of white leather, and looks like a sumptuous living room in a modern, minimalistic apartment, so far removed from the Rosie-and-Jim styled boat of my imaginings.

'Oh Mark, you are a star,' I drool, kissing him squarely on the lips.

'Thought it would make a nice treat,' he replies modestly.

We settle down for our trip amongst the luxury, feeling

like we've been transported away from this frightfully dull English spring afternoon to the glamour of the French Riviera.

Champagne refills ordered from one of the highly attentive (and not unattractive) waiters, I grab a menu and give it a quick once-over. I'm going to need something to soak up all this alcohol or I will be under the table, not at it, very soon. And what a waste of Mark's lovely, thoughtful treat that would be.

The waiter, who moves so fast I am convinced he is wearing roller blades, is back with us in record time, bearing the next bottle, which he promptly uncorks and pours professionally, not wasting a drop. Clearly he is hoping that the tip we will leave will be as generous as the price-tag on each bottle.

'Well, being slightly worse for wear doesn't seem to have dampened your enthusiasm for shopping. Good job it's a big boat.' Alex teases, throwing a glance at all my bags. She, of course, looks amazing, as usual. I dread to think what time she must have got up this morning, but she still manages to look effortlessly gorgeous. She doesn't go in for make up in a big way; she just seems to have that natural glow which gives her the appearance of having spent hours getting ready, when in fact all she has probably done is apply the tiniest bit of mascara and swish her hair up into a twist on the back of her head. If she wasn't so lovely with it you'd have to hate her.

Alex and Evie are my best friends. And I can say that sincerely. Despite the wealth of female friends I've been lucky enough to have over the years and the fantastic relationships I still have with my sisters, these two ladies are a cut above all the others. Maybe it's because in the relatively short time we've known each other we've been through so much. You see, Alex lost her husband to a brain tumour three years ago, just before her youngest daughter, Rosie, was born.

So we are a very close trio, how can there be any closer bond when we have shared such raw emotion? I would do anything for either of them and I have no doubt that the feeling is mutual on all sides of the friendship triangle.

'A toast, to our best friend, Grace, may she always be strong of limb and fair of face.' James, Evie's husband, raises his glass and we all chink, giggling at the little rhyme, of which he is inordinately pleased. We're back on real glass glasses now, and there is no danger of us spilling a drop as the yacht glides effortlessly along the river. I can imagine it must be turning a few heads; it's not the normal sort of river traffic you'd expect to see on the Severn on a Saturday afternoon. Even the swans look pretty bowled over. This is the life, I could get used to all this opulence and luxury.

'What are you two up to tonight?' Evie enquires whilst the others are still chortling and talking amongst themselves. 'Making a baby, if Mark has anything to do with it,' I reply, deadpan.

'Really?' she asks. 'I take it you're not so keen?' I catch Mark's eye across the table as he glances in my direction. He doesn't much care for me discussing our relationship and what he calls 'personal matters' with my friends. Come on guys, it's what girls do. Whilst you all talk about football, the size of your plasma TV's and who's going to win the Formula One Championship this year, we girlies are getting down and dirty on our private lives. It's what keeps us sane, given that we are either married to or living with emotionally retarded beings - otherwise known as men. He leans back into the leather banquette, arm stretched along the padded back, giving the impression he is craning his neck to see out of the window. I recognise it as a poorly-disguised attempt to pretend he is distracted, so that he can eavesdrop on Evie and me. Given that it's only the five of us here, plus a similar number of staff, plus a little light background music, there's every chance he will get the gist of what I'm saying, anyway.

'It's too soon for me,' I say, turning slightly in my seat in an attempt get outside Mark's radar. 'Maybe I'll come round to it. I just wish he'd suggested us getting married instead. God knows we've waited long enough.'

Mark and I seem to be having the world's longest engagement. If he'd announced that it was about time we finally tied the knot, then yes, it would have been the perfectly logical next step, and what fantastic timing it would have been to express such a desire on my birthday. But we aren't married, so wasn't he jumping the gun by talking about babies? The trouble is, we'd just seemed to kind of let the whole wedding thing slide a bit. I would love to make us properly official; that little piece of paper which sometimes these days is so devalued, means a lot to me, and although I know Mark is committed to me in his own way, and although

I am a career woman through and through, an ardent-ish feminist (when I need to be) and on the side of the sisterhood and all that, I still dream of miles of organza and lace, posies, and matching wedding favours, and all those enticing little wedding details. I wouldn't be normal if I didn't. But the longer it goes on, the less Mark seems bothered about us getting married. He thinks we are fine as we are, and clearly he thinks it's fine for us to go ahead and start a family without getting married first.

'Right guys, shut your traps for a minute, it's time we gave Grace her presents!' Alex interjects enthusiastically, in what I recognise as a diversionary attempt to save me from an awkward moment with Mark. Bless her, that's what friends are for. She trip-trips off in her platforms to the corner of the room or cabin or whatever it's called, where her own not so insignificant pile of shopping bags currently resides, and sweeps up an expensive-looking pink and flowery gift bag.

'What do you give the girl who has everything?' James chirps, grinning like a maniac again. I don't think I've ever met anyone who gets such a buzz out of their own jokes and amusing quips. I half expect him to jump up and give himself a round of applause.

'A baby?' I hear Mark whisper *sotto voce*, sort of behind his hand as he looks at the floor instead of at me. Did he really intend for me to hear that? Was it just his way of making yet another little (not so subtle but desperate) plea to my softer side in the hope that I'd give in? If he was a woman, I would say he was having a bitchy moment, but do men ever really have those? Whatever the reason, it just comes across as petty and a bit silly as we are in the company of our friends, especially given his usual secretive nature when it comes to the personal stuff. But if anyone else has heard it, or picked up on its significance, then it's not obvious, and the banter continues as before. Just me looking like I've been steam-rollered, then.

'Grace, my darling friend, happy birthday,' Alex says, handing me the bag, which is overflowing with artfully crumpled matching pink tissue paper, looking too good to open. She bends down to plant a kiss on my cheek before tiptoeing back to her chair.

'I love birthdays and I think I'm going to love them till I'm at least ninety-seven,' I giggle, forgetting Mark's snide aside in the presence of presents. 'Can I open it?' I ask, turning back to Alex.

'Well, it IS your birthday,' Alex giggles, in her best little-girl-lost voice. It loses a lot in translation, but Evie, Alex and I have to go through the ritual of saying that on all our birthdays. It cracks the three of us up but the men just never seem to get it, and we like that. We lost sight of why it was funny years ago, but it just is. Sign of a good friendship, I suppose, when you can still laugh at things even though you can't remember why they were funny in the first place.

I delve into the bag and pull out a gorgeously wrapped pair of long, black silk gloves. They look like something a nineteen-thirties screen goddess would have worn.

'They're beautiful, Alex, thank you,' I say, and I mean it, stroking the sumptuous fabric and almost purring with appreciation.

'Not entirely practical, I know, and rubbish in the snow,' Alex jokes, 'but I thought they'd be great for all those posh bashes you have to go to with Mark. Besides which, whoever wants anything practical for their birthday. Give me something I want, not something I need, any day!'

'My turn now,' says Evie. She hoists her handbag on to her lap, rummages around for what seems like ages – I'm such a kid, the anticipation is killing me – and hands me an envelope-sized present, wrapped in metallic gold paper and with a huge shiny bow. I destroy her beautiful wrap in one rip to reveal a pair of tickets to the opera at Covent Garden, for later in the year.

'Wow, what can I say,' I do manage to say, completely blown away by Evie and James' generosity.

'I knew you'd always wanted to go, and it is an excuse to get all dressed up and buy a new pair of shoes,' she says, 'not that you ever need an excuse to buy shoes!'

'Thank you all so much, you are so kind and I love you all to bits,' I say, grinning at my mates. I look across at Mark, but he is away with the fairies, probably in future-daddy-land, dreaming of those babies he so wants.

Mark had dumped the whole baby idea on me first thing this morning. I'd bounced down the stairs in my new white robe, Mark had poured me a coffee, and I'd sat down to enjoy the croissants he'd warmed up, savouring the doughy bakers-shop aroma filling our kitchen.

'Thanks, Mark, you're my knight in shining Armani', I

had joked.

'Nothing's too much trouble for the love of my life and the future mother of my children,' he'd proclaimed. I'd choked on my first sip of coffee, spraying a fine mist of the stuff all over my robe.

'Oh!' had been about the extent of my reply, the shock clearly evident on my face. Something along the lines of 'What would you like to do today?/ Is 9am too early for champagne? / Drink your coffee, I'm taking you back to bed for several hours of unbridled passion,' would have been a little more expected, and not so likely to make me choke.

I suppose I shouldn't have been surprised, really. Mark had been growing increasingly clucky over our friends' children in the past few months, but I'd been burying my head in the sand and hoping that it would go away, and that it wasn't a sign that he would like a few of his own. It was obvious, looking at it objectively, but I suppose I just liked to hope that he was being a nice friendly sort of uncle figure to the little angels. Hoping they'd ask him to be the new Santa for the village Christmas party this year, or something equally innocuous.

The trouble is, in all the time we've been together, Mark and I have been a bit lax about discussing our plans for having children, or not. We've always assumed (or at least he has, and I've never really contradicted him) that one day, 'when we grow up', maybe we'd have kids. I'm a teacher, you see, so one would tend to think that with my great love of children (I work with the little darlings, don't I?) I would want to start popping out a few of my own. But I'm a great believer in the correct order of things, and as Mark and I are still not married, I thought I had a bit of time before the question of parenthood would rear its not so aesthetically pleasing head.

Plus there's the issue of not wanting to put my parents through what they went through with my sister. Or myself, come to that. Or Mark.

'Wouldn't it be lovely?' he'd gone on, plugging away at it now that he'd started. He obviously felt that pacing the room whilst he put his case helped, but it just made him look even more like the lawyer that he is, let out of the courtroom on day release. I half expected him to say, 'I put it to you, Miss Connery…' He grabbed an apple from the fruit bowl on his way past and proceeded to half massage the poor thing to a pulp, like some sort of stress toy. There must be some kind of gene that gives lawyers that superiority edge over us mere mortals. Handy in the courtroom, I don't doubt, but not so pleasant when it's your other half giving you the third degree in the comfort of your own home.

'I mean, you're 33 now and I'm 36 and we're not getting any younger and we're financially stable and we have a lovely home and we have a lot to give a child and all our friends are doing it and you love kids, you're a teacher after all, and surely you must be ready… Aren't you?' No wonder I had been taken aback; he'd clearly been building up to this for a while.

'Wouldn't it be great to be a family?' He'd beamed from ear to ear, eyes gleaming like a small puppy with a new toy. I'd struggled not to let out one of those loud, comedy gulps, like they do in cartoons.

After lunch Mark gets up to stretch his legs and wanders out on to the small deck at the front of the boat. I feel a bit like I should follow him; he looks like a schoolboy at a disco, popping outside for some air to pass the time because no one wants to dance with him. How unfortunate it now seems that he had to bring up the subject of babies this morning. He had arranged this fabulous treat for me, and although it's brilliant and I'm loving every minute of it, I can't help the tiny bit of resentment that's brewing inside of me, and the cross feeling that he has in some way spoiled my birthday, despite all this.

'Are you free after school on Monday?' Evie asks before I have a chance to trail after Mark. 'Why don't you pop round for a cuppa and a natter? Sounds like you need a bit of girl talk.' She is doing her best to make me feel better; she's a great one for doing that without judging or expressing an opinion of her own.

'I hate this, it's the first major thing we haven't agreed on,' I explain. 'But we never set out the ground rules, so neither of us really knows how to approach it. You should have heard him this morning, it was like he'd prepared a sales pitch for me.' I hate slagging Mark off to her, to anyone come to that. But I need to get it off my chest. 'He wants us to talk about it tonight. I just want a quiet night in and a cuddle on the sofa.'

Evie will no doubt profess to understand, but having children has come so naturally to her, and she's everyone's idea of the press-inspired 'Yummy Mummy'. She adores her kids and cannot imagine life before they came along, but at the same time she's fortunate enough to still be able to maintain her glamorous lifestyle, hobbing with the nobs at James' work do's, off on regular shopping jaunts to London, and travelling with James on the odd business trip overseas - without the kids of course. She is always decked out in the finest designer clothes, her hair, make-up and nails radiating that 'just stepped out of the salon' look. She's the sort of woman who looks like she knows how to climb out of a sports car; knees together, swing to the side, don't get up until your stilettos hit the red carpet.

Evie not only seems to have it all, but to be able to make it work too. She has made one big sacrifice though, but this tends to be overlooked by those who come into contact with her, in the face of her outwardly charmed Modus Vivendi. When she met James she had been working as a project manager for a software company specialising in financial packages. She was outstanding at her job and destined for greatness. She and James' paths had crossed when she was overseeing an installation at his offices. Their romance had been pretty whirlwind - they were both hovering around thirty and on finding one other, seemed to discover from within an agenda which included settling down and having children before they got too old, despite an immense drive for career success from both of them. Maybe it was just a case of meeting the right person at the right time, and both of them realising that they wanted more than just job status.

So Evie had promptly married James and conceived their

first child, Imogen, on one of the many drunken honeymoon nights they spent in Bali. Not quite how they had envisaged starting a family - a year or so together first would have been nice - but they were both over the moon, if a little shell-shocked, when Evie discovered she was pregnant. There had been no looking back; Imogen had been followed almost exactly two years later by Anastasia, and the Brookes family was complete. James would have loved a son, but the symmetry of two adults and two children was just too comfortable for them, and neither felt the need to carry on reproducing beyond the arrival of their two gorgeous girls. The girls grew up, passed the toddler stage and started school, but somehow Evie never managed to find the time to go back to work. The loss of her salary was quickly absorbed as James' financial advisory business grew in stature and their net worth increased dramatically over the next few years.

If Evie misses the excitement of the career she has side-lined, she hides it well. But she is an extremely intelligent woman, and I sometimes wonder how she copes without the stimulation and the daily cut and thrust of the workplace. Her life as it is now doesn't involve a lot of stress; I can't think what she does for the large chunk of the day that isn't taken up with making sure the girls get to their various activities, or visiting some salon or other for hair styling or removal, but she must fill it somehow. Surely there is a limit to how many times you can realistically go shopping in one week? And that from me, Grace, Queen of Shoppers.

I couldn't imagine what it must have taken for Evie to

walk away from her career so easily, but then the call to motherhood must have already been heard by her - I had not yet been summoned.

As Mark comes back into the cabin, he whispers conspiratorially in the ear of one of the staff and suddenly the music changes pace and volume. Oh no, this has all the feel of the first dance at a wedding, only it's not my wedding and at this rate it's never bloody likely to be, and everyone is watching, and OH MY GOD, Mark is pulling me to my feet and suddenly we are spinning round to the strains of Lady Gaga's 'Just Dance'. I am relieved that at least it's not a 'slowie' and thankfully we can just throw ourselves around the dance floor and be silly and have a bit of a laugh about the whole thing. Fortunately the others come to my rescue and before long we are all strutting our funky stuff on the miniature dance floor. It's a long time since the necessity to dance has been foisted upon me mid-afternoon (except at weddings, it's always at bloody weddings, isn't it?) and somehow it feels really liberating and decadent. What a bunch of boozed up middle-agers we must look, but hey, who cares, we're having a brilliant time and letting off some steam.

All too soon it's over and we are back at the little landing stage and disembarking, heaving all our bags back onto dry land and saying our goodbyes. Those poor waiters, lining up and hovering expectantly for their tips; for some reason we three ladies feel the need to show our appreciation for a brilliant afternoon with more than just cash, so those gorgeous young lads are subjected to much enthusiastic kissing – cheeks only, of course. We just can't pass up an opportunity like that, can we? Evie and Alex have to get back to relieve babysitters, so we go our separate ways. I am very chilled out and more than a little tipsy, again. Still, today's champagne has completely killed last night's hangover, at least.

At home I disappear upstairs with my bags to unpack and try on. Mark always finds it hilarious that I can try all the clothes on at the shops, be happy enough to buy them, and then rush home and try them all on again, *because you can't tell properly in someone else's mirror if it really looks right or not.* Shop mirrors can be false witnesses and flatterers, not always prone to telling the truth. Anyway it's a woman's prerogative to change her mind, isn't it? No mirror but your own can be the proper judge of whether something makes you look fat, thin, whether the colour is 'you' or not, if those vertical stripes really are too much, and all those other fashion dilemmas that men just don't get. But then when all you can EVER wear is a derivative of trousers and a shirt, life must be pretty easy. A bit like having a uniform only in lots of different colours. How easy it must be getting dressed in the morning when you're a man. No fuss, but not much fun either. No wonder David Beckham tried to make the case for men wearing skirts. Poor chap was probably just hopelessly bored with his wardrobe.

Besides, I'm not just trying stuff on, I'm keeping busy in an attempt to put off our 'chat'. I've had a brilliant birthday thus far; we'd had such a lovely afternoon, and other than Mark's one-off snide comment, he had been his usual gorgeous and entertaining self. I don't know why I expected him to be any different really; it wasn't like we'd had a row or anything, just that we both knew there was unfinished business between us to be talked about. But we had managed to shelve that in the name of having a good time.

I slip into the first outfit – a turquoise silk dress – and parade off downstairs, sporting new heels and matching clutch bag too (Mark has to get the full effect, after all). I do a twirl for him in the kitchen with a 'Ta daaa!' and he pronounces the first outfit delectable, just as he had done in the shop. Poor thing.

Indulging in my eternally favourite pastime – shopping – this morning had given Mark another chance to produce an Oscar-winning performance for acting as though it is his too. Come on, we all know men pretend they are hard done by, being dragged from clothes shop to shoe shop, via that lovely little bag shop that actually stocks Mulberry bags *outside* London and that cute little boutique with the really unusual stuff where the staff are so helpful, you just *have* to buy something. What man in his right mind doesn't enjoy watching the love of his life have so much fun trying on clothes, shoes, bags, accessories, appearing to make a decision to buy the lot, then almost simultaneously changing her mind, handing it all back to the assistant and flouncing out of the shop, proclaiming that it just 'isn't her'?

I have to say I am reaping the benefits of Mark's fabulous new salary; there is no way on a teacher's earnings that I could indulge in my much-loved retail compulsion quite to the extent I have been, and he seems happy for me to do that. Ever since we set up home together there have never been any disputes over money, whose it is, who has earned it and who is spending the most (usually me).

'Does your mirror like that one?' he ventures bravely, as I head back downstairs in outfit number two.

'Mirror says yes,' I reply. 'Think I need a tan to go with this, though. Still, I won't be wearing it till the summer.' This dress shows more leg than I usually like, but I don't see Mark complaining. Luckily I have the sort of skin that only has to spot the sun coming out and it goes brown. Which makes me a bit of a bargain tanner, always useful when you live in a country where sunshine is a scarce resource.

Mark, bless him, sits patiently whilst I produce a full-scale fashion show of everything else. Enough to try the patience of a saint, I should think, especially as he has seen it all not a few hours earlier. I plant a big kiss on his cheek. 'Thank you for a wonderful day, you truly fabulous and gorgeously handsome and sexy man,' I drool. Mark pulls himself up from reading the paper, which he has been doing between fashion parades, straightens his back and clears his throat nervously. 'So,' he starts. 'Can we talk about this?' Uh-oh, here we go.

And talk we do. Mark is quite convincing in his argument, to give him his due. It turns out that he just really genuinely wants to be a Dad. He feels the time is right; we are earning enough to afford for me to take time off work. We could even employ help if we wanted to, he says, especially as our families live so far away. And practicalities aside, I sense in him this real urge to be a father, not just because that's what people of our age do, or because all his friends are doing it, but because he loves me and he wants us to be a family and the idea of having a baby with the woman he loves is the best thing in the world he can possibly imagine.

I tell him that's all very lovely and noble and all those kind of things I know he wants to hear, and then I say that I would want us to get married first. That's where we always hit the barriers. To be honest, we haven't talked about it for a while; we had no reason to whilst parenthood wasn't on the agenda, and it was only ever just going to be the two of us. Mark goes very quiet.

'Why is it such a big deal to you, Grace? You know I love you, and isn't this proof that I want us to be together forever?'

'Yes, but in that case I don't understand why you won't commit to me,' I push.

'I am committed to you, I told you I was, didn't I, and having a baby together would reinforce it.'

'Yes, but being an unmarried mother is something I never saw myself being,' I say. I get up and wander towards the window, gazing out at the garden.

'Why do you have to be so old-fashioned about it?' he whines. 'Co-habiting partners these days have much the same rights as married women, you know that. You make it sound like you'd be stuck in a council flat on a sink estate with five kids by different fathers.'

'Don't throw all the legal jargon at me, Mark, just because you can,' I say, spinning round to face him. I know my body language is defensive, but I feel as if I've been backed into a corner. 'If you don't want to marry me, just say so. I'm not being old-fashioned; I just want some security, if I am going to even consider having a child with you. When we got engaged all those years ago, I thought it was because you actually wanted to marry me one day?'

'God, you're starting to sound just like your mother,' is his really helpful reply, still evading the question. At that point I leave the room. It's my birthday, after all, and I'm not hanging around to be spoken to like that.

Mark's hurtful comments really stung me. He has always admired my family, and compared my childhood favourably to his own - he was the typical latchkey kid, in the days when it was acceptable to leave children under fourteen at home unsupervised. He'd let himself in, do his homework and get the tea started before his mother got home from work. We on the other hand used to arrive home from school to the smell of freshly baked muffins and a hearty casserole in the oven.

My childhood was a happy and safe one. My parents created a wonderful world for us of cosy family life, and lots of love. Our summers were spent mucking around in the garden or traipsing off across fields on a trek, backpacks full of jammy dodgers and Tizer. My sisters were more like friends than siblings; both older than me although not by much, we never fought, pinched each other's toys or pulled hair, as little girls sometimes do. We shared our toys, then shared our boys. When the talk turned from Sindy dolls to snogging, we went through it all together. There was forever a pool of young men hanging around our home, and one of us was always either in love, heartbroken or 'giving up boys'. Looking back on it, it must have been hell for my Dad. He was so protective of us all, and no man ever being good enough for his girls, he was very tolerant and managed to avoid decking any teenage lad who upset his daughters. I think my Mum quite enjoyed having a house full of males after years spent amongst raging female hormones. I used to love watching her face light up when the latest blue-eyed lothario was sweet-talking her to get to one of us. She would fall for it every time.

    I really respect my parents; that generation had it right in raising their families; there wasn't the focus on material things like I see in the kids at school now. We were happy with what we had, and that was enough. The summers were long and hot and our house was filled with love and fun.

Mark and I have had a long engagement, a very long one. It had been two full years into our relationship before we even thought about settling down together, and then we were largely propelled into it by the circumstances at the time. Our engagement was therefore pretty unromantic; we hadn't even lived together properly at that stage, but there we were suddenly being pushed by events surrounding us into what we knew we would always do but hadn't yet managed to get round to. So it had been more of a 'Perhaps it would be the right time to…' sort of conversation, and we both knew it made sense to make things more permanent at that stage. Funny how they are no more permanent now than they were then. If only Mark had managed to keep up that level of commitment and get me a wedding ring to keep my engagement ring company, which has for so long languished alone on my fourth finger.

And here I am now, several years later, still only engaged, and just not convinced that motherhood is for me – yet, at least, and I tell Mark that. I can't see myself as a mum, not right now, even though I always thought I might be at some point. Putting it into words makes me realise for the first time just how strongly I feel about it. I'd heard my friends say time and again how the urge had suddenly kicked in, after years of child-free heaven, to fill their house to the brim with offspring, but surely that urge must have been there all along, just latent, hidden under the career prospects and cracking salaries, waiting to be unleashed. When I think back, I can't remember ever really feeling that urge, even a dormant one. I had never played the Mummy role through in my head, never rocked imaginary babies in my arms, looked longingly at maternity clothes, or gone all soppy over a teensy weensy babygro. It had just never happened for me in that way.

I try to explain all of this to Mark, but it comes out as a jumbled mess and not as the balanced opposing side of the argument that I'd hoped. Not that I'd really known what I would say, didn't have anything to say, given that it was not something I had been working up to as it had been for him.

I'd had no time to prepare my case for the defence, other than today, and then I'd been busy having a birthday.

Mark can't understand why I'm not jumping at the chance to get down to some baby-making with him. But he is also failing to see why I feel I have to get married first. Then I start to wonder if this really is just my delaying tactic – will tying the knot suddenly make me want to have babies?

At that moment I am hit by a failure to understand something fairly crucial. How could we have come so far in our lives together, without ever discussing this properly? No more than as a dismissive wave towards the future, anyway. Mark is pretty upset, but he's also ignoring my side of the argument. It's not only my fault that we have never talked it through in any depth. I think we have both arrived at this point in our lives equipped with a set of assumptions about each other, some right and some, quite obviously, way off course. I don't know what to say to him next.

Three

As I pull up outside Evie's house, the faded Cotswold stone radiates a warm and mellow glow in the late afternoon sunshine. Hers is one of those lovely inviting homes where you know the hall will always be clutter-free, the toilets recently cleaned, a scented candle burning and the coffee machine primed and ready for action. Evie will always be beautifully turned out too – I have never yet managed to catch her out, slouching around on a Sunday morning in tatty old joggers and one of James' tee shirts, no make-up, or pre-shower with her hair not washed and straightened to perfection. I don't know how she does it. Well, actually I do. It probably has something to do with Suki, the Nanny-come-Housekeeper whose quiet presence means that Evie is free to get on with the finer things in life, whilst the tat and toilets are taken care of for her.

This time though the smell of baking greets me; Evie has given Suki the afternoon off, and she and the girls have spent most of the day baking, by the look of it. The surfaces are piled high with every sort of kiddie-friendly cookie and cake imaginable. It looks like she has worked her way through the Domestic Goddess handbook and out the other side, like a busy little cooking bookworm with an urge to bake for Britain. 'Are you having a party or something?' I ask, wide-eyed, only needing to sniff the air to get a hit from the sugar-sweet aroma.

'Well they will last the girls a few days, and they have some friends coming over for a sleepover tomorrow night. You'd be amazed how much cake eight girls can eat between them,' she replies. Evie has clearly had a great time, judging by the flour on her nose and cheek, her cake mixture-streaked Cath Kidston floral pinny, and the hugely satisfied grin on her face.

'We don't get to do this sort of thing often enough,' she enthuses, wiping her hands on a tea towel. 'Term time is hopeless, I'm always so busy ferrying them around to one thing or another. And weekends are full of homework, or pony club, or whatever. It's been so lovely today just to kick back and cook with them. We've had a ball. They've really talked to me, too. Properly.' She sighs happily and flops elegantly and with an exhausted but contented sigh onto one of the bar stools tucked under her granite-topped kitchen island.

Imogen and Anastasia, sensing a grown-up 'chatting session' coming on, take advantage of the moment to slip out of the kitchen and up the stairs, no doubt in the avoidance of clearing up more than anything else.

Evie is usually hard to pin down on a school day, but the girls' exclusive private school flushed them out a week earlier than my school, so the three of them are at home, with time on their hands and varnish on their nails. Imogen and

Anastasia are lovely girls, ten and eight respectively, both very different, but both with their Mother's expensive tastes and desire for the finer things in life. Watch out boys, in a few years' time these girls will be snaffling around for affluent boyfriends who can keep them in the style to which Daddy has allowed them to become accustomed. Yet to say they are spoilt would be wrong. They both have their heads screwed on pretty firmly; Evie has done a good job raising them with high moral standards, and has brought up two bright and sensible girls, even if she can't help herself from splashing a little bit of cash on them now and again. I think it's lovely for her that she can.

I wonder if Evie will attempt to extol the virtues of motherhood upon me? But she knows too how I feel about getting married. I can imagine her trying to appeal to my retail addiction with promises of the as yet unchartered waters of baby shops – clothes, shoes, prams, cots, all the paraphernalia needed to get one very small person through the earliest stages of its little life. Some serious shopping to be done.

When my sisters' children were born, I remember being completely floored by the amount of equipment their homes were suddenly filled with. A once spacious three-bedroomed home now heaving at the seams with giant pieces of baby stuff. And the oddest thing of all, a whole bedroom fully decked out to house the little monster, with a beautiful cot, matching curtains and bedding, gadgetry, teddies, the works, only none of it being used because the little darling is sleeping (or not) in the master bedroom, as close to the mother's side of the bed as it can possibly get, in some kind of wicker thing that looks like a dog basket, propped up on a spindly little frame, because babies (apparently) sleep better near the mother and the risk of cot death is reduced. It sounded like some kind of government propaganda to me, put about to keep new mothers so knackered through lack of sleep that in no way could they return to the workplace until the child was at least twelve, thus leaving all those wonderful, abandoned positions available for the men to snap up.

Evie will see things from my side too, I am sure of it. She knows just how much my career matters to me. I am never going to earn megabucks, like she could have done, or like Mark is starting to now, but my whole sense of self-worth and persona is defined by what I do, and it makes me who I am. I can't imagine myself doing what Evie does, I need something for me – not just to be defined as someone else's wife or mother.

I've always wanted to teach, since those days as a small child when I would line up my teddies and 'learn them their lessons'. I couldn't imagine having to give it all up for long enough to even give birth, let alone taking maternity leave for ever and a day, which seems to be the norm now.

My job is wonderful; my school is in one of those unbelievably perfect Midlands villages, the sort of place where people have either been forever, or return to after 'gallivanting off' for a few years to get an education, get married, see the world or all of the above. We're a bit different because we did the whole gallivanting off thing from London *to* here and then stayed.

The children I teach are fantastic, too. I know a teacher's lot is to repeat the same stuff year on year with a different set of kids, and how dull does that sound. But it's the things they say and do which leave me never ceasing to be amazed by the human brain in all its diversity. I could laugh or cry in equal measures at some of the wild stories and fantasies, the misinterpretations and mispronunciations I hear on a daily basis. For a bunch of eight and nine year olds, they are remarkably perceptive and mature. I can see in most of them the caring, considerate, inquisitive and interesting adults they are going to be in the not so distant future.

My school is in a very comfortable catchment area, so there are no real rough and tough kids, the worst are the handful from the less well to do homes in the village and a couple from the very small cul-de-sac of local authority housing, but even they are 'nice' compared to some of the children I came across in London, and their parents can at least string a sentence together. Not a single ASBO in sight at this school; in London some of the kids saw it as the only qualification worth having.

So babies just don't feature in that happy teaching equilibrium of mine. The nappy, puking and sleepless nights stage is not what I find rewarding about children. Give me a six year old with a fully formed set of functioning parts and a willingness to learn, and I am away. If children came ready-made and fully housetrained then maybe I could buy into the whole thing a little easier. I need to have conversations with kids, not babble in that jammy-wammy, oochy-coochy sort of way that new mums (and dads, come to that) do. Mark doesn't get that. On Saturday evening he just kept ranting on about the feel of a newborn dozing on your shoulder, and something about the sweet little snuffling sounds they make. All I could envisage in that scenario was the trail of puke down the back of your top when they produced a rip-roaring liquid burp which belied their tiny frame.

I thought Mark and I were happy as we were, and I don't see any real reason to upset that. We both have great careers, loads of friends and a fantastic social life. We tick along nicely; he doesn't inspire in me any extremes of emotion; I love him, I usually like him, rarely hate him, occasionally resent him. Although the latter is usually related to his inability to put the lid down on the toilet or his failure to grasp the fundamental difference between the laundry basket and the floor. But from conversations with my friends, it appears their other halves are just the same, so I suppose it must just be a man thing. Blame the genes not the jeans, when I find them hanging out of the laundry basket yet again. All that and yet I live with a relatively tidy and fastidious man, who once had his own place and actually kept it clean. It would appear then that all men, after that bachelordom period of living on their own and fending for themselves has elapsed, are programmed to think that dirty dishes levitate to the dishwasher and the washing machine is voice activated and only responds to the lady of the house. Don't get me started.

'Just imagine it Grace, lots of little mini-me's and -you's

running around all over the place, think about it.' Mark had been straight back on the attack at the breakfast table this morning. Whatever had happened to a quiet and peaceful breakfast in this house? He'd caught me at a moment when there wasn't a diversionary tactic in sight. I was trapped at the table with him; I wasn't running late for school so couldn't just make a dash for it, I'd made my sandwiches the night before, and the car was already loaded with the marking I needed to take in. Bugger it, I was stuck. He hadn't mentioned the subject at all yesterday, and I had naively hoped that maybe it had gone away. Just a little bit. Fat chance of that. He is renowned for his persistence, it's what makes him such a good lawyer.

I had just thought about it, for the whole of a nano-second. Lots? Running around? Help. I love my cream sofas and carpets just the way they are.

'Yes but before you get to the running around stage, and even during and after the running around stage, you have to go through the pooey nappies and no sleep stage. Not to mention being pregnant and actually giving birth in the first place. Have you thought that through?' I had reeled off, barely coming up for air.

'I have,' he replied, smugly. Were there any aspects of parenthood he hadn't considered in his in-depth analysis? I could imagine him drawing up some sort of business proposition entitled 'Having a Baby – the Pros and Cons of Parenthood,' and coming down firmly on the side of the Pros. I half expected to be presented with it, neatly bound in an A4 folder.

'If you give up work now you would be so rested and relaxed by the time things happen that you being as strong as you are, you would cruise through it all, and you'd hardly notice all the getting up at night and no sleep. Plus stay at home mums can sleep in the daytime too. Even if you have to get up six times in the night, you could sleep when the baby sleeps during the day.'

Give up work? Stay at home? Be a full-time mum? What planet was he on? Not the same one as me, quite obviously, but I decided to let that last comment slide in the hope he wouldn't come back to it.

'So how many times a night would you be getting up then?' I'd boldly ventured.

'Well, of course, as the only breadwinner it would be important for me to get a good night's sleep.' He's not a lawyer for nothing – he's so good at evading questions. Next stop politician.

'So not at all?' I'd asked. My mouth fell open, my eyes wide with disbelief. Help, someone had stolen my fiancé and replaced him with a relic from the nineteen-fifties, who thought a woman's place was at home, barefoot and pregnant.

Not feeling the urge to fight any more, and not knowing what else I to say, I decided to bring the meal to an early conclusion. I stood up and started clearing the table.

'Look, we had a great weekend, Mark. Can't we just let this drop for a while? Now's just not the time.' I'd said, my body language dismissive as I put away cereal packets and wiped the table.

Mark's persistence had whittled away in my mind, though, as I finished getting ready for school. Why *didn't* Mark think things were OK just as they were, and more importantly, why *was* he still evading the marriage issue? I couldn't bear the thought that he felt there was something missing from our lives, a gap which could only be filled by having a baby. *He is enough for me,* I thought; *my life is full and complete with only him in it, I don't feel I need more.* Although at that moment, some space and a partner who hadn't got a mind like a one-track record would have been nice.

Evie's kitchen is a mess – I don't think I have ever seen it without everything in its proper place, shiny and waiting – but today the house feels like a real home, buzzing with life, and love, and… kids. I wonder if an element of that is for my benefit. No, I am just being cynical, I reassure myself. Evie is not trying to show me how warm and fuzzy family life can be, she is just having a lovely day with her girls, a break from the daily grind.

'It's made me realise how much I miss my girls,' she goes on. 'OK, I know they are always here, they never board like some of their friends do. But life is so hectic, we hardly ever get a chance to chat like this. It's amazing how much they'll talk when they're distracted. It makes me a bit worried that they bottle all this up normally. I wish they would talk to me like this every day.'

'Well they are growing up,' I offer. 'They will start to keep things closer to their chests.' I may not be a mother, but I do understand pre-pubescent girls, and boys, pretty well. More than ten years of teaching has given me that, and far more. 'Was there anything worrying in what they told you?' I probe.

'No, not worrying in the true sense, it just made me realise there are huge chunks of their lives I know absolutely nothing about,' she replies. 'Like the things they and their friends talk about. Weight issues for one, which was scary. They talk about ways to stay stick thin, even at their age before their bodies have started developing. I mean, you and I would never have seen things like that as a worry at their age, it's frightening really. I know they're in with a good crowd, but there's nothing to stop the most well brought up girl from becoming anorexic. It's made me realise just how I need to keep my eyes open,' she sighs. I can see her thinking how her daughters are growing up and slipping away from her already, despite their still young age.

She pulls herself together again. 'Anyway apart from all that, we've had a lovely day, lots of giggles, and eaten a TON of cake!' she says, her tone brightening. Somehow I can't imagine Evie eating even an ounce of cake. She doesn't maintain her tight size eight figure by snacking and eating 'naughty' treats. No wonder she worries about the girls discussing dieting, it must make her wonder what sort of role model she is creating for them.

'So how are you? How was the big chat with Mark?' Evie asks, turning the focus back to me. She pours me a cup of tea, beckons to the kitchen table and slides a plate of flapjacks towards me. I know I have come here to confide in her, but slipping into the warm and cosy feel in her home in a way makes me not want to have to regurgitate all the ups and downs of the past couple of days. But not telling is no good either. I need to talk it through with someone and I have to start somewhere. I try to explain how Mark feels; Evie listens patiently, and doesn't interrupt or pass comment as I tell her.

'Where have I gone wrong?' I ask her afterwards. 'Am I abnormal? I seem to be missing all these genes that make me want to be a mother. Does that make me a really bad person? I just don't seem to be able to stir up a single maternal bone in my body to feel anything positive about having a child. I can't hate kids, can I, look at what I do for a living.'

'Maybe there is an underlying issue here,' Evie ventures. 'But you and Mark are happy, aren't you? Everything else is OK? '

I explain to her that I feel very strongly about getting us married first, but I can tell I don't convince her that marriage will change my mind on whether we have babies, or not. I explain to her, not for the first time, how disappointed I am that Mark doesn't see marriage as an important issue.

'Yes we are OK, or were. No, that's wrong, we are. Nothing changes that, apart from this ongoing dispute about marriage, of course. But he's really determined he wants to start a family. It's scary.'

'He probably wasn't expecting such a negative reaction from you, either. This is the first big dilemma to hit you both, isn't it? Think about it, you've never had to go through any real crisis together, have you? You're just bobbing along, enjoying your happy and comfortable lives, not a care in the world. Then one of you veers off at a tangent and 'bang', it stirs up a whole can of worms. You have to be able to take the rough with the smooth. I know I sound a bit like a walking cliché, but sometimes you just have to compromise to keep things on an even keel.' How could she manage to make it all sound so logical and be so cool about it? My clever and sensible friend.

'Yes, but compromise for me at the moment would mean giving in and saying yes to starting a family. There's no midway in all this, you can't be a little bit pregnant or give a baby back if it doesn't work out. It's all or nothing, which means one of us having to cave in,' I reply.

There is a scrunch of gravel on the drive, and the sound of tyres skidding as James' Aston Martin pulls into view. He treated himself to it for his fortieth birthday nearly two years ago, and a gorgeous beast it is. Even I, from my position of not being a car person in the slightest, can see that. It's almost exciting enough to convert me. But not quite – I won't be watching re-runs of *Top Gear* on *Dave* just yet.

Not only that, but Evie is pootling around in a lovely shiny new midnight blue Merc, a convertible, four-seater of course so that they can fit in *en famille*. Now that the kids are older, she has ditched her huge four-by-four in favour of a more sporty little number, and it suits her personality; compact and racy, with a fully automatic soft top and plush leather interior. There is never a speck of dirt on it either, not like some of the cars the mothers at my school deposit their offspring in. OK so a lot of them are farmers, and it's real country dirt, and most people can't afford the weekly valeting costs like James and Evie, but they look like they have taken the off-road route to school sometimes. I couldn't imagine all that mud going down well at Imogen and Anastasia's school; there a four-by-four is meant to gleam, and is simply an indication that you meet the minimum wealth requirement to send your daughters to that school.

'Hiya Connery, are you up the duff yet?' James explodes into the kitchen, planting kisses on each of our cheeks. Evie's face turns white.

'I'm so sorry Grace,' she says, looking mortified and fixing an evil-eyed stare on James. 'Excuse my husband's lack of tact, won't you, he can be such a pig, sometimes,' she spits out the last four words through gritted teeth, continuing to glare at her husband, eyes wide.

'I sense you ladies are in the middle of something,' he continues, totally unaware of the effect of his social gaffe. 'I'll leave you to it. Mmmm these look nice, just pinch a couple and some tea from your pot and I'll be off to my study if you need me.' He grabs a plateful of cakes and leaves the room under the same whirlwind that had carried him in.

Evie seems to visibly collapse. She sighs and apologises again. 'I'm so sorry Grace, I can't believe he can be so unsubtle. I did tell him that you and Mark were planning to have the baby chat the other night. I wish I hadn't now, I'm just mortified'.

'Don't worry about it, Evie,' I reassure her. 'Of course you're going to tell him, it's not your fault he blurts things out. That's just James for you,' I try to smile and shrug it off.

James is renowned for speaking his mind, to the point of rudeness sometimes. It seems to have done him good in his career though; his extremely high net worth clients might be well-blessed in the wallet department but aren't always gifted with the brains or common sense to match, and need a hard-talking financial advisor to keep them on the path to continued *richesse*.

'I think sometimes he forgets to switch off his work brain before he comes home, it seems to take him a while to mellow when he first gets back. He's never like that with the girls though, he's completely soft where they're concerned. It's only ever me that has to cope with the fall-out, which I'm glad of, I suppose. The worst is if he has a day working at home, then I try not to be here, as he's like it all day.' Uh-oh, a flaw in the perfect Brookes marriage? Maybe I have been looking at the world through rose-coloured spectacles, only seeing all the good things in everyone's relationships, including my own.

Evie is right about Mark and me though. We've never had to go through any major ups and downs in all the years we have known one another. So you could say we are in trouble here. But I can't see a way through it without major capitulation on one side – it's impossible to meet half way on something like this, isn't? What do I do, have one baby instead of Mark's desired two, jump straight back into my old life immediately post-partum, leaving him to be a house husband? That wouldn't work either, there is no way we could survive on my salary alone; I would have to be the one to do the vast majority of the childcare, as I do the lion's share of other things around the home.

I know I am mad about my career, and wouldn't give it up for anything, but it imposes nowhere near the stresses and demands on my life as Mark's career does on him. I work five minutes away from home, I am home by five most evenings, six at the latest, and OK, yes, I do have to spend a fair bit of time marking and preparing, if I don't stay on at school to do it. And yes, I do get stressed, I don't see how anyone who takes their job seriously can ever avoid stress. You'd have to be in a catatonic state not to get worked up about something – what proof is there otherwise that it matters and that you are making a difference?

But Mark's career is on a different plane altogether. He can be totally at the beck and call of his clients, with evenings and weekends no exception. Yet he loves it. He thrives on the pressure, even though it means he isn't at home as much as either of us would like. And because of that, a lot of the roles that would have been traditionally male a generation ago fall to me; taking the bins out, dealing with the post and admin, paying bills, minor DIY jobs, organising anything that needs attention, all that sort of stuff is my domain too. I'm sure it must be the same in many households these days, as the working day gets longer and the demands of a career take precedent more and more. At least Mark appreciates that I do more than my fair share at home. Sometimes I feel a bit like a housekeeper, especially after yet another evening spent alone, but Mark is generally quick to redress the balance and let me know he values what I do, just as I value him. And that he misses me and would still rather spend the evening with me, despite the satisfaction he takes from his career. It's not always a case of buying me another gorgeous bunch of flowers (although it would be churlish to turn them down, wouldn't it?), just a few kind words here and there to make me feel loved and appreciated, and not taken for granted. Both of us know that Mark couldn't do that sort of job if he didn't have a supportive partner; not one who is necessarily home all the time, but who is at least around a lot more than he is to take the pressure off on the domestic front.

So there is no way that fabulous career is being sacrificed in the name of parenthood, is there? No, once again, it would all largely fall to me. Which makes my decision that much harder. Mark would get to keep his career and independence, and cluck over his new baby when he wanted to, congratulating himself on his prowess in fathering a child, but the moment the going got tough he would have the luxury of retreating to the spare room, or work, or late meetings, and would be able to cherry pick the finer points of fatherhood as they fitted in with his working life.

'So what am I going to do?' I ask Evie.

'It's a tough one, darling. I wish I could just wave a magic wand and sort out everything for you. Do you really think it would be that bad? I mean, wouldn't you at least like to see if you *can* get pregnant, for all you know, it might never happen. Maybe you could agree to give it a try, just for a little while and see what happens. You never know, you might just get into the whole thing and think it's not so bad after all?'

Somehow I had guessed Evie would come down on the side of Mark, pro-baby. Even though she herself had gone down the conventional route of marriage first, babies later, if only just. Had I come round here, subconsciously wanting to be talked into it? I can't imagine for one minute Evie wanting to talk me out of it. Maybe I need someone like her to help me see both sides? I'm in turmoil. Arghhh, help.

'But what if it doesn't happen and Mark can't cope with it and it puts a huge wedge between us and all sorts of other awful things like that?' I ask her. 'Or what if we start trying, then I want to stop – can you just stop a roller coaster ride like that and it not have a catastrophic effect on your relationship?'

'It's going to put a wedge between you if you don't want to try, ever, isn't it?' She really is the voice of reason, spelling out in simple English all the things I know in my head I need to address.

'I'm so scared,' I wail. Evie comes around to my side of the table and gives me a huge hug.

'You love Mark, he loves you. One of you has to agree to change your mind, and can you see a way forward if that person isn't you? Or if you don't manage to persuade him to get married first?'

'Why did I know you would say that?' I ask. 'You're my sensible friend, you're so sorted. I don't want to drive him away, Evie. But it scares me that if I don't give him what he wants he might look elsewhere. At the same time I can't lose sight of the 'me' in all this. Why should I be the only one who is prepared to compromise to save our relationship?'

'I can't see Mark being the sort of person to do that, but I know what you mean. It would leave you feeling a bit exposed. And you're not at the point of 'saving your relationship' yet, are you? It's not that bad, is it? I can't tell you what to do, but I think you really do need to talk to Mark about this a lot more. It's obviously very important to him; you need to work through this as a couple, not see each other as opponents with a battle to win.'

'I know, you're right, as always.' This time, I give her a hug, glancing at my watch. 'I really should get back, dinner to cook and fiancé to talk to, and all that. Thank you honey, as always you're my very brilliant friend, and I love you to bits,' I say, giving her a squeeze and a kiss on the cheek.

'Awww that's OK sweetheart, let me know how you get on, won't you?'

'I'll call you soon as,' I reply. I yell a 'Goodbye' to James and the girls and head for my car. Usually when I leave Evie's house I feel cosseted, looked after in a way a similar to when I visit my parents, all cosy comfort and warm and fuzzy. This time I leave with a churning stomach; I'm dreading getting into discussion with Mark again, but I know it has to be done. One way or another it's crunch time.

Four

The phone is ringing as I open the front door.

'Hi honey, it's me,' Mark's voice trills. No sign of any lingering bad feeling. 'How was your day?'

'Oh, you know, the usual. Good actually. Made some real progress with that boy I was telling you about at the weekend. His mother's coming in for a chat later in the week, I'm sure we'll be able to sort him out.'

'Good, good, good, tell me all about it later, won't you?' As brusque as usual when calling from work, he doesn't have time to chat. Not meaning to sound dismissive, he's just phoning up to impart a message.

'Have you started cooking yet, I thought we might go out tonight?'

'Nope, just back from Evie's so haven't even starting thinking about dinner. That would be great, I'm not in a cooking mood tonight. Where do you fancy?'

'How about that new Chinese in Purbrook, I know they're open Mondays, give them a call, see if you can get us a table. I should be home by seven thirty, so eight would be good.'

'Will do, see you later, don't work too hard.'

Great, I really don't fancy cooking. Only trouble with going out is the lack of distractions; no fiddling around with food or clearing the table to divert us from the subject which will inevitably be on the agenda for discussion yet again this evening. Just full-on eye contact for the whole time and lots of talking. We did say we needed to, after all. We'd managed to avoid the subject for the remainder of the weekend, both seeming to quietly agree that we needed time out from it to think, and we had a fairly normal weekend, in spite of everything. And being in a restaurant means that we will both have to stay calm. Not that we ever do the whole shouting and slanging match thing, but there will be no scope for storming off, or taking five minutes away from it. Not without making a spectacle of ourselves in one of the smartest eating places Purbrook has to offer, and neither of us are the sort of person to do that. We want to go back again if the food is any good, after all.

I remember when Mark and I ate out in White's Restaurant in Worcester one night, some special occasion or other, a birthday or anniversary probably. Definitely not Valentines, I know that, as both of us hate the rows of tables for two all lined up and squashed in, the set menus with lots of aphrodisiac foods for 'lurve', and the cheesy background music, it's all so naff and commercialised. Anyway, whenever it was, the couple nearest to us had been having a simmering row all evening, and finally by the time the cheeses arrived, it had exploded. I remember at the time thinking if that had been me, I would have just left; what could be more awful than trying to have a row, quietly and discreetly, whilst the rest of the restaurant knew exactly what was happening, and ears were flapping all over, trying to pick up juicy titbits of conversation. It had looked fairly terminal for them by the end of the evening, poor things, but they had provided all the other diners some free live entertainment in the process. No, Mark and I will definitely not be giving such a performance tonight.

Better find something to wear then. The upside of a night out is an opportunity for spending some deeply satisfying moments browsing in my wardrobe and choosing something to wear. Fantastic, and on a Monday night, too. Get to it, girl, there's a date with your fiancé to prepare for, outfit and accessories to choose. Important stuff to attend to.

I stare in the bathroom mirror as I dab at my eyes, gently taking off the evening's make-up. Reflected back at me is a woman of more than average looks, nice hair, shoulder length light brown and layered, with some reassuringly expensive-looking highlights. Good skin, but… hang on a minute, are those the beginning of some crow's feet I can see, etching themselves in around my eyes? Didn't notice those last week. Does my skin know I've just had a birthday, and so it feels it has to suddenly adjust itself overnight to look like it belongs to a thirty-three year old woman?

I remember my mum saying about old age suddenly creeping up on you, but it's easy to be dismissive of that when you still have youth on your side. And when you are young, you can't imagine ageing, or the horror of being an old person, you think youth will last for ever. Sometimes I struggle to imagine old people ever having been young, firm and sprightly, thinking about and doing all the things my generation is doing now. My grandmother, for one; I had seen the photos of her as a young woman, and she had been truly beautiful, tall, slim and blond with a cracking pair of legs and a glowing complexion. I struggle to reconcile that with the woman I know and love now, shrunken, gnarled and weathered by life, almost as though she had been born old, and the woman in the photo was someone else entirely. I suppose it's all part of that inability we have to imagine life before we entered the world; her generation were happily getting on with things having survived a war and all its heartache, falling in love, having babies, for several decades before I even entered the world. It's the whole mortality dilemma isn't it – how can the world have been turning before we were born and continue to do so after we die?

I know I'm not old, far from it, but there is no way even with a thorough skin care routine (and I have always been careful) and good genes that the little lines and wrinkles can be staved off indefinitely. I don't want to lose that enviable glow of youth, but here we are, it's being eroded before my eyes, little by little. I still think I look young, but compared to the firm and even skin tone I remember having as a twenty year old girl, yes, I do look a lot older. Nothing more I can do about it though than I already am, but a bit depressing nonetheless.

Is it that desire to keep the world turning and leave something behind when you depart that drives people to have families? Or is it really just an inbuilt urge to have someone to nurture, to pass on all you know to, someone who looks a little bit like you and a little bit like your other half, or like other members of your family, who you hope will inherit all your good points and none of the bad? I am always fascinated but the way we are all made up of little bits of so many people; a mother's bright blond hair, a father's piercing blue eyes, a grandparent's talent for music, an auntie's artistic skills... Everyone says I look a lot like my mum; I can't imagine having a child who looks like me. Something a bit spooky about it. It makes me feel a bit queasy, actually. Maybe because we never really know what we look like, do we? How many times in real life do we pull the same expressions as the ones we see in the mirror? Mirrors never show us the frowns of concentration, the strange pensive expressions when we are daydreaming, or the open-mouthed trancelike TV-watching face. And neither do they show us amazement and surprise, or happiness, or how our eyes dance when we smile? That's why most adults hate having their photos taken – it's just that they don't recognise the person in the picture as the one they see with the neutral dead-pan expression in the mirror every morning. This twenty-first century obsession with looks and being perfect gives us such a lot to live up to.

It's a good job Mark can't see himself in the mirror right now. His current facial expression is fit to shatter the toughest mirror, even for one who is so handsome by day. He had gone up to bed as soon as we got home, pleading exhaustion. I had fiddled around for a while downstairs, going over the evening's conversation in my head and trying to come to terms with it, under the pretence of locking up and making myself a last cup of tea.

He looks as though sleep had come the instant his head hit the pillow. Uh-oh, he's on his back though, which doesn't bode well for a peaceful night's sleep for me, as it generally presages higher decibel levels of snoring. His mouth looks as though it has been propped open with a matchstick, and with his face bereft of colour as he sleeps, he looks like a slightly chubbier version of Edvard Munch's *The Scream*. Maybe that is what he is doing – screaming in his dreams trying to resolve some work issue or other, or screaming at me, trying to make me see reason in a domestic argument dream. Or maybe he is just so tired he had passed out and lost all control of his facial muscles. Poor thing, he works so hard and really needs his sleep, and luckily for him, he generally gets it. Sleeping like a log is definitely an expression invented for Mark. He does brilliant log impersonations.

Actually, the evening had gone heaps better than I had hoped, although I would never have guessed at the outcome being what it is. Mark had been thrilled to arrive home and see me all glammed up for an evening out, a beaming grin on his face as he ran his eyes appreciatively over my new Jigsaw dress and latest pair of LK Bennett patent leather heels. 'You can take the girl out of the city but you can't take the city style out of the girl!'

'Well, you know me, any opportunity to get them out. The heels, I mean,' I'd said, feigning innocence and waving one leg in the air to show off my gorgeous footwear. My very intentional innuendo had had its desired effect as the corners of Mark's mouth turned up into that wayward come-hither smile of his. Mark liked to see me with a bit of cleavage; he wasn't one for keeping me under wraps, for his eyes only, like some men could be. I often saw him clock other men's reactions on seeing me, and enjoying the thrill he got from recognising that they found me attractive too, smugly congratulating himself that I was his. Well that had lightened the tone for the start of the evening, at least.

'As you are looking so gorgeous, I suppose I had better spruce myself up a bit too. Can't have the glitterati of Purbrook thinking I'm not worthy of you, can we?'

'For one thing I don't think there are any glitterati in Purbrook, and secondly, you look gorgeous, if a little day-worn.' I plant a kiss squarely on his lips, and tweak him on both cheeks. So we can still flirt, despite our recent differences. That's encouraging.

'How long have we got till we need to be there?' Mark asks, curling himself around me. I know where he is taking this.

'Not long enough,' I reply, gently prising him off me and nipping in the bud his idea of a little pre-dinner appetiser of the bedroom kind. I protest that my hair and make-up have taken far too long to mess up, lovely and spontaneous though it would have been.

'Oh you're just too sensible,' he complains, but still with that languid smile of his. 'So I'm having a shower on my own then. Boring.' Laughing, he disappears up the stairs, leaving me to pour us a little drop of something nice and cold to whet the whistle before we leave.

Mark and I did actually have quite a nice evening, amazingly enough, given my initial dread of it. He had come home from work in such a good mood, and our early-evening flirtation had done a lot to temper the feeling of the occasion. The restaurant had been gorgeous as well, which helped. With the arrival of the starters – a mixed finger-buffet of Chinese delicacies – we could tell the food was going to be of a standard to make us want to come back. The staff were lovely, hovering attentively in the wings in that easy way that only the Chinese seem to be able to manage with any aplomb. English waiting staff always come across as either too ingratiating or downright unbothered, with no happy medium. So we had launched ourselves into the food with abandon, voraciously eating sticky ribs and sesame toasts and licking our fingers (not each other's as we used to in restaurants in the heady days of our youth – we have matured a bit since then), totally caught up in the wonderful taste sensations.

So when Mark turned serious it had come as a bit of a bolt out of the blue, God knows why, and I was caught with sticky fingers mid-air. How much time had we spent talking about babies over the past few days? We went over everything yet again; my career and how it mattered to me, how I felt about the baby issue, and marriage, and this time it actually seemed to come out right. I felt like I was making a good case for the defence, so to speak, and Mark seemed to be listening to me and taking it all on board, but at the same time, the lawyer in him coming out to put his own views across.

But then something really weird happened. I looked at Mark and suddenly wondered why I was sitting here making a case against something that was, for the majority of people, the most natural thing in the world. Maybe I was drunk – I was certainly more than a little bit tipsy – but all of a sudden I found myself making an about turn and not so much giving in to Mark, but agreeing to maybe, just maybe, give it a go.

I wasn't quite sure what had happened to me. It felt like an out of body experience – there I was, hovering in the air in this fancy Chinese restaurant, watching a woman who looked and sounded like me tell her partner how she had not so much changed her mind but could see where he was coming from, and how maybe she would be OK with a teensy-weensy bit of trying for a baby, just for a while to see what happened and how scary it felt once she threw her pills in the bin. How, if she didn't feel too uneasy about that, she might somehow be able to get her head round the whole idea. How, although she thought she wasn't in the least maternal, the rational side of her mind must be kicking in and telling her to do the right thing. How she must like kids seeing as she spent so much time with them, day after day. How she didn't know where all this had come from but suddenly she felt compelled to say it. Provided of course he kept his end of the deal and they could start planning their wedding, too.

Maybe Mark had laced my wine with some kind of baby-loving hallucinogen? It hadn't felt like me in that restaurant, saying all those things, but, there, I had said them and I couldn't take them back. Mark had looked as overjoyed as the day he had popped the question. His whole face had lit up, eyes sparkling, and was that a tear I detected in the corner of one eye?

As I reach for the moisturiser I pause and scrutinise myself again in the mirror. Had I really said all that? Was this it, were we really going to start trying for a baby? I am terrified, but in a different sort of way to the terror I had felt when I had been the opposition. Almost like now that I know the enemy, as it were, I can come to terms with the battle ahead a little more and prepare myself for it. Not that it will be a battle, I hope. Maybe a couple of pill-free months of wild abandonment, rampant sex at all hours of the day? It sounds like fun from where I am standing, or from where I would be lying, I should say. Then maybe nothing would happen, no bump would materialise, and Mark and I would be happy to return to our 'DINKY' days, accepting the fact that children weren't going to be on the cards, but that we would be enough for each other and be blissfully happy for ever and ever. OK? That was the plan, for me anyway.

I'd had a major breakthrough on the wedding front, too. Mark had said of course, it was only fair, if it mattered so much to me, that we should get on and do it. Hardly romantic, but at least he was prepared to do it for my sake. I am acquiescing to please him, after all, and what I am giving in on is far more life-changing. So I think it's only right that he does something for me, too.

My plan is all fine, of course provided I don't actually go and get pregnant in the process. Just imagine it, all those years of dreaming of walking down the aisle, and when I finally do it, I have to wear a wedding gown the size of a small marquee to accommodate a baby bump.

On the other hand I would never dream of tricking Mark into pretending I was off the pill, whilst secretly popping it every morning as a precaution. No, I don't do deception. I am going to throw myself into both of these major events with the commitment they deserve. I will plan my wedding down to the n'th degree, give trying for a baby my best shot, and if it doesn't work out, then we have a fantastic (married) life without kids to go back to, don't we? I have my plan, and provided all goes my way, there will be minimum disruption and normal business will be resumed as soon as possible. No problem.

By the time I crawl between the sheets ten minutes later, I have managed to convince myself that what I had promised Mark was not a house full of children to rival the Von Trapps, but the merest whiff of an attempt at starting a very small, very-unlikely-to-happen family. It's enough to convince me and to stop me lying awake all night dwelling on all the various possibilities. I fall asleep instantly. All that wine probably helped.

Five

I arrive at school the following day with a spring in my step, and a spring breeze blowing my hair. I had made a big ceremony of the 'pill disposal' at breakfast that morning, throwing the remaining few in the bin with a flourish and a 'Ta..Da..' and Mark, still glowing from the previous evening had held me like I was a precious casket, all ready to receive and nurture his future offspring. I am surprised at how 'up' about the whole thing I feel too. It all seems quite exciting in a way, a new chapter in our lives, even if I do envisage it as a fairly short and temporary one. I'm not going to make the mistake of mentioning that to Mark. I will deal with that when the time comes, several months after our amazing wedding ceremony and extravagant honeymoon, feigning disappointment at the children we will never have, and quickly helping him get back on his feet and appreciate what we do have, and how good it is.

I have a packed day ahead of me. Preparations have kicked off for the summer play, and the kids in my class being the major contributors to that, most of the work falls to me. But I love it. Auditioning the children for the major roles, they amaze me with all the hidden singing, dancing and acting talents that lie dormant all year, suddenly shining through. A shy child who blossoms into a shining star on the stage, a class clown who turns out to have a voice like an angel. It's always worth every minute of the extra work I have to put in. This year we are doing '*Joseph*' – I still remember all the songs from when I had been in it myself as a child, and I've seen it on the stage in the West End twice since then. Jason Donovan had been gorgeous – I still remember drooling over his smooth, toned and tanned six-pack with the bunch of girlfriends I had gone along with. No sexy abs in our production though; just lots of kids working really hard to have a great time and produce an amazing show, and our '*Joseph*' will no doubt be just as spectacular in its own way, and his coat just as Technicolor as the slick London version.

'Morning Grace, how are the rehearsals coming along?' It's Tom, my head teacher, bounding into the staff room, arms laden with books.

'Good thanks, we're going to try and finish the auditions today. Everyone seems to have picked up the songs really quickly – well, how can you fail to, their parents probably all know it well enough to sing along with them at home. I've been waking up in the night humming *Any Dream Will Do*!' I laugh.

'Great, I will try and pop in on you all later,' he grins, his eyes twinkling 'I'd love to see how it's going and watch my brilliant director in action.' Is he flirting with me? His smile implies a little more than just a professional interest in what I'm doing. Surely not, I pinch myself, we are great friends and colleagues who work very well together, but I have never detected any other vibes from him. No love-interest antennae needed around him, normally. It is great to have a boss who is so dynamic and involved, though. And young. At my old school in London, the head had been just a head, an ancient fuddy-duddy who was ensconced in his office most of the time, barely making contact with pupils, teachers or parents, other than through all the formal channels. This school is so small, Tom has to do a bit of teaching as well, which means that he knows each and every one of the pupils by name, and given that he is always out in the playground at drop-off and pick-up times, he is familiar with most of the parents on first name terms as well. The children love the easy way he has with them, and the quiet sense of respect that he engenders in them is lovely to see.

But flirting? Perhaps I had imagined it. Surely my hormones aren't kicking in already; I only threw my pills in the bin just this morning. Tom and I have become friends in the four and a half years I've been at the school; Mark and I don't socialise with him directly but he is very friendly with Evie and James, who knows him from way back when, and he and his ex-girlfriend had often been at various Brookes' parties and functions. I know he broke up with Sophie about a year ago, and we haven't seen much of him outside school since. They had lived together for ages and had planned to marry, but something major had happened, I don't know all the details, and they had split up. I remember how distraught Tom had been, poor bloke barely holding it together some days at school, but he had pulled through it and as far as I know had been single since. James probably knows all the ins and outs. But why the sudden interest in the love-life of my boss, on the back of one semi-flirtatious comment? None of my business really, unless he decides to talk to me about it himself, which somehow I doubt. I shake myself back into the real world. The bell is about to go and my class will be waiting for me.

Three o'clock comes and I wander into the playground, availing myself for any parent who wants to nab me for an informal 'chat'. It isn't a concerned or pushy parent who corners me though, but Alex, there to meet Archie and Millie, and it isn't a school matter she wants to talk about.

'So how did it go with Mark?' she asks, excitement in her eyes, grabbing me by the arm and dragging me off to a less populated corner of the playground.

'You two, just play over there for a minute, and keep an eye on Rosie for me, will you? I just need to have a quick word with Grace.' She motions to the children to run along out of earshot, knowing they will gladly grab five more minutes of tearing round the playground with their friends.

'I must be mad but we've decided to give it a go,' I announce, pulling an 'I'm not really sure and I'm a bit scared' sort of grimace.

'Wow, Grace, that's brilliant news. So you changed your mind then? Clever old Mark, talking you round, you won't regret it, you know, it'll be the best thing ever, you'll see.' She is so enthusiastic, just like Evie. Hopefully some of it will rub off on me eventually.

'I'm not sure, but I've said we can try, and we'll see what happens. It's all a bit scary really. I feel like I'm being picked up by all this and carried along. We'll just have to see how it all turns out.'

'Oh, it's brilliant Grace, you'll love it, you'll see. And you can always come and talk to me, you know that, don't you.'

'Thanks Alex, I think I am going to need a bit of propping up over the next few months – especially if it works and… Oh my god, what do I do then?'

'You'll cope, you'll be fine, look at you, superwoman with all these kids here. Oh Christ, look at Rosie.' Rosie, Alex's three year old daughter, is standing on top of the bicycle racks, arms outstretched like a miniature tightrope walker, her older siblings egging her on as she walks precariously along the metal bar.

'Time to go, I think,' Alex says, shouting back to me as she runs to save Rosie from imminent danger. 'But can you and Mark come for supper on Saturday night? Nothing fancy, just a bit of a get together, please say yes, I haven't had you both round for ages.'

'That would be lovely,' I reply. 'Let me know if you need me to bring anything.' I know she won't need anything; Alex is the world's best coper, and always manages to put on a fabulous spread, despite having no man around the house to help with all the little practicalities that a dinner party entails.

People throw the word 'tragedy' around so much these days that it has become devalued, but Peter dying really was a tragedy. It makes me sad that I never got to know him that well; my friendship obviously is with Alex, and in the year or so that I knew her before he fell ill, he had been away a lot, doing research for his latest book. Another tragedy; if he'd known he had such a short time left to spend with his family, would he have spent it away from them, working on something he would never actually get to finish? They had been the perfect couple, with the idyllic life, beautiful children, the works. Theirs was a 'together forever' sort of marriage; childhood sweethearts, married young but then travelling for a few years, doing the chalet season in the winter, he the host, she the chef, earning enough to fund their skiing, spending the summer months somewhere hot and exotic, teaching scuba diving or hiring out surfboards, whatever it took to pay the rent and fund the lifestyle.

Once the travel bug's grip had lessened, they returned home, their lives enriched by the wealth of people and experiences they had encountered. It seemed a bit tame for them just to settle for the rural lifestyle as both sets of parents had done before them, and they considered moving away permanently to London. But then Alex's grandmother died, leaving her a slightly crumbling but nonetheless beautiful manor house nestled in the Worcestershire countryside. Suddenly the two of them were transformed from shorts-and-walking-boot-clad backpackers into, if not pillars of the local community, then at least into the local folk's expectation that that was what they would become, with a bit of coaching. They were fairly unconventional village 'gentry'; they had no money for one thing, and they were young, beautiful and trendy. Alex's grandmother had lived in the house, barely touching it for the past forty years, but Alex had not been left the funds to bring the house back to the standard it merited, let alone maintain it going forward. So the roof leaked and the walls crumbled, but still they thought the house was a fabulous place to live, and eventually to raise children, which was what they both wanted.

Then Peter had a surprise visit from an old school friend who changed their lives in two ways. Hugo, who had managed to track Peter down after years of trying, was a wine broker in London. Given he knew more about wine than anyone Alex and Peter knew, they had asked him to chose a bottle from Grandma's cellar for their meal, but instead of returning with a slightly dusty bottle of Chateauneuf de Pape, he had returned empty handed but open-mouthed and stunned. Apparently Grandma's collection contained several unopened cases of 1961 Chateau Latour, worth best part of two grand per bottle. Once the shock had worn off, and on Hugo's advice, Alex had had the wine validated and then auctioned and it fetched enough not only to re-roof the manor, but to get a builder in to fix the damp problem, re-plaster and even fit a new kitchen and two out of the three bathrooms. Suddenly the house was looking less like a cross to bear and more like the gorgeous family home they had envisaged.

Hugo's second revelation was to do with Peter's career. Not that he really had one at this stage; newly returned from travelling, he had dabbled unsuccessfully and unhappily with one or two office jobs, none of which really appealed or at which he seemed to be any good. It seemed that the wanderlust had not made him an attractive prospect for many employers – too much independence, they said. So much for travel broadening the mind.

So Hugo suggested that Peter turn his hand to becoming a travel writer. After all, between himself and Alex they had seen enough of the world and experienced the true character of so many countries to give him a good starting point. Provided he could get it down on paper in an engaging enough way, and captivate his target market. There were tons of travel writers out there, not all of them good. And Peter had never had anything published. He had read English at university, but studying the language does not by default make a good writer. However given the other options open to him, more office jobs or something more manual – he was by employers' standards unskilled – he decided to give it a go. Within a year he had turned out 'Work to Ski, Ski to Work', aimed at a young market looking to do exactly what he and Alex had done. Writing was something that he seemed to have a natural aptitude for, and the manor house provided him with the inspiring location, and the space, to get on with it and put pen to paper. He had no trouble finding a publisher, and after a few months of his first book selling like hot cakes to the gap year contingent, he was tipped as the next Bill Bryson, his publishers crying out for more of the same. His career went from strength to strength, as book after book filled the shelves.

When Peter returned from Mauritius complaining of headaches, he and Alex thought it was just the pressure of work; he had been packing it in to try and meet his publisher's tight demands. It took a while for them to realise that something was seriously wrong; forgetting things, people's names, dates, not remembering to collect the children, all those kind of things that are usually the domain of the old and absent-minded. When the tumour was diagnosed, it rocked their world. It wasn't the sort of thing that happened to people like them. They were young, only in their thirties, with two healthy, happy kids, and another, a second little girl, on the way. His condition deteriorated so fast, no one really had time to make any plans. The tumour was inoperable, it was just a case of making him comfortable, the doctors said. It was all so wrong, Alex thought. Those were the sort of comments you expected to hear about your parents – sad enough, but at least the right order of events in the circle of life. Not about your fit, healthy, gorgeous and energetic husband of thirty-eight, a young father.

Of course we were there for her, Evie and me. It was awful for us to see her and Peter preparing to separate, till death do us part proving it was not just something people said blithely at weddings for tradition's sake. But the really heart-breaking part was seeing Alex having to prepare the children for what was to come; they were only tots, but old enough to understand that Daddy would be going away, forever. We did what we could, although we felt so helpless. Just physically being there for her was all we could do, plus take care of the more practical things whenever possible. Her eldest, Archie, had not long started at my school, so I was able to keep a close eye on him, plus ferry him to and from school whenever I could.

And then the inevitable happened. It seemed that Alex had mourned Peter even before his death, that much did he change over the last few weeks, and once he died, she dealt with it stoically and almost without emotion. But the grief and desolation was all on the inside. She needed to keep going for the sake of the children, and her unborn baby. I cannot begin to imagine what must have been going through her head as she pushed that baby out, a mere three months later. A child that would never meet, let alone know, its father. Tragic, I can't say it enough.

Peter's death catapulted his books to the top of the non-fiction charts and made him a worldwide sensation overnight. He had done very well financially from them during his lifetime, but posthumous sales and continued royalties meant that Alex would never struggle for money again. Which was one less thing for her to worry about; she had enough on her plate, what with raising the children single-handedly, and trying to fulfil a father's role as well as a mother's. And she did a brilliant job too – her kids were well-balanced and happy, and she herself was not one to mope and think about what might have been, instead she channelled all her energies into enjoying life and her children as best she could.

I am always full of admiration for how she copes. Since Peter's death she has been a tower of strength for the kids; she has to be, really. They are still so young, and the eldest two obviously miss their Dad so much, but she manages to provide for them a happy, loving and stable home. She does enlist paid help, I don't know how she would manage otherwise, and Peter's royalties give her the freedom to do that. She devotes her life to those children and is a brilliant mother to them.

Can I see myself doing that? Being so selfless as to be able to put someone else's needs before my own? I'm still not sure. Having someone else in your life who depends totally and utterly on you, can't do one single thing for themselves, and whose continued health and existence depends on you remembering fairly basic things like feeding them, changing them, and strapping their car seat into the car and not driving off with it still sitting outside the house. Ohmygod. I love what I have with the children at the school – during the day they are mine, I pump them with knowledge and experience, then send them outside to their parents who remember to turn up and collect them and do all the responsible bits. Plus the fact they are all of an age where nappies and poo no longer feature (with one or two minor exceptions over the years which I won't go into – they nearly made me change professions).

Alex dashes off, surrounded by her gorgeous brood; blond, spiral-haired little Rosie clinging to her leg and begging to go back to the bicycle racks for some more adventures, tall, dark, Archie, the living embodiment of his father, swinging his violin case around like a whirling dervish, in a complete world of his own, and Millie, with her long, straight blond hair in two plaits which had presumably started the day looking a little tidier than they do now, trotting along contentedly beside her mother, chatting away, no doubt filling her in on the finer points of the day. I smile at the picture they make as they wander out of the school gates; a real unit, a family, despite the lack of a father figure. But his presence is still so tangible around them all, like he is walking alongside them, unseen.

I retreat back to the now empty school building. Much as I love the children being around, there is a strange kind of serene, surreal feel to an empty, out-of-hours school. The children's presence is always there, in the artwork and photos which adorn the walls, the abandoned PE kits hanging limply on their pegs. If you stand quietly you can almost hear a ghostly rush of children whizzing from classroom to playground and back again, an imagined sense of another presence in the building. In the holidays it's the weirdest, when the walls are bare of work and the building is merely a shell, waiting for its occupants to come home. Tonight though it is homely and familiar, and I take my place at my desk to wrap up the day's marking and prepare for tomorrow.

Six

I wave to Frannie as I turn my car into our drive. The old lady is in her front garden, pretending to weed the flower bed, although I know her gardener will have been in today and there won't be a weed in sight in her immaculate little patch. She uses it as a pretext for nabbing passing villagers for a chat, bless her, and for keeping tabs on the comings and goings in our road, which on some days, in this quiet little corner of England, are few and far between. But who's going to blame her for seeking out a bit of company in the best way she can. Life round here must seem awfully tame for her, after the heady days of her youth.

Francesca Blakely-Smith has been our neighbour since we moved here, four years ago. She's not the sort of dear old lady who has lived in the village all her life, with children and grandchildren settled nearby. Oh no, Frannie's life had been far from that sort of ordinary. She'd lived the high life in London at the heart of the rocking fifties, swinging sixties and beyond, done all the flower power stuff and been engaged to, and scandalously lived with, all sorts of gentrified and wealthy young men. She'd had her picture in Country Life, on the arm of some eligible bachelor or other, more times that I'd had hot dinners. She'd never managed to permanently secure any one of them, and swap the engagement ring for a wedding ring – and boy didn't I know how that felt – but that suited her. And as she put it, she'd had a 'bloody good time' with each and every one of her past conquests, no strings attached, and now was living out her dotage in a more sedate manner. She couldn't be doing with being shackled with some old codger now, she says, someone who had been so handsome and charming in his youth, but whose wealth is dwindling along with his marbles, needs help getting to the loo, and is all her responsibility. No, she says, much better to be on her own and mistress of her own destiny. I admire her, she's a grand old bird and has some fabulous stories to tell, which she does in her own richly colourful way. For one so frightfully posh – she is by far the poshest person I have ever met – her use of expletives is unexpected but hilarious, provided there is no one under the age of eighteen within earshot. She swears so much that Mark calls her 'Frannie the F word'.

'Good afternoon, Grace, how was school today?' She calls up to me, clean, shiny, unused trowel in her hand.

'Hello, Frannie. It was good thank you. How are your lupins? Your garden is looking beautiful, I must say.' I always find myself picking up my own diction and use of the English language when speaking to Frannie – I feel so badly spoken in comparison, with my odd mix of mild Estuary vowels and slight Worcestershire twang.

'Have I asked you yet if you would like a ticket for the school play?'

She pulls herself up off her kneeler with a click and groan of tired old bones.

'Now, my dear, I'm glad you mentioned it. I saw the poster and thought I might ask that delightful Mr Pearson if he'd like to come along with me. Bloody gorgeous he is, for a man of his age. He still has all his own teeth, too, so he says. If we were both fifty years younger I'd give him a run for his money, I can tell you. Fucking old age, Grace. My mind still wants to do all those things I used to do years ago, just this old carcass of a body that won't cooperate.'

It always amuses me to hear Frannie speak. Her crystal clear, silver-spoon-in-the-mouth accent is so pure, unlike much of the vocabulary she uses. She had been educated at Roedean and had all the breeding and class of a minor member of the royal family, and when dressed up in her finery, looks a bit like one of them too, with her back-combed hair, high forehead and strings of pearls. God knows where, or whom, she had picked up her colourful language from, but it makes her a bit of a character and she is popular with all ages in the village; they treat her as a something of a local dignitary.

'Shall I put you down for a couple of tickets then Frannie? Good luck with asking Mr Pearson, I'm sure he'll be bowled over.' I make a move towards my front door, but Frannie starts to follow.

'He reminds me of Edward de Wintour, you know. He was my second fiancé.' As she comes over all dreamy-eyed I can see she is settling into one of her stories, and I don't have the heart to brush her off and make a quick escape. I could well be the only person she has seen all day.

'He was quite exquisitely beautiful, looked a bit like your Mark, actually, tall and dark with real come-to-bed eyes. A shame, though, those eyes were full of such promise, but when we actually got down to it, he was absolutely fucking useless in bed, didn't know what to do with the damn thing, my dear. There's a limit, you know. It's all very well being able to get a girl excited, but you have to be able to complete the deal.' Typical Frannie. I couldn't imagine standing there and discussing the dreadful price of cod these days, or what the local Flower Arranging Society's annual fund-raiser was going to be.

'So I had to let the chap go,' she goes on. 'Release him from his obligations to me. Our parents were disappointed, of course. It would have been a fortuitous match from both sides, but a girl needs a chap who can satisfy her, I'm sure you understand, dear Grace.'

I'm not sure I want to reply to that and feel myself blushing. It's one thing for Frannie to regale me with stories of her days as a bright young thing, but I don't really go in for reciprocal stories of sexual encounters. Not with someone who is as old as my own Grandmother, anyway. It's just not right.

I manage to extricate myself from Frannie's clutches after a few more stories of the escapades that she and this Edward fellow had got up to. Good on her. How fabulous to get into your late seventies and have so many stories tell. You only get one shot at life and she has certainly lived hers to the full, even if in her latter years things have become a little more sheltered.

Supper at Alex's house tonight – should be fun. A lovely, relaxed evening, lots of champagne, great conversation, light flirtation with other male members of the party, all totally innocent and harmless of course, and lots and lots of laughs. You really can't beat it for a way to spend an evening. Especially when the whole group are people you know well; no introductions needed, no worrying about being seated next to someone you had never met before and the small talk drying up.

Actually, I'm not entirely sure who is going tonight, other than ourselves and Evie and James. Presumably Alex has invited a few others – she can seat ten quite comfortably around the beautiful Queen Anne table in her dining room.

Mark has nipped in the shower whilst I'm rifling through my wardrobe, deciding what to wear. It's that funny time of the year when you feel like you should be casting aside the winter weeds, but the weather hasn't really caught up with that idea yet. Early spring, no longer winter, the sun keeps trying really hard to break through, Mother Nature is bursting into life everywhere, and here we are still walking around in drab and dreary browns, blacks and greys.

Tonight I am determined to add a bit of colour to the evening and so plump for a pair of pale linen trousers and pretty pale pink and cream wrap-around top I bought last week. I think I need a little strappy vest underneath to avoid one of those embarrassing un-wrap-around moments that can happen with these sorts of garments. Wrap-around dresses are the worst in my experience; they have that nasty habit of coming untied at inopportune moments, so that as you sit down, everything just falls apart, and your modesty with it. Handy in a romantic clinch, I suppose, if you need to get naked quickly, but not so great for looking professional at a staff meeting.

Oh yes, it happened to me at my very first meeting at Cropley School, and extremely embarrassing it was too. Tom hadn't seemed to mind the expansive flash of thigh that came his way, but I'd blushed scarlet to my roots, and vowed never to wear that dress to school again.

I quite fancy wearing a pair of shoes that haven't had an outing for a while, so I spend an indulgent few moments gazing at the rows of neatly stacked boxes. Yes, real people like me really do put them in clear plastic boxes with a photo on one end, just like that scary, skinny posh woman with the glasses on that TV show tells you to do. If my shoes are tidy then life is good.

I am so lucky here to have so much space to keep my stuff. When we moved in, we had the smallest bedroom converted into a dressing room, just for me, and I now have everything a fashion-loving girl could want. Plus a whole side to the wardrobe just for my shoes. I remember going to see *Sex in the City* at the cinema with the girls. When I got back Mark had asked me what the best bit of the film was, and I had raved enthusiastically about her wardrobe, or rather her closet. He was a bit perplexed to say the least, but anyone who has seen the film – and loves clothes – would agree as to how eye-poppingly fabulous it was – there was an audible gasp from the entire cinema (largely female – or gay) when Carrie revealed her newly designed closet. I had mine first, though. It's not quite as grand or extensive as Carrie's, but to me it's fabulous and I love spending time in there, ogling and touching all my pretty things.

I do have a lot of shoes, I have to admit, but that doesn't quell the hunger for more. I can't walk past a shoe shop without just a little trip inside, on the very slight off-chance that there might be something there a bit unusual or special. You never know what you might come across. And generally if I do go in, I don't come out empty-handed. Ahh, there are the shoes I was wearing when I met Mark, a bit old and worn now, but I have kept them, they are the head of the wardrobe, a lucky mascot. They were what brought us together; to get rid of them would only be a bad omen.

Mark and I met seven years ago when I was living in a flat-share with a couple of girlfriends and taking the train up to London each day to my job in South London. He would set off in his smart suit and designer tie; I would be dressed as best as I could on a junior teacher's salary. I couldn't afford designer clothes in those days, but would still spend every penny I could on shoes. I even managed to save up for my first pair of Jimmy Choos in the first year I started work.

The shoes I was wearing the day I met Mark made an impression on him, quite literally. As the train pulled into the station that morning, there was the usual scramble to get onto the already busy carriage. Not a fist fight or anything, just some polite-ish jostling to make sure everyone got on (sometimes they didn't and there was a half hour wait before the next train came). My sale shopping experience always came in useful at moments like this. I was used to sharpening my elbows and foraying into a crowd of shoppers, all set on the bargain of the moment. Getting on our train was a bit like that, each man, or woman, for himself. Or on that morning, each three inch heal for itself.

I could run for the train in those shoes too, despite the heels, and without looking like a circus act. And run for the train was what I had to do that morning. Giselle, one of my flat-mates, had used all the hot water (again) so I'd been desperately boiling up water to have some sort of a wash and tidy my hair up a bit and at least pay some homage to hygiene. Not a great start for the morning, unbeknown to me, that I would meet the future love of my life. So that had made me late. I bolted to the station at break-neck speed and reached the platform just as the train was pulling in. As I did the whole polite jostling thing I felt the heel of one of my shoes land on something soft and this was followed by 'Argghhhh, watch what you're doing will you?'

'Sorry, sorry,' I mumbled. I looked up into the face of the man whose foot I had impaled and did a double take. Not that I knew him, or anything, I had never set eyes on him before. But I looked at him and recognised him, and had to stop myself saying 'Oh, it's you'. I recognised him in that strange kind of subconscious way that must only be what they call Love at First Sight. It wasn't a Coup de Foudre and there weren't thunderclaps or anything like that. It was a feeling of being home, the total recognition of another person who is going to have a profound effect on your life in one way or another. Our eyes locked and I knew he had felt it too.

'Are you OK, I'm so sorry', I ventured.

'Did you sharpen those before you left home this morning?' he asked sarcastically, bending down and rubbing the front of his foot. Clearly it had hurt rather a lot.

'Are your shoes OK?' I asked. There was a nasty scuff on the top of one of his expensive looking work brogues.

'It's my foot I'm more worried about'. By this time all the other passengers had got onto the train and we were left by the open doors, 'But don't miss your train on account of me'.

Wow, such politeness in the face of such pain.

'No, really, it's fine, I'll be OK, I want to make sure you're OK first'. He hobbled onto the train; miraculously, there was an empty seat. I followed him and kept close by. If it had been anyone else I would probably have done a runner by now, out of sheer embarrassment. But I felt I needed to stay with him. Some greater force was at work here. I just needed to find out what it had in store for me.

He sat down just as the train pulled away from the station. I grabbed hold of the overhead rail to steady myself. I was totally shaken. He took off his shoe and rubbed the patch between his second and third toes.

'You certainly made an impression', he ventured at a joke. 'I'm Mark, by the way.'

'I'm Grace. Grace Connery,' I replied 'although I probably shouldn't be giving you my full name, you might be some big City hotshot lawyer and sue me for every penny I've got, now that I've ruined your budding side-line as a professional dancer'.

'Well, I am a City lawyer, as it happens, but not so hotshot as yet, maybe one day. Don't worry I won't be seeking damages, and I may probably never dance again, but that could be doing the world a great favour.' This guy had a sense of humour. I loved it.

It turned out that Mark did the daily commute as I did, usually from a station further up the track, but on that occasion he'd been out with a friend (male, I had managed to ascertain almost immediately) and stayed over. How he could manage to look so immaculate after a night spent on someone's sofa I couldn't fathom, but then he'd probably had the luxury of a hot shower, unlike me, I suddenly remembered, and no annoying flatmates to get in the way.

Mark worked in the City for a big commercial law practice, Clayford Chalmers, in their property law department. It all sounded very glamorous but he explained that he was actually still training, and would be for another three months, finishing his last six month 'seat' before becoming fully qualified. Well he could finish my seat any time, or sue my pants off, come to that. The chemistry between us was electric. I loved his scent, a heady, gorgeously clean-smelling mix of fabric conditioner and musky after shave, which I inhaled deeply as he leaned in closer to talk to me over the hubbub of the train carriage.

I was mesmerized by his huge brown eyes, and although I was trying to play it cool, he must have noticed how I hung on his every word. He seemed genuinely captivated when I told him about my own career, laughing with unfeigned sincerity at the stories of recent escapades in the classroom.

The train pulled into Waterloo. I honestly hadn't noticed the time passing; we had been so absorbed in each other. Suddenly there was a scramble for the doors and an awkward moment between us, neither of us sure what to do next. 'Please don't just walk out of my life', I prayed silently. 'How's your foot?' I asked instead.

'I think I'll live, but I may need to keep you posted on my progress,' he said. Relief. Big inward sigh. He wanted to see me again. Hallelujah.

'Of course,' I replied coyly, trying to hide my sheer jubilance. 'My nursing skills aren't up to much but I do have a lot of experience in playground injuries.' We walked side by side along the platform, with him still limping slightly, and through the barriers into the station, both heading for the underground.

'Here, I'll give you my card. Will you call me? I'll be very disappointed if you don't.' He added this with a fake stern voice, his eyes downcast, but a teasing smile playing at the corner of his lips. He knew damn well I would call.

'I'm afraid teachers don't carry business cards, but yes, I promise I will call you,' I replied. He leaned towards me and his lips brushed my cheek with the faintest of kisses. I thought I would pass out. I felt delirious. How was I to concentrate on a day's teaching after that? I wanted to go home, lie down in a darkened room, and put all my senses back into order. Each one felt heightened, more acute somehow; the station was dazzling in all its colours, the noises were like a cacophony of out of tune musical instruments, and I noticed every smell around me, from the heavenly aroma of coffee from the nearby vendor, to the fusty, unwashed smell of the dread-locked man selling the Big Issue.

And of course I did ring Mark, that same evening in fact. There was none of that 'Should I, shouldn't I, will he think I'm too keen, should I make him sweat, keep him waiting' type dilemma like I'd had with boyfriends in the past. We both seemed to know that whatever was going to happen was inevitable and we just had to do as fate instructed us to bring it to pass.

Mark and I had a wonderful courtship, to use that word at risk of sounding like my Gran. But that's exactly what it was. Because we both seemed to recognise that we had forever, there didn't seem to be any rush. The just holding hands and kissing stage seemed to last for an eternity, and that was lovely. We were young and in love and we enjoyed each step as it came. He would send me flowers and I would buy him those corny little teddies with the love messages attached.

Our weekends were spent walking hand in hand anywhere and everywhere; in parks, around the shops, along the river, it didn't really matter as long as we were together. And in the evenings we would sit in pubs, still holding hands, and deliberate on where to go and what to eat, whether we wanted to meet up with friends or just be alone and go home and curl up in front of a DVD. It was blissful and uncomplicated.

When we did eventually take things further, which amazingly was a whole six weeks into our relationship, it was perfect. Mark had banned his housemate for the evening and transformed his home into a love palace. I arrived there expecting to meet him and have a quick drink before going out, but the house was in darkness even though I knew he was home. He opened the door and was silhouetted against a backdrop of candlelight. There were little tea light candles everywhere I looked, illuminating the hall, and leading a path through to the kitchen. Without uttering a word, he put his finger to his lips, beckoned me inside and led me by my hand through to the kitchen, where he presented me with a glass of champagne. 'To us and to forever,' he whispered, and it didn't even sound corny like it should have done. Wow, this was the stuff of Mills & Boon, I thought. No one had ever done anything this romantic for me before. Wait till the girls hear about this. 'To us and romance,' I replied, equally cornily, kissing him on the lips. 'Why are we whispering?' I asked, 'Is Joe upstairs?'

'God, no,' he replied. 'I paid him no small amount of money to go out for a meal with that girl he's been seeing from work. I'm really hoping he'll make a go of it and not come back. At least not until much much later. That leaves us all the time in the world.' He curled himself around me with a groan of longing and kissed me again. It looked like tonight was the night. I had wondered when Mark would want to take things further, but even so hadn't felt the need to push him. I would enjoy each moment as it lasted.

Just as I began to lose myself in his kiss he pulled away. 'Right, dinner,' he said. 'Everything is ready, please sit here madam.' Like the best trained maître d' he pulled my chair out and as I sat down, placed my napkin in my lap with a flourish.

'I didn't know you could cook, let alone all this,' I gestured to the table and the waiting food in amazement.

'I'll tell you all about my student job some time,' he replied. I knew he'd worked in a smart London restaurant during his student years – he must have picked up more than just washing up skills from clearing tables and doing dishes.

Our meal was delectable. After the main course, Mark stood up and cleared away the dirty dishes before saying 'Excuse me a minute, I just need to get dessert ready.' He threw me a mysterious glance and one of his flirtatious smiles over his shoulder, grabbed a box of matches from the ledge and headed for the hall. I could hear him striking match after match and smiled as I knew what he was up to. He was lighting all the tea lights that he had placed on the stairs, I presumed leading up to his room. I sat quietly and waited for him; he had planned it all so carefully I didn't want to spoil his moment. I knew how he wanted me to be amazed by all this, and I was. Completely bowled over in fact. It gave me a chance to take a deep breath and think about our relationship. I knew where things were heading tonight and I was totally and utterly happy about that. Both of us were ready and I wanted it more than anything. Being with Mark was the best thing that had ever happened to me. I knew I had found 'the one'.

Mark came back to the kitchen to fetch me. 'Would madam like to walk this way, please?' He held my hand and led me slowly towards the stairs. 'Dessert this evening will be served in my room, would madam care to partake?'

'Yes please, madam would,' I replied in my best fake posh accent as he led me gently up the stairs. I had never actually been in Mark's bedroom, that chaste had our relationship been until now. There was none of the blokey bachelor pad feel to it that I had half expected, or that musty smell that seems to linger around men's rooms. Not wishing to sound like I have 'got around a bit', I have experienced a few of my ex boyfriends' bedrooms, and it has not always been pleasant. Instead Mark's room was decorated almost totally in cream, with tasteful brocade curtains draped at the window, matching cushions on the bed, and amazingly for a man, no clutter and no dirty boxer shorts or odd socks peeking out from underneath. I should have known, I suppose, he was always turned out so immaculately, his room simply mirrored his personality and appearance. Unless of course he had blitzed the room half an hour before I arrived, and his wardrobe was stuffed to bursting point with all the detritus that usually accumulates on a bedroom floor. Even mine. Oh yes, we women are not immune to a bit of bedroom clutter and dirty laundry about the place. Just as long as no one else sees it.

I liked the fact that I still didn't know everything about Mark; there was still such a lot to discover, and not just the secrets of his wardrobe. There were more candles up here, and scented ones too. The smell was intoxicating and so was

Mark.

And of course our lovemaking was as delectable as dinner. Mark's technique displayed all the attention to detail his cooking had demonstrated, ensuring we had all the ingredients for a perfect, romantic and exciting first liaison, and mixing them together with an expert's hands… and lips, and fingertips, and tongue, and… well. I have to admit I had been slightly worried that things were so perfect between us on all other levels, emotional, spiritual, intellectual, we might not match that degree of flawlessness on the physical side, and in a way I had been prepared in my own mind to settle for less than full marks in the bedroom as we had such a brilliant relationship in all other aspects. You couldn't have it all, could you? Or maybe you could. I needn't have worried. Mark was kind and caring, warm and loving, and above all damn sexy with it. As he kissed and teased, caressed and nuzzled, he brought me to the extremes of endurance before I finally let go and gave into my senses. As I came again and again I clung to him knowing I would never want or need anyone else.

'Why did we wait so long?' I asked as I lay spent in his arms, my hair trailing across his broad chest.

'Anything worth having is worth waiting for,' he replied, as I felt him stir again. 'I wanted it to be special. I've never met anyone like you, Grace, you bring out the best in me. I love you so much.'

Right, that was it. I could start writing that romantic novel I've always been promising myself. I now had first-hand experience of all the emotions felt by the heroines of love stories back through the ages, and been the recipient and deliverer of all the soppy, corny lines. Lizzie Bennett and Mr Darcy had nothing on us. Only they weren't corny lines when the man I loved so much said them to me and I knew he really meant them. I had never been one to wear my heart on my sleeve, but in Mark's company those little endearments just seemed to pop out unbidden. It was all so perfect, you couldn't have scripted it any better.

Mark jumps out of the shower, all pink and scrubbed and glowing, and smelling of the gorgeous Molton Brown body wash I had bought him. He walks around the bedroom in that struttingly confident way that only men seem to have when naked. It must be something to do with the freedom of the swinging bits that gives them more of a swagger, but I could never bare all with such confidence, and I didn't know any other women who would want to either. We girls can't wait to at least get some undies on. But I suppose men don't have all the hang-ups about their bodies that women do. You only have to look around on the beach or at the pool on holiday – lots of fairly fit and toned women, reaching for their sarong to tiptoe the few steps to the pool, discreetly casting it aside as they slip into the water. The men on the other hand are happy to strut about, whether muscled Adonis or paunchy flab-wobbler. And it always seems, the bigger the belly and bum, the smaller the trunks. Yuk. There should be a rule about Speedos only being worn in the Olympics; anyone who breaches that should be locked up on the spot. And as for thongs, the sight of a piece of string disappearing between the wobbling buttock cheeks of a middle aged tattooed heavy-weight is enough to send anyone running for the shade.

'My turn now,' I say, heading for the bathroom and peeling off layers as I go.

'Not so fast, young lady,' Mark says, grabbing my arm playfully as I make to get past him. 'We're not in any rush tonight are we? What time is Alex expecting us?'

'She said about 8.30. I think she was running a bit late – the children needed collecting from some party or other.'

'Well then, we have ages, don't we?' I know what he's planning, and this time I have no excuse to dodge him, nor do I want to have one.

'But you're just out of the shower, you're all lovely and clean. Me, on the other hand, I could do with a freshen up,' I joke.

'We can jump in together then, I don't mind another dousing. I'll scrub your back if you scrub mine,' he grins.

And that is it. Before I can say another word he has turned the shower back on and is pulling me through the glass doors into the huge cubicle.

'I always think what a waste of space this shower is without someone to share it with,' he laughs. We'd had a huge shower installed in the en suite before we'd moved in. It's one of those fabulous ones with a massive shower head which can emit anything between a light rain shower and complete deluge.

Mark unhooks the shower head and begins gently soaking me, wetting my hair, my back, my buttocks, then he adeptly hoists one of my legs over his arm and directs the full force of the water at the most sensitive part of my body. I can feel myself succumbing quickly, the powerful vibrations of the water lifting me and waves of lust coursing through my veins. He hangs the shower head back on the rack and kneels down, his tongue taking the place of the jet of water, and licking and caressing me as I press back against the glass for support, the water pouring down over both of us as we are caught up in our lust. I lift my head to feel the water cascade over my face as Mark's tongue and fingers bring me to a climax. We slither together to the floor and I climb onto Mark, who is more than ready for me, lowering myself down onto him and riding him like a powerful water horse until he groans with ecstasy and it's all over.

It was the briefest of encounters, but I am totally spent. Mark had been more forceful and commanding than usual, fired up by the desire to make his longed-for baby, no doubt. I have never seen him so driven during our lovemaking. We have always had a very lively imagination in the bedroom (and all around the house, come to that), trying new things and generally having a bit of a laugh whilst we're at it. Our love life is fun, giggly, romantic and sexy. But this is on a different plane; Mark had the look of a man on a mission, his eyes had been glowing with lust and a determination that I'd not seen before. I'm not complaining though, if he can make me feel like that in the space of a few minutes, then I am all up for more of this supercharged Mark.

'Wow,' is all I can manage as I stumble from the shower, dazed and a bit pink.

'You are gorgeous and I love you,' he says as he wraps me in a huge fluffy towel, straight from the warm towel rail, planting a kiss on my forehead.

'We'd better get ready,' I say, breaking the atmosphere of the moment, and needing to. I will be dragging him back into the shower for a repeat performance otherwise, and then we really will be late.

I dry myself quickly and head for the bedroom before Mark can say any more. I sit on the side of the bed to get my breath back and catch sight of myself in the mirror. I look so alive, eyes and cheeks flaming, the usual post coital red blotchy patch forming on my chest.

With a deep breath I pull myself together and set about making myself presentable for the evening ahead. Hair and face to fix up, but I don't think I will need quite as much makeup as usual – the glow of lovemaking has put the blush in my cheeks and the sparkle in my eyes.

Seven

As we walk up Alex's driveway, the house is ablaze with a warm welcoming light on this crisp spring evening. It's a sort of back to front house, with the grand Georgian facade facing away from the road, towards the hill and, in our opinion, some of the most stunning countryside in Britain. We are no locals by anyone's standards, having only been here a few years, but I cannot imagine ever leaving this little corner of Worcestershire. It has swallowed me up and tied me in and now it is my home. I think it is as much to do with the people who live and work around here as with the countryside itself, but we all consider ourselves very privileged to inhabit our cosy little world.

There are a few cars on the drive; we aren't the first to arrive then, despite the fact that we probably live the nearest. Not surprising given our earlier antics in the bathroom. It had taken me a while to pull myself together, calm down a bit and get dressed and ready, and I still feel more than a little spaced out now. A dark green Range Rover – looks like Susie and Graham's, a couple from our wider circle of friends. I haven't seen them for a while, so it will be good to catch up with them. James' Aston Martin – I guessed he and Evie would be here too - great, no evening is complete without them. And a third car, a small, dark coupé which I don't immediately recognise until I see the number plate. It's Tom's car; so he is the one making up numbers tonight by the look of it.

How difficult for Alex, being on her own, planning supper parties always with an odd number of people. Makes things tricky when it comes to seating, as the usual boy/girl/boy/girl seating plan doesn't work quite so well. Not that any of us mind, and most importantly Alex doesn't mind either. It's very admirable of her to put on such fabulous evenings as she does, as the sole host, taking on the role of chef, wine waitress and hostess. Quite a challenge for anyone, but then she knows us all well enough for it not to be too daunting, I suppose, and she does usually enlist the help of a local teenager or two, to assist with passing round the plates, clearing dishes, and washing up. A nice round number for her tonight, though, a cosy eight which is a lovely size for a dinner party, I always think. A small enough group to all engage in the same conversation around the table if that's the way things are going, but also enough people to be able to turn to one side and have a cosy conversation with your neighbour for a while, without feeling like you are ignoring the rest of the party.

Amongst our friends we have this lovely unwritten rota for entertaining, so it's always somebody's 'turn', but then no one takes offence if someone misses their turn, and we just do it when it suits. We have a huge circle of acquaintances, largely people I have met via the school, from the village, and a few who live round here that Mark also knows from work, plus a large circle of those we consider our true friends. It's nice to mix them all up now again and see what happens as the evening wears on. But then on other occasions it's great just to have a really relaxed evening, with close friends only, some Marks and Sparks canapés, a quick lasagne, and a pud from one of the delis in Purbrook.

Alex opens the door to us looking radiant in a silk Karen Millen dress. There are all the usual 'mwa mwa' kisses on both cheeks. I hand over my floral offering, and Mark his alcoholic one, and she leads us through to the drawing room. Alex has done herself proud; even for a simple evening as this the house looks immaculate, stunning arrangements of flowers, presumably from the garden, dotted around in huge urns, and elegant antique candelabras, all lit and brilliant, an inheritance from Grandma, evoking a warm and comforting sense of stepping back in time to a more genteel age.

Evie turns to greet us, away from her conversation with Susie, the latter full of apologies for not having seen us in 'such an age'. More 'mwa mwa's'. James and Tom are deep in conversation in front of the fireplace, where a roaring fire is burning in the huge inglenook. This house is such a surprise on the inside, the beams and cosy fireplaces doing battle with the elegant facade and more gentrified Georgian exterior. It has been added to so many times over the years, it's is now a mixture of all centuries and all styles in one, but they sit together perfectly.

James and Tom know each other from way back. James' younger brother had been at high school with Tom, in

Malvern, where they had all grown up. The three boys, and Tom's younger brother too, had all been firm friends, despite the age differences which at the time seemed huge, but as adults were inconsequential. James and Tom had been the ones to settle back in the area after going off to do the necessary training for their various careers over the years, and their friendship had reignited. When Tom had secured the headship at Cropley School, James had been thrilled to have his old chum back working nearby, and they had started to see a lot more of each other again. James remembered feeling disappointed that he had moved his daughters into private education a year or so earlier – if he had known his friend would be at the helm of the local school he would probably have entrusted them to the state system for a lot longer.

They are clearly discussing something deep and meaningful. Graham seems to be hovering on the outskirts of the conversation, not wanting to butt in, nor wanting to inveigle himself into the conversation that the women are having on the other side of the room, and so is looking a bit left out. It's funny how the sexes naturally gravitate towards one another for this initial part of an evening. No wonder many hosts stick to the alternate placing of the genders around the dinner table, otherwise it would be possible to spend the entire evening without speaking to a single member of the opposite sex. And the dynamics of an evening always seem to work better when everyone is mixed up – no one too near or next to their own partner, but with some 'fresh blood' on either side to talk to, secure in the knowledge that your partner is not too far away, should you need back-up or his or her version of a story.

Mark in his usual ebullient manner strides across the room to greet the male members of the party, greeting and kissing the women as he passes. Graham takes advantage of the moment to reintroduce himself into the male conversation. Poor chap, he probably doesn't know the other men as well as these three know each other, and is in danger of being left out of the conversation completely if he fails to make his move now. His wife on the other hand is one of those women who have the innate ability to monopolise the conversation, no matter what the subject matter is. She is in full flow with Evie, but is happy to include me in her conversational eye contact, whilst extolling the virtues of her children's never ending weekend activities and how good they all are at them. I can't pass comment there, but I do at least nod and make the right noises, and look interested, until the conversation moves onto something a little more stimulating.

Alex is on the periphery of the conversation, being the busy hostess. She has Lucy, an eighteen year old girl from the village, passing round the canapés and topping up glasses, but being the true hostess that she is, she is on constant watch to ensure that this is running smoothly and no one is going without.

The greetings over, the two parties settle back into their respective corners of the room, like boxers awaiting the start of round one. Alex and Lucy flit in and out with various intricate looking canapés (presumably a skill acquired in

Alex's days as a chalet girl). The evening looks promising, I think, surveying the attendant guests. It has been a while since we have seen Susie and Graham, so it will be good to catch up with them properly, once the topic of conversation turns away from Susie's kids, and ages since Tom has been at the same social event as us.

I am always conscious of how different people are away from their working environment; none of the constraints of work talk, a little bit (or more) of alcohol, and free and easy conversation, no holds barred. I find myself hoping, in a strangely guilty kind of way, that I might be seated near to him at the table. He looks very handsome tonight. Next to Mark's dark good looks, he is completely different; in as much as Mark is dark and brooding in his appearance, Tom is the complete opposite, preppy, blond, curly hair which is usually verging on the long, bright blue eyes, tall, but with a much more muscular physique than Mark. Both extremely good looking men, I think, and I have the good fortune to be engaged to the one and to work with the other.

So few men are truly good looking, although men have the advantage of getting better looking with age, I reckon. They kind of grow into their looks and physique as they progress through their thirties and into their forties, a few grey hairs and the beginnings of some crow's feet merely adding to the character of their appearance. You only had to look at George Clooney. And, even older than him, what about Harrison Ford and Sean Connery? Really old men now, in the great scheme of things, but still utterly gorgeous. If only the same could be said for women. We have the misfortune of fading with age, unless blessed with extremely good genes or rich enough to have some 'work' done. Mark and I have a number of middle aged friends (and I consider middle age to be forties rather than thirties, although that will probably shift to fifties when it's my turn to be forty) who are roughly the same age as each other, but the man is starting to look a few years younger than the wife, unless she is lucky enough to have either been an absolute babe in her youth and have bone structure to die for, or has had the benefit of the surgeon's knife to give her a bit of a lift in her middle years. And let's face it, not many of our friends fall into that category.

Funnily, I find myself thinking about age a lot these days; something to do with where we are in our lives, I suppose. The possibility of impending motherhood has suddenly made me realise that in fact I am no longer the younger generation; there are millions of people out there of my age or younger with families, doing the responsible parent thing and having to behave like adults. I can't actually imagine feeling like a grown up, maybe it's just something you never do, whatever your age. Perhaps I will have to hit fifty or sixty to realise that this is it, I am the parent (or even grandparent) generation now.

Alex calls us through to the dining room for dinner, and we drift through slowly, the men holding back and allowing the women to get to the table first, all of us hovering in the doorway and waiting for Alex to tell us where she wants us, according to her seating plan.

'I need to be near the door, so Grace, you go over there,'

she says, directing me to the opposite side of the table, by the fireplace. 'James, can you go at the head of the table next to me, I might need to call on you later to carve the joint, if that's OK. Mark you're next to me here, Graham down the other end, and Evie next to you. Who does that leave?' As everyone takes their places, just Tom and Susie remain unseated.

'Looks like you are there then, Tom, next to Grace,' Alex says, pointing to the place next to mine. 'And Susie on your other side, here. That's sorted. Sit down everyone, please.' Everyone takes their places and Lucy appears to top up the glasses and start serving the food.

'Cheers guys, and thank you Alex for inviting us all, and here's to what looks like being a lovely evening.' My other half, doing his gracious guest bit, raising his glass and toasting Alex and the assembled friends, before the conversation kicks off again in earnest.

'Thank you all for coming, and here's to friends,' Alex raises her glass again in response and there is more clinking before everyone settles down and tucks into the soup, which Lucy has been busy putting out.

I feel a warm glow of excitement as I look forward to the evening ahead, most of that due strangely to Tom's placement at my side. He turns to me with a huge smile.

'Are you sure you don't mind being stuck with me for the evening, Grace?' he teases. 'Isn't it enough for you having to put up with me all week, then you come out for a lovely evening, only to get stuck with me at the table? I won't be offended if you don't speak to me all night, honest,' he says, although his body language contradicts his words.

He sidles fractionally closer to me as he speaks, turning his back slightly on Susie, his arms folded on the table and his elbow brushing lightly against my sleeve. I get a whiff of his aftershave. Something musky and very sexy. Good job he doesn't wear that to work; with an all-female staff, there is the possibility of several of us being incapacitated at once, too weak at the knees to stand, let alone teach, with all those strong pheromones wafting around.

'Don't be silly,' I giggle, slightly cross with myself for being so girly. 'It's lovely to see you away from work.' I feel light-headed all of a sudden and know I am blushing. Must be the champagne. I always seem to be blaming it for something these days. But how nice to be blaming champagne, rather than the cheap cider of my teenage drinking years and then the equally cheap wine of my student days. At least champers doesn't leave you with such an almighty hangover in the morning, even if it does still cloud your judgement and hinder sensible behaviour in much the same way at the time of consumption. Or turn me into a giggling wreck in the face of a handsome man who happens not to be my fiancé, just like now.

I have always been fond of a little flirting, and Mark is the same. Fortunately both of us are of the opinion that it's just a bit of fun and doesn't do any harm, and if we do ever feel that one or the other is going too far then we have a special little code of conduct for bringing the other back into line. Seated as we are across the table, opposite but one, we can hear what each other is saying, or not, depending how deep in conversation we are, and Mark is currently engrossed with Evie, recounting a story about one of his clients, by the sound of it, and not making eye contact with me at all. Which is a relief, given the puce colour of my face at the moment.

'You look rather lovely tonight, Grace,' Tom continues, not quite *sotto voce* although I get the impression he isn't entirely sure he wants Mark to hear his comment, especially when he adds, 'Really hot', leaning in even further. If only he knew that the glow on my skin and the sparkle in my eyes was due to the post-coital rush of blood to my head, and that only an hour or so earlier I had been writhing in passion in the shower with my fiancé. No, I don't want him to know that. Unless he has guessed, of course, recognising that unmistakeable look of sheer satisfaction in my eyes, that just-had-sex rosy glow that is completely impossible to hide. I remember trying to conceal it from my parents, many years ago, after nights out, coming home, attempting to look like I had had a squeaky clean evening. Not that I could ever be classed as an old slapper in those days or anything, I was far from it. But I'm sure my parents would like to think that I at least left home still a virgin, and not that I had ever had seedy (but actually pretty inventive and lovely) sex on the back seat of whichever boyfriend of the time's car. They wouldn't have cared to know just how bendy I could be when it came to finding a comfortable position to fit into on the back seat of a Mini Cooper.

'Lovely top, reminds me of that meeting...' He screws up his eyes and leans towards me again as he waits for his words to take effect. Now I really am blushing. I'm not imagining it, he is flirting with me. And I am finding it hard to be the 'career flirt' I normally am; detached but amusing and flattering. Seeing how flustered I am, he makes an attempt to change the subject, but as he starts to engage me in serious conversation, his knee brushes against mine and it is as though someone has wired me up to the mains. I feel the jolt go through me. I wonder if he felt it too.

I glance worriedly across at Mark again to check for a reaction; he doesn't appear to have noticed how flustered and pink I am looking. Fortunately Evie has him captivated.

Actually I am really enjoying the feeling, now that I have overcome the initial intense embarrassment and my face is starting to cool down. It reminds me of when Mark and I met; that buzz of excitement and anticipation, only this time it's tempered with guilt, as I know I shouldn't be feeling it. Sitting opposite me is my gorgeous fiancé, who I love and worship with all my heart, and with whom I am trying to have a baby. What is happening here?

The evening wears on, Alex produces some beautiful food, and much wine is consumed by all. As Mark and I have the advantage of being able to walk home later, we are both drinking copiously. At some point I give a vague shrug of recognition to the fact that maybe both of us should be cutting down our alcohol intake, if our fertility stands any chance of succeeding, but then I think, oh well, it's only early days, plenty of time for all that later, what the hell, and carry on drinking. Besides which, I'm not pregnant yet, am I? I never drink to excess really these days anyway. Gone are the student days of drinking myself into oblivion and not remembering how I got home. Nowadays I tend to slow down or stop completely when I can feel myself going too far. I love the buzz of having a few drinks and the way it makes me feel, but when that starts to turn sour I like to stop.

We reach that point in the evening where the music gets turned up, stories get more drunken and revealing, and confidences and confessions are revealed. Tom has spent the evening talking almost exclusively to me, apart from the moments when we have been obliged to join in the whole-party conversation or risk looking rude. I have had Graham to my right, and the end of the table, and I don't always find him stimulating company, although tonight he has been very pleasant and we've chatted a bit. So, frissons and flirting aside, I am grateful to have Tom to my left, and he has been witty, amusing, and more than a little bit flirtatious. Only now I am getting used to this new flirty Tom and giving as good as I get. He's not my boss this evening, just someone I can have a bit of fun with at a boozy dinner party. I've overcome my initial shyness and am enjoying every minute of it. I wonder if maybe a bit too much?

 Tom tells me a lot more about his ex-girlfriend than I'd ever heard before. He tends to keep things fairly close to his chest at work, and is generally every inch the professional head teacher. I'm the same though; I hate people's dirty laundry being aired in public at the best of times, and a school is no place for that. It turns out he had lived with Sophie for over a year; they'd talked about getting married, having children and buying a house together, but had never made any definitive plans in terms of a timescale for it all. Then they had started to drift apart for no apparent reason, she was spending more and more time away from the flat they shared, and he had found out, via a friend of his, that she had been spotted with another man in a restaurant nearby. The friend had broken the news to him that it had looked a bit more than just platonic, and Tom had confronted her. Apparently she had been having an affair with this man, someone she worked with, for over six months. He was distraught to find out that she had been cheating on him for more than half the time they had lived together, and that it had all started round about the moment they began to discuss settling down permanently.

'I don't understand how she could do that to me,' he tells me, the signs of pain rearing their ugly heads once more as he rakes over old wounds.

'It completely threw me, I couldn't cope. I withdrew from everything, friends, family, the lot. It was only work that kept me going, I had no option there but to carry on as normal.'

It has made him very untrusting, he says. He has started to see someone, he tells me, but only recently, and he's taking that very slowly, one step at a time, and not rushing into anything.

At that bolt of unexpected news, I feel something contract inside me, like someone has grabbed hold of my stomach and squeezed. I realise I am jealous of her, this new woman in his life, whoever she is. Why should he be single for one minute though; he is a complete catch, young, gorgeous and with a good job that, OK, will never make him rich, but will set him up more comfortably than most, and it's a secure career path, too.

I wonder what she looks like? I had only met Sophie the once, and she had been a real stunner, equally matched to Tom on the looks scale, but there had been something about her that was at odds with the beautiful exterior, a side to her that I could not quite put my finger on. When Tom tells me how she broke his heart, somehow it doesn't surprise me. She obviously had it in her. I probe gently to see if I can find out any more about the new girlfriend, carefully so as not to look too interested. Apparently she is a teacher in Worcester; Tom met her at a conference and they have been friends for a while, with the relationship gradually developing into a bit more than that. But he is very wary, he says, he won't be moving in with anyone or making any serious plans for a long time yet. So he can't be that keen on her then, can he? That's reassuring to know, for some strange reason. I manage to convince myself it's purely because I wouldn't want him to see him hurt again.

'So what about you and Mark, then Grace? Are marriage and babies on the horizon for you?' Tom asks, successfully deflecting interest from his own love life, but without realising how close to the wind he is sailing.

'Should you be asking me that as my boss?' I reply. 'I don't want you marking that up on my file and lining up my replacement if I say yes!'

'No chance, Grace, you are irreplaceable, and a very special member of my team, you know that. Whatever you decide to do is fine by me. I'm just interested to know. I'm not contingency planning or anything!'

I hope I haven't offended him. And that hope makes me want to confide in him. I tell him that Mark and I are just thinking about starting a family, and about the marriage issue. I explain how Mark is really keen to get cracking on having kids, and how I want to get married first. I try to explain to him how I had never really imagined myself as a mother.

'I just don't know if I have it in me,' I confide. 'I love the children at the school, but being a parent yourself, well, it's all a bit scary and grown-up.'

He puts his hand on mine, looks into my eyes and smiles, and that is enough. He's right – he has definitely cast his headmaster's hat aside for the time being. The vibes he is transmitting are not of the professional variety.

That aside, I'm not really sure exactly what he can say to me at this point; he doesn't have the woman's perspective on things that my close girlfriends do, so isn't qualified to offer advice or experience. And although he may not be acting like it, he is my boss, so obviously he doesn't want to lose me to motherhood when my career is so well established and I'm part of a very small team. Whilst I am talking, he is focussed on me the whole time, intent on what I am saying, as though there is no one else in the room. Mark is absent from the table; he was last spotted carrying a pile of plates into the kitchen with Alex, so fortunately is well out of earshot. I'm not sure he would appreciate me sharing all this personal stuff with another man, not least my boss. Tom doesn't attempt to offer an opinion on it all though, and I am grateful for that.

He lightens the tone with his next comment: 'Have you ever thought about what your name would be if you marry Mark, Grace? You'd be Mrs Hopper, Grace Hopper, that sounds a bit like Space Hopper, doesn't it!' he laughs.

'You'd better not wear orange with a name like that!' he goes on. 'At least you are lovely and slim, so there's never any chance you could look like a space hopper, you're far too gorgeous.' His eyes twinkle mischievously.

I laugh, but he is back to the flirting. I feel like I need a break from it so I excuse myself and head for the loo. Nearing the kitchen door, I can hear Mark and Alex talking, and when I grasp the topic of conversation, I stop short, just out of their line of vision, before it's too late and I'm spotted. Although eavesdropping isn't generally my thing, I feel compelled to hear more.

'She doesn't really want to do it, you know,' I hear him saying to Alex. 'I wish I had known that sooner.' I feel a jolt go through me. How can they be so openly discussing Mark and me starting a family? And what does he mean? Would he never have settled down with me if he'd known how reluctant I am to bear his children? I consider whether the same could be said for me and his inability to commit?

'I really hope she comes round to it. She's said we can go ahead and try but I don't really think her heart is in it. I love her and everything, but this is so hard.' I am startled; this is more than Mark has ever revealed to me. He'd made his views known and is good at doing the whole lawyer thing of putting his case forward, but when it comes to disclosing his feelings, he is pretty reticent.

I feel betrayed by both of them. By Mark because of what he had just revealed to my friend, and by Alex too as she doesn't immediately leap to my defence. I know she cares for us both, but she is *my* friend first and foremost, not Mark's. Shouldn't she be saying something to make him go back and talk to me, not be nodding sympathetically and making all the right noises to show that she understands how he feels?

I am glued to the spot, and although I don't like what I am hearing, I have to see it through. Not only that, if I move now, they will know I have heard everything. I can't just breeze past innocently.

'Poor you,' I hear Alex say to Mark. 'I can see how it must be hard for you. I couldn't imagine life without my kids. I can't remember what it was like before they came along. I do remember Peter and I both suddenly wanted to get on with starting a family at about the same time, so we never really had these issues. You can understand to a degree though where Grace is coming from.' Finally my best friend is sticking up for me. 'She loves her career and feels fulfilled with what she has already. And that must mean she is blissfully happy with you, Mark, otherwise she would want more to fill her life, wouldn't she?'

Whether Mark is mollified by this or not I don't know, I

can't see them and therefore can't judge the body language or see the expression on his face. I'm still struggling to understand why he has chosen to confide in Alex. Why can't he open up to me like that? I'm his fiancée for goodness sake. I didn't realise that he and Alex ever had such deep and meaningful conversations. I didn't think he would consider he knew her well enough. But then maybe he is missing the lack of a male friend to confide in. His closest friend from his student years still lives in the South East and we don't see as much of him and his family as Mark would like. But then men never really seem to open up to each other anyway, do they? It's all back slapping and talk of mundane day to day things, sport and work, rather than emotional heartfelt conversations. Sometimes it takes a woman to ask the direct questions that get a man talking.

Although all sorts of thoughts are doing battle in my head, in a way I am relieved for him that he can talk to *someone*, but I just wish that someone could be me. Up until now I had always thought Mark told me everything; now I'm not so sure. Maybe Alex has just been the catalyst he needs to make him talk; a case of being in the right place at the right time.

I can't hold out any longer, I need the loo and I'm not sure I want to hear any more. Breezing past the kitchen door trying to look as though I have only just left the table, I smile at Mark, who is propping up the Aga, whilst Alex loads dirty dishes into the dishwasher. They look very cosy together. He jumps to attention guiltily on seeing me, and starts stacking some of the dishes on the huge kitchen table.

Hopefully neither of them will suspect that I have heard a thing, but that doesn't stop them looking like a couple of rabbits caught in the headlights.

On my way back, I pop into the kitchen. Mark has disappeared, but Alex is still there, adding the final flourishes to one of the puddings. It's a huge pavlova, homemade of course; it would be no less than a punishable offence for the owner of an Aga to even consider serving up bought meringue to her guests. Besides which, it always tastes like sugary cardboard compared to the home made stuff. I have lost my appetite though and the sight of all that cream turns my stomach. I don't want to let on to Alex at this stage that I overheard her chat with Mark – she will keep. If she has anything to relay back to me I hope I can trust her enough to do so in her own time. If I know her as well as I think I do, then she will. I offer my services to help carry and we head back into the dining room together, laden with bowls, more cream, and the huge fruity pavlova, to a rapturous reception from the remaining seated guests.

'So, Grace, where are you off on your holidays this year?' I mentally shake myself down, trying to put what I have overheard to the back of my mind. It's Graham; he is just being polite and helping to fill a lull in the conversation, whilst Alex heaps vastly generous helpings of puddings into bowls.

'We haven't planned anything yet,' I confess. 'It's a bit of a pain that with my job, even though we haven't got children,' and here I nearly add a 'yet' but manage to restrain myself in time; I don't know him well enough to go into all that, 'we still have to travel at peak time. Can you imagine, with all the holiday we teachers get, if we then asked for more time off in term time?' I roll my eyes, in a self-deprecating manner. It's a common bone of contention amongst those not in education that those of us who are get such long holidays. We end up spending half our lives justifying it, and telling people that we do work extremely hard in term time, and it is very intense and all that, and that we do have to do quite a lot of planning in our own time too. Sadly it never really convinces them, and many are just jealous, but I can't see most people swapping their lovely fat private sector pay cheques and bonuses for public sector salaries and two percent annual pay rises.

'We'll probably just end up taking a last minute break late summer,' I go on. 'It seems to fit in quite well with Mark's work as a lot of his big clients are on holiday in August. We'll go for a late deal on the web, or something. At least as there are only two of us it's usually quite easy to get sorted. We're easy to please – just a warm climate and a five-star hotel needed. How about you?'

'Oh I leave all that to Susie normally. We have to go in peak time, too, with the kids, but this year it's easy, we're going back to exactly the same place we went to last year, lovely villa in Tuscany…' I drift off a bit as he pontificates in great detail about all the fabulous things they all got up to last year, but manage to nod and mutter in the right places to convince him I'm listening.

'Sounds gorgeous, you lucky things,' I smile at him. I

don't think he noticed I wasn't paying attention. Hopefully he won't test me on it later.

Meanwhile Tom is quietly working his way through a second helping of Alex's delicious apple pie, over my left shoulder, detached from any conversation in particular, but nodding and smiling as though he is taking part in any one that threatens to come his way. I recognise a classic case of 'bionic ear syndrome', as I have the feeling he is trying to listen in on my conversation above all the other noise. Mark and I invented the term for those moments when one of you is talking and the other not really paying attention, but tuning in instead to a conversation taking place nearby. All whilst attempting to give the impression that you really are listening to your partner. But it's usually the glassy-eyed expression that gives it away, and Tom is displaying all the classic symptoms. I suspect he is waiting for Graham to disengage so that he can move in on me again.

Mark and Alex have slipped back into their places at the table as though they haven't just shared the most private of conversations. Mark is back talking to Evie, the two of them do get on very well, and just seem to laugh all the time. Alex is talking to James, and it sounds like both Brookes are recounting the same humorous tale about one of their recent holidays, but in two very slightly different versions. Neither of them has realised, so hearing it across the table in almost-stereo is quite amusing, as each of them is at a different stage in of the story.

'So Grace, how did you and Mark meet? I know you're fairly new to this area,' Tom asks. 'Were you an item when you came to live round here?'

Good effort, Tom. The very minute Graham stops talking, he sees a window of opportunity and goes for it, turning towards me to make sure I am his captive audience, yet again. Safe territory though, talking about my partner to another man, the latter who, as of this evening, I am finding uncomfortably attractive.

So I set about regaling Tom with the story of how it all happened. Our story needs no embellishment; it had been an unconventional meeting, and is always an amusing tale to tell. He roars with laughter at the shoe thing; one thing he does know about me is my love of shoes, and at school he frequently teases me about the number of pairs I must have.

'Oh Grace,' he laughs, wiping genuine tears of laughter from his eyes, 'that really is a corker of a story. It sounds like something from one of those sex and shopping novels - 'She tripped and fell into his arms, realising too late that it was his foot she had stepped on. As she gazed into his pain-stricken face, his eyes were like deep-brown pools, and she knew they would be together forever. It was love at first sight'. You could call it *Head Over Heels* or something like that.' Tom reels this all off with one hand on his heart and a theatrical flourish, and this time it's my turn to laugh.

'I suppose it does sound pretty funny when you put it like that,' I reply. 'And it's all true too. That's just as it happened.'

'I think that's lovely, Grace, how romantic, and so much nicer than having to admit to pulling each other in a bar, or something like that. It's a great story. And are you still as madly in love now as in those *Head Over Heels* days?'

What a question! I know I must look shocked, and feel more than a little put on the spot by his question.

'Of course we are, Tom,' I protest, just a little too defensively, and look down at the table, averting his gaze. 'Mark and I are soul mates.' I can tell the dreaminess has gone out of my voice, it's all matter-of-fact-ness now. Who am I trying to convince here, him or me? I don't know what's wrong with me tonight; feeling disconcerted but quite excited about sitting next to my attractive boss, revealing to him our plans for starting a family and my reservations about it all, telling him about how we met, and then finally not being able to say convincingly that I still love Mark as much as the day we had met. Something to do with the conversation I had overheard in the kitchen, possibly?

'What are you two gassing about over there?' Great timing for James to cut into our conversation and spare me any more blushes. Susie has nipped off to the loo, Alex is busy getting the cheeses ready in the kitchen, and he finds himself marooned at the head of the table with no one to talk to.

'I was just hearing all about Grace and Mark's first encounter,' Tom replies, grinning. 'I assume you've heard how she goes round the country, spearing men on her spiky high heels and luring them back to her den of iniquity for hours and hours of illicit sex?' What was that about me being spared more blushes? I feel myself turning as pink as the roses in Alex's hearth.

'In your dreams, Tom, I think,' Mark cuts in, freeing

himself up from his ongoing discussion with Evie to leap to my defence. 'It was much more romantic than that, wasn't it Grace? I still have the scar to show for it, mind you, but it was worth all that pain.' Mark smiles at me, but there is a slight hollowness in his eyes I haven't seen before. I am more used to him looking at me as though he can't resist reaching out and touching me for a second longer.

'I think it beats the rest of us on 'how we met' stories, don't you?' Tom continues, throwing the topic of discussion open to all, much to my relief at no longer being the centre of attention.

'Well, Susie and I met on holiday in Spain when we were young, free and single in our twenties,' says Graham, picking up the baton. 'We were the classic corny holiday romance, both staying in the same hotel with a bunch of mates, then it turned out we didn't live that far apart back home. We got very drunk on Sangria one night, and the rest is history, as they say.' There was a collective ahhh around the table, then Alex, who is back at the table with the cheese board, chips in with her story.

'Peter and I were at school together, so we go back even further,' she starts, passing round the plates and cheese knives. She is brilliant at talking about Peter as if he is still around; well, he is in a way, as his children are so much a living embodiment of him. Some people who have lost a loved one either never speak about them in polite company, or make everyone else feel awkward if they do, as their sorrow is still so apparent. Alex does neither. When she speaks about Peter it's with a lightness of tone, as though he has just popped out of the room, and although she is very pragmatic about his death and its consequences for her and her children, she works hard at keeping his memory alive, for her sake and for theirs, too. They remember so little about him as it is.

'He used to throw things at me in Maths lessons,' she says. 'I thought he hated me and I didn't like him very much to start with, then when I told my mum about it, she said that boys that age have a funny way of showing it if they fancy someone. They get all defensive and react strangely around the girl. So I kept an eye on him which wasn't difficult as he was soooo gorgeous.' She flutters her eyelids dreamily at this point, lifting the mood, and raising a laugh from everyone assembled. 'But it wasn't until the end of term dance that he made a move. None of his mates were watching, so he stopped throwing cheese puffs at me and sidled up to me and very shyly asked me to dance. And the rest is history there too! We were married by the time we were twenty, while we were still students, so at least I had him for a long time before… everything else. Fate must have brought us together young as it knew we wouldn't have much time.' She says this with a smile and without showing any sign of the heartbreak I know she still feels, but it leaves a feeling of melancholy around the table as everyone thinks of the friend they have lost.

Someone needs to pick up where she leaves off to avoid us all getting maudlin, and James steps promptly into the limelight with his story.

'I spotted this hot babe who came in to sort out our

computer installation at work,' he says, grinning from ear to ear at Evie. I notice her roll her eyes. Poor girl is probably wondering how much mileage he will get out of the story this time. Some double-entendre references to sockets and mother boards as usual, no doubt, so she braces herself for the worst he can do, preparing to laugh it off if the need arises.

'She was grappling around with some wiring under my desk when I realised she was the one for me.' James can never tell the story straight. Evie had been far too senior at her software company to do the grappling around herself, she had merely overseen it from a project manager's perspective, which had meant lots of meetings with James. The meetings turned into lunches out, and then dinners, 'And the rest is history – again,' James finishes with a flourish, just to end his story in the same manner as everyone else, and looking up to ensure he has a rapturous reception from his audience.

'The only story we haven't heard yet is yours, Tom,' probes James. Very insensitive of him, I reckon, given that Tom is here on his own, and he knows how heartbroken his friend was after Sophie.

'But I haven't found the love of my life yet, so that doesn't count. When I do, I'll regale you all with stories of how it was,' he continues happily enough, not seeming bothered by James' gaffe.

'Whether it ends up being a chance encounter across a crowded room, a holiday romance that turns into true love or a good friend and colleague who I suddenly realise is more than just a mate.' I gulp. Tom can't be talking about me, can he? No, that would be silly. He must be talking about his new girlfriend, she's a teacher, too, after all. Tom and I have had one evening of some fun but fairly outrageous flirting, plus a couple of electrically charged accidental brushes against each other, and besides which, I'm spoken for, and he knows that. I had told him all that personal stuff about Mark and me, and he is sitting bang opposite Mark, too. I must be imagining the slight sideways glance that comes my way, then, after his final comment. Not eye contact as such, that would just draw attention to what he was saying. Although no one else around that table has any reason whatsoever to think that the person he is referring to might be me. No, I just have an overactive imagination, that's all.

Eight

'Bye, Alex darling, thank you for another fabulous evening,' I say, kissing my friend on both cheeks, and giving her a warm hug.

We are the last to leave Alex's house, though not by much. The others have left in dribs and drabs over the past half hour and Mark and I, being the most local, and with no babysitter to rush back for, offered to stay behind and help stack the dishwasher, now on its umpteenth run of the evening. Neither of us could bear the thought of Alex coming downstairs to all that, single-handedly, tomorrow morning. She had sent Lucy home a while ago; the poor girl is in the middle of exams and needs to get some sleep before getting back to her revision tomorrow.

The kitchen had still been a mess; most of the dirties had been brought through from the dining room, but the kitchen table had been piled high with dirty cheese plates, glasses, and crockery. I know Alex doesn't put her best crystal in the dishwasher so I had rolled up my sleeves, and reached for the marigolds and fairy liquid. 'You really don't have to,' Alex had protested. 'Yes I do,' was my fake-stern reply. 'Besides which,' I'd continued more cheerily, 'I always love a post-match analysis after dinner parties, so we can have one now. I'll wash, you dry, you know where everything goes.'

'So, how did you get on with Tom?' Alex enquires as we are washing up. 'Was it a bit weird sitting next to your boss all evening?' She knows where to hit the nerve, albeit unintentionally. Mark has been dispatched to the end of the drive with the rubbish, which needs sorting into recyclable and not, so I know he will be gone for a few minutes.

'No it was fine, lovely actually,' I reply, keeping my head down over the sink so she can't read anything in my eyes. 'He was really good company and we talked about all sorts. He got quite personal, but somehow I seemed to be able to open up to him. We talked all about the baby stuff, too. I was quite surprised really, we always get on well at work, but we've never talked like that before.'

'Well that's really nice,' Alex replies. 'You're both very professional people, you don't air your dirty laundry at work and I can't imagine Tom does either. Did he tell you much about Sophie? She really messed him up, poor thing. It's such a shame, he's a lovely man and he has so much to offer. Peter always thought really highly of him, you know. He knew him years ago. They weren't at school together or anything, but their families were quite friendly. I like to have him round now and again just to keep that connection going. Not to mention the fact that he's also our esteemed headmaster, and it's always nice to keep a finger on the pulse of the children's school!' she adds.

'How about you, how was conversation at your end of

the table?' I enquire, changing the subject quickly.

'James and Mark were great fun, as always,' she laughs. 'Although I got the feeling that Evie and James had a bit of a something going on. Did you pick up on that?'

'No, I didn't notice, what do you think it was?' I enquire. I had been so engrossed with Tom, I hadn't really tuned in to any subtleties in the relationship stakes between anyone else.

'I think they might have had a bit of a ding-dong before they arrived,' she continues. 'Something to do with a comment he had made about her parents, you know what an unsubtle brute he can be sometimes.'

I want to ask her about her conversation in the kitchen with Mark, but I can see the light from his torch coming up the garden.

'You and Mark seemed to have a lot to talk about,' I probe quickly, before he comes back into the kitchen. 'Was he OK?'

'I'll fill you in some time in the week,' she replies, also spotting him approaching. 'He's OK, just a bit confused, I think.' Alex has that knack of reassuring me with just a few simple words, and although she makes light of it, I am still concerned that it was her he had turned to instead of me.

'Hi ladies, how's the clearing up going in here then?' Mark comes striding through the back door. 'It's a beautiful night out there, loads of stars. Are you ready to go home then, my love?' He sidles up behind me and squeezes me around my waist, nuzzling into my neck.

'If Alex says I can go then yes, I am,' I reply, freeing

myself from his grasp. His clinches seem incongruous with his earlier attitude and I'm not in the mood for public displays of affection right now.

'Thank you both so much,' Alex says. 'You've saved me hours of clearing up in the morning. See you guys in the week. Have a good lie in tomorrow, and think of me up early with the kids!' she jokes.

It's just past one thirty as we wrap up in our warm coats, grab our torches, and head out of Alex's drive. Mark was right, it is a beautiful night, crisp and chilly, and here in the countryside, with no light pollution to spoil the view, the stars are out in full force.

'What a lovely night to be walking my beautiful fiancée home to bed,' Mark chirrups. He seems to have changed in temperament since the hollow-eyed look he had given me across the table earlier. He's probably had a bit too much to drink, which usually leaves him feeling more amorous than normal, but often with the inability to deliver. When he's like this, he will invariably whisper sweet nothings for ages, be all over me like a rash, then pass out in the deepest of sleeps as soon as his body hits the bed. Normally I find it quite endearing and funny; tonight though, I have his earlier words of doubt buzzing round my head and I'm not in the mood for even gently fighting off his advances. I plan to take myself off to bed as soon as we get home, to sleep and nothing more.

True to form, when we get back, Mark reaches for the brandy bottle, pours himself a large slug, and by the time I have returned from depositing my numerous items of outdoor apparel on the coat rack, he is snoring in the comfy armchair in the corner of the kitchen. I grab a warm throw from the back of the sofa, and place it carefully over him, planning to slip off to bed. But as I reach over to tuck it under him, he seizes me by the wrist, startling me with the suddenness and with the strength in his grip.

'Ow, you made me jump,' I say, 'I thought you were asleep, I didn't want to disturb you.'

'Not so fast, young lady,' he replies, for the second time this evening. 'Come here and give me a kiss before you go.'

I lean over, planning a quick pursed lips affair before shooting off to bed, but he pulls me onto him and in a quick movement somehow manages to flip us both over, so that I am the one in the armchair, and he is leaning over me. He kisses me hard, thrusting his tongue between my teeth, the bitter taste of the brandy harsh on his lips. His hands reach for my breasts, squeezing, pushing me back into the chair as his tongue thrashes around in my mouth. I find it anything but a turn-on and try to gently push him away. He isn't having any of it though; with his knee he succeeds in prizing my legs apart and I know that if I don't act now to stop him, what he is about to do is totally out of character and both of us will suffer in the morning, when realisation of what he has done hits home.

'Mark, please don't,' I plead, 'I'm tired and I need to sleep.'

I push him as hard as I can, and it is as though a light suddenly comes on in his head. The whole thing had only lasted a matter of seconds but it had felt like an eternity.

'Grace, I'm so sorry, I didn't mean to hurt you,' he says. 'I don't know what came over me.' He stands up and runs his fingers through his hair, and begins pacing the floor, trying to pull himself together. It's not like him to be brutal with me, or to ever try to force himself on me. He reaches for me and pulls me into his arms, gently this time, stroking my hair. I stand inside his embrace, arms by my sides, not wanting to reciprocate. 'I'm so sorry my darling, I would never hurt you, you know that, don't you?'

But I am scared at the glimpse of the man I have just witnessed. He is usually so gentle with me; when we make love it is a two-way thing and always a mutual decision. If one of us isn't so keen, the other is always prepared to back off. How can we have gone from our passionate encounter in the shower, only a few hours earlier, to this?

Nine

I wake late to sunshine streaming through the curtains. Looks like another gorgeous spring day. I turn over to find Mark's side of the bed empty, but still warm. He has been to bed then, at least. After the events of the night before, I'd taken myself off upstairs as quickly as possible, needing to put some space between myself and Mark, and had left him pacing around the kitchen, beating himself up over the way he had treated me when we had arrived home. I still can't quite get my head around the whole evening, there is so much flying around in my brain.

It's tempting to pull the duvet back over my head and sleep for a few more hours, avoiding having to think about it and trying to make some sense of it all. Also, I'm not really ready to see Mark yet, I can't begin to imagine what sort of frame of mind he will be in today, and whether there will be an uneasy atmosphere between us. I can't see how everything can just slot back into normality, as if it had never happened. We certainly have some issues to talk about, and it's going to be hard work. Mark and I have always been two halves of the whole. At this moment in time, I couldn't feel less like that matching half, and I need some reassurance that everything is OK and can get back to normal, if that's what we both want. I'm not used to all these emotional ups and downs. So much seems to have happened in such a short space of time. I find it unfathomable that by agreeing to try for a baby with Mark, only a matter of days ago, we have stirred up so many strange emotions and created something of a barrier between ourselves already. Is that a sound basis on which to start a family? Somehow I don't think so.

I shower and dress quickly, the warm water coursing over my hair and body waking me up and giving me a little more courage to face whatever is waiting for me downstairs.

On the kitchen table there is a note, and a bunch of daffodils from the garden in a vase. 'Grace, so sorry. Love you. PS Gone out for croissants, back soon,' it reads. The coffee machine is on, the table set; Mark is obviously planning a conciliatory breakfast. No sooner I read the note, I hear his key in the lock, so there is no quick escape back upstairs to bed. He comes into the kitchen, bearing a paper bag from the deli, and looking somewhat sheepish. He doesn't say a word, but puts the bag on the kitchen table, comes over to me, puts his hands on my shoulders, stands squarely in front of me and kisses me gently on the cheek, stroking my face with the back of his hand afterwards. He bends down a little to look into my eyes for some sort of reaction.

'How are you feeling today?' I venture, peeling away from him and trying to keep the topic of conversation in neutral for a while, 'Alex had some nice wine last night. I think I had a bit too much.' I attempt a light-hearted laugh.

'My head is pounding, but I don't think it's the wine,' Mark replies, pulling out a chair and sitting at the table. 'I feel so bad about last night, Grace. I don't know what came over me. You know I would never try to force you to do something you don't want to, don't you?'

But isn't that exactly what is happening in my entire life? By agreeing to try for a baby despite my better judgement? And Mark daring to suggest that I should give up work to help make it happen? I am starting to feel that Mark is trying to control me. Things haven't exactly escalated into full-scale control-freak level but I feel we have gone from a couple on completely equal footings to me caving in to Mark when I don't really want to. I am just glad I'd pushed him away from me last night, and stood up for myself. God knows where we would be now if I had let him go ahead.

'I thought we'd just have a nice lazy Sunday today,' Mark carries on, changing the subject and attempting to lighten the tone. 'How about some fresh air later, a walk up the hill maybe? Exercise is supposed to be good when you're trying for a baby, isn't it?' He is starting to sound like a broken record. And to mention trying for a baby when there are so many other issues going on between us shows a distinct lack of understanding. Also whatever happened to me having an opinion on how we are going to spend our Sunday? It would be nice to be asked.

'Actually, I just fancy a quiet day reading the papers, thanks,' I reply. Let him go out and climb the hill if he wants to, clear his head and his conscience. A bit of distance between us and time on my own will do me just fine for today.

So Mark goes out on his big hill-climb later that morning. Given my unwillingness to budge from the sofa and therefore his lack of a walking companion, he has rounded up James and another friend, and they plan to make a bit of an afternoon of it, stopping off at a local hostelry on the way back for a spot of 'hair of the dog'. Let them have their boys' afternoon, I am completely happy with my decision not to go. I stoke up the fire in the living room, get a good blaze going, and settle down with the Sunday papers and a book I've wanted to finish for a while. I have a fleeting and vaguely guilty notion that perhaps I should be doing some marking at some point, but only for about five minutes and it soon passes. Work can wait till tonight if needs be. Right now I need a bit of indulgent me-time. I know it's a beautiful day outside, if chilly, and there are all manner of useful things I could be getting on with, but I need a bit of escapism, a good book to get immersed in and help the afternoon float by without having to engage my brain too much.

The 'beep beep' of my mobile gives me a start. I must have nodded off mid-page; the fire is roaring, my book open on the floor and my phone flashing with its 'message received' alert. I sleepily pull myself up and reach for the phone to see who could be texting me on a Sunday afternoon. Probably just one of the girls wanting to chat. It's Tom. My heart misses a beat and suddenly there is that strange churning sensation in my stomach again. How dare he shatter the peace of my Sunday afternoon? Why is he texting me today? I will see him tomorrow. What can't wait until then?

'Had really gr8 time last night, thx 2 u u were fab company, cu mon,' the message reads. Here it comes again, that warm and fuzzy feeling, and I smile to myself as I read the text for a second time. Should I text him back or just wait till I see him tomorrow? Dilemmas, dilemmas. But personally I hate it if I text someone and they don't reply within some sort of reasonable timescale, even if it's just to say 'OK' or 'thanks'. I am a mobile phone company's dream, I think to myself, as I type in my reply.

'Me 2, luvly eve, thnks, enjoy ur w/e,' I send back, nothing too bland, nothing too encouraging, and quite final I think – I'm not expecting anything back. I still haven't really got my head round what's happening here, but I do know that Tom is inching his way into my thoughts more than he should do on a normal weekend. Is it just a knee-jerk reaction to what I am going through with Mark? Surely it can't be more than that? I must have imagined the chemistry between us last night. I am spoken for, after all, and don't make a habit of spending my time thinking about other men or enjoying frissons of excitement when they accidentally brush against me. I'm not actively looking for attention elsewhere, so why is it seeking me out?

Beep beep. There it is again. Another message. Surely not Tom again? I reach to pick up my phone from the floor, but this time it's from Evie.

'Howz ur head? U & T have gd chat last nite?!!' it reads.

Oh God, had it really been so blatantly obvious to all around the table that Tom and I had spent pretty much the entire evening engrossed in each other? I hope it hadn't looked too bad. Funny how Mark hasn't mentioned anything about it, in spite of all that has happened between us since then. I suppose he thinks it's natural that I should sit and chat all evening to a man who is my boss. After all, we have heaps in common, probably lots to talk about, and see each other every day, so there is nothing unusual in that from where he is sitting, is there? He wouldn't be setting out consciously to look out for any signs of flirting. Nothing above and beyond the way Mark and I flirt normally, anyway. There is no reason for him to suspect that I might have enjoyed being seated next to Tom just a little more than I should.

I reply to Evie, just to shut her up if nothing else.

'Head fine, having lazy day on sofa. T good co thks.' There. I will leave it at that, and I press the 'send' button quickly. I don't know why Evie is digging around. After all she had spent most of her evening monopolising my partner, to the extent that when he wasn't pouring his heart out in the kitchen to one of my best friends, he had been deep in conversation with my other.

Beep beep. Not again. I am starting to think turning off my mobile would be a good idea this afternoon. So far I have managed to read one section of the Sunday Times, given that up as it's a bit large and unwieldy to read in a position of horizontal-ness on the sofa, had two little naps, and re-read the same paragraph of my book several times over. Not very indulgent for a self-indulgent afternoon which is already halfway through. Being idle seems to take an awful lot of effort. No wonder I don't do it very often.

I check my phone again. This time it is Tom. I wish he wouldn't keep creeping into my thoughts, and it's not helped by him making himself a physical presence in my living room by virtue of modern technology. There he is, blue light flashing away, *Read me, read me*, you know you want to really. Why doesn't the world outside recognise that I am working really hard at having a lazy afternoon here? Might as well have got on with that marking after all, then all these texts would have been a welcome diversion rather than a pain in the backside.

'Look fwd 2 c u 2moz. Wear THAT DRESS?? xx'. This is getting dangerous. Next he will be telling me what underwear to wear, and to meet me in his office at 10.50 for a quick bit of hanky-panky before the bell rings for the end of break. No, no, no, calm down woman, that's my fantasy. (Is it?) I astound myself at how easily that thought popped into my head. Tom's texting is straying beyond the friendly and chatty, off the straight and narrow and back to the flirty and downright naughty. He can't possibly know I'm on my own. For all he knows, I could be sitting across the table from Mark, eating Sunday lunch in some country pub or other, and there are his texts, popping up and interrupting our quiet afternoon *à deux*. But then I suppose I could have done the sensible thing, chosen not to be interrupted, switched off my phone, and ignored it, in order to spend some quality time with my partner. It almost feels like Tom knows I am alone this afternoon, like he can see me lounging here on the sofa in front of the fire, all by myself. Perhaps he is in the garden, watching me through the window like a stalker. Now I know I'm being silly, he just isn't the type. But still I feel like getting up and closing the curtains.

I take the decision not to reply to that last text; to do so is asking for trouble. Perhaps Tom is just waiting to see how far I will go. Well that's it, I'm stopping now. The end. I won't give him the satisfaction of knowing he has me twisted in knots. I switch off my mobile and throw it across the room onto the other sofa. No more interruptions, just me-time now. Mark can always call me on the land line if he needs me, which of course he won't. I lay back on the sofa, staring up at the ceiling, arms folded across my chest, trying to make myself relax. I try doing that thing they sometimes do at the start of a massage; making you consciously clench all your muscles, from feet up to neck, then release them all one by one and relax. It doesn't work. I still feel tense and my brain is working overtime. I don't hold out much hope for any more reading, I'm not sure I have the concentration. Too many distractions early on have put paid to that and now I just don't fancy it. I lay gazing upwards, finding shapes and faces in the stain left from when the shower had leaked last year and soaked through the floorboards and down through the ceiling. It has been painted over a couple of times since, Mark hates any imperfection, but still it seems to creep back, as though it has decided it wants to be a permanent feature of the house, not just a blot on the ceiling. Mark would go bonkers if he knew it was still showing and blame the painter for a bad job; he doesn't do much lazing on the sofa and gazing into space, so probably hasn't noticed it. I will give our painter-decorator a call on Monday.

I wake to the click-click of Mark's footsteps on the ceramic tiles in the kitchen. I didn't hear him come in. What time is it? I must have dozed off on the sofa – again. I am no good at this lounging around lark; either I lay on the sofa feeling anxious or like I should be doing something more worthwhile, or fall asleep, with no happy medium. The fire has burnt down quite a bit and the sun has lost its glow, so I guess it must be late afternoon. Oh well, I haven't wasted too much time dozing then. It takes me a few minutes to pull myself up and lose the disoriented feeling that falling asleep in the daytime always gives me. I have to work out where I am, what day of the week it is and what's going on. No different to any normal morning then, Mark might argue. Waking up isn't a thing I do easily at the best of times.

Mark comes into the living room. 'Ahhh, you're all lovely and sleepy,' he smiles. He leans over the back of the sofa to give me a kiss; I make sure it lands on my cheek, but he doesn't seem to notice what I think is my obvious slight turn to one side. It looks like the walk has done him good; his cheeks are glowing, although that could be from the cider in the pub rather than the fresh air from a tough hill climb. His eyes are sparkling and he looks as though he has had a thoroughly enjoyable time.

'You look happy,' I pipe up, rubbing the sleep from my eyes. 'Good walk? Where did you end up?'

'Well James wanted to head over to the Crown at Cherington but then Tom suggested a pub he knows over the other side of the hill so we headed there for a late lunch, then hacked back over the hill afterwards. It was great, we saw deer, foxes, even a badger, you would have loved it.'

I don't really hear what he says after the word 'Tom'. So Tom had been the third person to go with them. That means when Tom was sending me provocative texts earlier, he'd been either walking, eating or drinking alongside my fiancé. Sneaking off to one side to send me flirty little text messages, secure in the knowledge that my partner was safely out of reach and that he could text me without Mark accidentally picking it up. Not that we ever share phones anyway, but I wouldn't have wanted to risk it if it was the other way round. I can't believe the audacity of it. No wonder I'd felt he knew I was alone this afternoon; what sort of weird kick did he get from texting the partner of one of the friends he's spending the afternoon with? It's just too bizarre. It makes me go all funny inside. But somehow it's exciting too. I can't work out what's going on with my emotions. Part of me is disgusted that Tom is behaving like this, but on the other hand it makes my knees turn to jelly with excitement and anticipation. I am torn between thinking he is a complete pervert and an absolute charmer. How close the two are, really.

'So Tom was the third man today,' I probe. 'How was he? Did he enjoy last night?' I try not to sound too much like I am interrogating him.

'Yes, he said you were scintillating company,' Mark

replies. 'He was up to something today though, kept texting someone, probably that new girlfriend of his I should imagine. He was very cagey about her, couldn't get much out of him. He must be quite keen, by the look on his face when he was texting her, he had a right old glint in his eye.'

Gulp. That was me then. Unless of course Tom had been doing the dirty and sending flirty texts to me AND to this new girlfriend he had told me about last night. That would really take the biscuit. In that case he *would* fall into the pervert category and not charmer. I'm not sure how I'm going to deal with seeing him tomorrow. Play it cool and act completely normal, that has to be the strategy. And on no account wear THAT DRESS.

Ten

Monday morning is a weird one. I feel like a teenager with her first crush, nervously waiting to see how the object of her desires will react when he sees her, reading things into actions, words, that aren't really there, looking for signs that he likes her too.

I remember when I really did have my first crush. Ironically it had been on my science teacher, but then teacher crushes must be so common amongst hormonal teenage girls, I suppose. He was a gorgeous, strapping, athletic sort of chap, probably less than ten years older than I was, almost fresh out of teacher training. I can't have been the only girl to fancy him; he was the sort of bloke who could silence a classroom of fifteen year olds just by walking in, pulling out his chair, glancing round the room with a lazy smile and sitting down. Even the boys seemed to be struck dumb by him; he was that much of a god he had them all aspiring to be just like he was, bright and funny, fit and muscled. He used to wear fairly tight-fitting tee shirts which showed off his perfect form, hard, well-worked out pecs bursting forth and triceps displayed nicely where his short sleeves ended. It still makes me go weak at the knees just thinking about him now. I succeed in bringing myself back down to earth when I calculate that by now he is probably forty-something, most likely married with a gaggle of kids, no time to work out any more, and all that lovely muscle has probably turned to beer belly and flab. It may well not have done but it calms me down, at least, and stops my pulse racing.

I brace myself for seeing Tom. I have to try to act normally, not give him any indication that he is sending me into turmoil. For all I know, it might be all in a day's normal behaviour for him, just that I haven't been the object of his attention until now.

Our school day generally starts with a brief staff meeting; more of a quick roll-call really to make sure we are all up to date with what's going on in the school, and to discuss any issues ahead of us that day. Tom breezes into the staff room in his regular high-energy way, filling the space more than I usually notice with his tallness, his wide shoulders and athletic demeanour. I had never really noticed how big and powerful he is. We are a bunch of fairly petite women; today he seems like a giant in comparison. *Pull yourself together woman*, I say to myself, *take your eyes off his muscles and his lovely blue eyes, they have never distracted you before. Focus on your class and the day ahead. Stop being so girly and so easily swayed by a handsome face and a fit body.*

'Morning all, hope you all had a great weekend,' he begins. He glances round the room at all seated, making eye contact with every one of us, and smiling in that warmly welcoming way he has. His eyes meet mine and hold my gaze for a few seconds. Then I cough self-consciously and look down at the documents in my lap, my hands nervously going to my hair, then back to my lap, pretending to rifle through my papers to disguise how they are trembling. How on earth am I going to work here like this? Is every day going to be full of highly-charged sexual tension from now on? Gone is the relative peace and tranquillity (this is a school, after all) of my normal day; every moment I'm not standing in front of my class will now be spent either avoiding Tom or reading things into his every word. I need to switch this schoolgirl crush off before it gets the better of me.

Meeting over, we set off in the direction of our respective classrooms to prepare for the onslaught of the children, who will be arriving in the playground in ten minutes or so.

'Grace,' Tom calls behind me as I make to leave the room. 'Can I have a word?' Oh dear, here we go. All the others have carried on so I am alone with him.

'I hope I didn't make you uncomfortable yesterday, I just wanted to say how I really enjoyed your company on Saturday night. It was great to spend some time with you away from this place and get to know you a bit better.' There is no sign on his face of the flirtatious Tom I had seen at the weekend. He looks every inch the professional. Gone is the teasing twinkle in his eye, and the overtly flirtatious body language. So maybe things will be OK after all. Perhaps it's all in my head. Well, if he can bottle it up and remain professional, then so can I. I sigh inwardly with relief. Maybe it won't be so bad after all.

'I need someone to help me with a presentation for the next Parent Information Evening, Grace. I thought you would be the perfect man, or rather woman, for the job? What with your creative talents and how brilliant you are with PowerPoint. Do you fancy it?'

'Um, yes, fine, OK then,' I stammer. Barely over the return of Tom from flirty to professional, I feel a little put on the spot and can't think of any good reason why I shouldn't work with him on this. Other than the fact that he flirted with me so outrageously at the weekend, of course. So I find myself accepting the challenge, or rather acquiescing for lack of a valid excuse. *No, I can't possibly work with you, I find you far too attractive and dangerous, and I'm afraid of being unfaithful to Mark,'* wouldn't really be an appropriate thing to say right now.

'Let's have a quick chat after school then, shall we? Quarter past three in my office? Great, see you then.' He doesn't wait for a reply, and as it's only a few minutes from the bell going, I have to scoot off back to my classroom, again wondering about what his real agenda is. But then he has enlisted my help on numerous pieces of work like this, and I've never normally given it a second thought before jumping in and offering my assistance. Why should today be any different?

The day passes busily but without incident and three o'clock comes all too fast. Luckily for me and my addled emotions, I barely have time to give Tom a second thought all day, and our paths haven't actually crossed much. Six full hours packed with literacy, a bit of history, numeracy and spelling tests, a visiting governor to entertain, and I am exhausted but satisfied. I love my job and I love days like today, where the children have been warm and responsive, fresh back after the weekend and ready to learn; all the things I love about teaching and find so fulfilling. Days like today make me feel like the brilliant teacher I know I am.

All children departed, the school enters into that quietly eerie state of limbo that I find so comforting. I sidle into Tom's office and plant myself on one of his two comfy chairs. He is on the phone, to what sounds like a parent, so I tune out and gaze out of the window as the last few stragglers leave the playground.

'Hi Grace,' he says, freeing himself up and focussing his attention on me. The intense blue of his eyes is unnerving. They seem to bore into me as he smiles, and it's a very warm smile. It lights up his whole face. 'Good day?' he asks.

'Great. The kids were fantastic today,' I reply. 'I love days like today when it all seems so worth it.' Keep talking, girl, just keep talking and it will all be fine, I tell myself, and then there won't be any time to think or to spend gazing at him in awe like a love-struck teenager.

'I know what you mean. Sometimes I wish I was still in the classroom more, not tied up with all this admin and bureaucracy,' he confesses, waving an arm to gesture at the piles of paperwork forming mountainous peaks on his desk. 'Still, it's all in the name of career progression, I suppose. Do you think you'll want to move up the ladder, Grace? Do you fancy being a head in a few years' time?'

'I don't know really, part of me would love to, but I do get such a kick out of teaching, I think I would miss it too much. And I'm spoilt too, I suppose. Mark's salary means I don't have to earn megabucks. So I suppose all the time I'm still happy doing it, I'll carry on, and deal with it when the urge takes me.'

At the mention of urges there is a twinkle in Tom's eye. Or am I imagining it? Perhaps this whole attraction thing really is all in my head. I certainly hope so as I need to put it completely and utterly out of my mind and concentrate on what it is he wants me to help him with this afternoon.

But that's easier said than done. As Tom talks me through his ideas for the presentation, I find myself drifting off and staring at his arms. He has rolled his sleeves up and removed his tie; a more casual look now that pupils and parents are no longer around. I have always had a thing about men's arms, and find a good well-formed forearm more erotic than some of the more obvious erogenous zones. His are muscular and sinewy, and covered in a fine blond down, not the sort of wiry, dark hair that men usually sport on their bodies. He clearly works out, as the muscle definition is perfect. As he gestures with pen in one hand, I can see the sinews and tendons moving and working, and I wonder what it would be like to stroke them. How soft would they be? Or to have those hands stroke me. His hands are large and strong, I don't know why I haven't noticed before, and perfectly groomed. They are soft, office-boy's hands; clearly he doesn't spend too much of his spare time doing the garden or chopping logs. His nails are smooth and clean, and cut neatly, and the skin on the backs of his hands is totally unblemished. How have I managed to work with this man for so many years without noticing how physically perfect he is? The trouble is, now that I have noticed, it's just staring me in the face and it won't leave me alone.

I can't help but wonder what his chest is like. There is no sign of any hair peeping out the top of his unbuttoned shirt. Probably just as smooth and soft as his arms. And as muscular and defined? Probably. I wonder what it would be like to run my hand over it, feel the muscles flexing, stroke that broad expanse of hairless skin. I shift uncomfortably in my chair, trying to disguise just how sexy I find this man sitting in front of me and how turned on he is making me feel. For goodness sake, I am an engaged woman, and far from starved in the passion department. Anyone would think I was a lonely housewife, in need of a good romp, eyeing up any handsome male who happens to be in the vicinity.

'Grace?' he asks. 'Are you OK?' I snap out of my reverie.

'Sorry, I'm fine,' I mutter, 'just a bit tired.'

'I lost you there for a moment. You seemed to glaze over. Everything alright?'

Does he really think that now we have shared a few confidences at Alex's, I am going to pour my heart out to him just like that? My new confidant? I wonder what he would make of me saying 'Actually, if you really want to know, I was just gazing absentmindedly at your beautifully honed physique and wondering what it would be like to touch you.'

Maybe not. I wouldn't like to guess at who would be

more terrified, me or him. The odd thing is, I *don't* want to be unfaithful to Mark. I have never spent time ogling other men or checking out what else is out there. It just isn't me. I've always been content in the knowledge that Mark is mine, he is gorgeous and everything I could want, and we are together forever. My eyes have never strayed beyond the two of us. But something has rocked that world though, and I find it hard to reconcile to the idea that Mark's proposition about having children has been the only catalyst to spark this progression from devoted fiancée to potential adulterer. It makes me question how strong our relationship was in the first place or whether there is some underlying layer of dissatisfaction that has now been uprooted, after only a very small amount of digging.

Somehow I manage to get through the rest of the meeting, and grasp the gist of what Tom wants me to do. I am tasked with writing the first draft of the presentation and we will get together again in a couple of days to go over it and bash out ideas. When we finish, I hastily gather together my things and beat a speedy retreat out of his office and back to my classroom. I have quite a lot I still need to do, loose ends to tie up from today and material to prepare for tomorrow. I need to get them done as quickly as I can and head back to the relative safety of my home, remind myself that that is where my life is, that Mark will be home from work in a couple of hours, and that life is totally normal. And put some distance between myself and temptation.

Mark comes home that evening in a vile mood, after a

horrendous day in the office. When he's like this I find the best thing is to offer comfort and provide a sounding board if that's what he wants, or keep well out of the way if he just wants space, which he does sometimes. Apparently there had been a serious hitch with one of his contracts, and it looks like they potentially stand to lose one of their larger clients. So fairly major, really, I can't blame him for being a bear with a sore head.

He doesn't want to talk, though. What he does want is a stiff drink; he manages to knock back half a bottle of wine within ten minutes of arriving home. The first glass disappears without touching the sides and he quickly refills his glass and carries on, sitting at the kitchen table and staring into space. I try to be supportive, try to offer a shoulder to cry on, but my efforts are rejected. He doesn't mean to be nasty, or to push me away deliberately, ' sure; it's just his way of dealing with tough times. He will bottle it all up and stew on it for a bit, drink a lot, get a sore head, then maybe talk it all through with me tomorrow when he's had a chance to calm down.

I'd had a brilliant day at work, and despite the meeting with Tom and my mixed emotions when I'd left his office, I am still on a high from my day. I know Mark is suffering though, and it's difficult not to be dragged down by his all-pervasive foul mood. But it will pass. He will be fine and he'll talk to me when he feels he needs to. In the meantime, there isn't much point my going to a lot of trouble over dinner, as undoubtedly he won't touch it, and will later slope off to his study with the bottle of wine (and possibly a second one too) to drown his sorrows. I don't feel that hungry myself; my stomach is still churning from earlier, with that strange feeling of not needing to eat that I remember when I first met Mark. Almost as though I am on an adrenaline drip; excitement buzzing through my veins and overriding the need for food. I settle on some cheese and biscuits for myself, check Mark doesn't want me, or sustenance, or anything else, and leave him to it. I take myself off to watch a bit of early evening TV, plate of food in one hand and glass of wine in the other, feeling a bit guilty that I have abandoned him in his hour of need, but I've tried. What else am I supposed to do?

'Beep beep'. My phone is going off again – another text. I seem to spend my life texting. Most of our social life is arranged via text; I wonder now how we coped in the days when all we could do was pick up the phone and speak to someone, or, heaven forbid, send a letter.

'Thanx 4 ur help this pm, have a luvly eve xxx'. It was from Tom. He's never been one to text me much in the past; only if it was something work-related, such as a meeting reminder, and that would have been sent to the other teachers too, not just me. We don't do personal texts generally; we are colleagues, not text buddies. And now he is sending me messages out of school hours. AND with three kisses too. Those kisses suddenly seemed to jump out of my phone at me, flashing ALERT! ALERT! ALERT! This is more than just a professional thank you, isn't it? Besides which, I don't feel I have done anything exceptional this afternoon, above and beyond what is expected of me in the name of my job. A thank you isn't really necessary. So why all the attention all of a sudden? It doesn't really help with my attempts to rationalise what's going on between me and Tom. Well, what is going on exactly? So far the trail of events as I see it is like this:

- boss sits next to me at a supper party and flirts heavily
- he gives off lots of signs that he fancies me, even though he knows I am happily engaged, AND trying for a baby
- he sends me texts whilst he is out for the day with MY partner
- back to normal at school on Monday and is professional and detached again
- he asks for my assistance on a project and I spend the meeting ogling him
- he texts me to say thank you for my help and adds three kisses

So nothing that condemning there then? Nothing that could in any way be considered especially naughty or dangerous. Is there? The trouble is that I have never suffered this kind of conflict in my adult life before. I am usually a paragon of virtue, always have been a 'one-man-woman'. So why am I feeling so up and down and all over the place, unable to concentrate in the face of his physical presence, analysing everything he says, trying to interpret his feelings from his words and actions? I can only equate it to being a teenager again, only this time I already have one man, and I'm going through all this soul-searching over another. Something isn;t right here and it's starting to worry me just a bit.

Now I have a choice; either to ignore Tom's text, or send a reply. Well, that's an easy decision. I pick up my phone and type 'No probs, will get 2 work on it 2mrrow, u have a nice eve 2.' Now, do I add kisses as he has done or just go for the nice but professional approach? I normally end almost every text with just one 'x', and never think twice about it, so it seems odd not to put one in here. It's just a friendly way to end a message, after all, as text messages can sound so blunt sometimes. OK, bite the bullet then. In goes the 'x' and I hit 'send' quickly before I can change my mind. Done. Sent off into the ether with no turning back. Let him make of that what he will. Somehow I doubt he will even give it a second thought. Men don't tend to analyse all the various nuances of expression in the same way as women do, they just take it all at face value. It's just one little kiss after all.

Mark emerges from his study around ten o'clock, looking a little worse for wear. Clutching an wine bottle and his glass, he makes for the kitchen and flicks the kettle on. I offer to make him a coffee; God knows he looks like he needs it. I put out my arms and he comes across for a hug, that universal cure-all with the ability to make us feel so much better about anything. He nuzzles into my neck. People all over the world and of all rank and file can hug and it's a fabulous thing, takes no time at all, costs nothing and yet makes all the difference. I can imagine Dennis Thatcher giving Maggie a big hug just after she declared we were at war with the Falklands, and even Prince Phillip giving the Queen lots of hugs when she was suffering her 'annus horribilis'. But I struggle with the thought of ANYONE wanting to hug Gordon Brown, although I'm sure the poor chap must get his fair share too. Sarah is a brave woman.

'Sorry Grace, I'm a grumpy old git sometimes' he mutters into my neck. His hands are roaming and starting to find my bottom, pulling me close, and I can feel his arousal through the fabric of his trousers. A drunken fumble is the last thing I fancy; there is nothing worse than snogging someone who has had far more to drink than you have, and smells like a pub during happy hour. He is a bit stinky; usually he will come home from work and jump in the shower, changing into something fresh and comfortable. He is not the most enticing proposition at this moment in time. I offer to make him something to eat, hoping that he can be distracted from my physical attributes by the rumbling of his stomach. Fortunately for me, it works. He is clearly starving, and the prospect of a sandwich, which he doesn't have to make himself (someone that drunk should never be put in charge of a bread knife) seems to cool his ardour. He struggles over to the table to watch me and wait whilst I prepare his supper.

And finally Mark talks to me. He takes me through the day's events, how things all started to go pear-shaped, and what is at stake. The wine seems to have done wonders for his thinking power amazingly enough; whilst he was ensconced in his study, he devised a plan of action for the following day, so suddenly things aren't looking so bad after all. Or at least he can see a way in which the problem might be overcome. He has such an amazing brain on him; he always astounds me at the schemes he can cook up from nowhere, but then he isn't paid a London lawyer's salary for nothing. He is a superstar. Suddenly I feel really proud of him and a huge surge of warmth runs through me. I know we have had our ups and downs recently, but he is still my Mark and I have an awful lot of love and affection for him.

I go into work the next day feeling like I have sorted everything out in my head. Mark and I had talked for about an hour; he had straightened himself out a bit and we felt so close it had helped to dispel the wandering paths in my mind about Tom. I have packed Mark off to work this morning with a bit more of a spring in his step than he'd come home with, and that makes me feel a lot better about our relationship. I feel we have a bit more direction as a couple, and we are gelling more than of late. Sometimes you just need a big upset like last night to force you to sit down and have a really good talk, and listen properly to each other.

As I pull into our road later that day, there is an ambulance parked outside Frannie's house, lights flashing. A sense of panic and foreboding taking hold of me, I hurriedly park my car and run over to her house. I can't bear the thought of her collapsing, or having a fall, and the poor old lady being carted off to hospital with no one to hold her hand in the ambulance. Bracing myself for the worst I approach one of the paramedics, to try to find out what has happened. As I am about to open my mouth, Frannie suddenly appears on her doorstep and I heave a sigh of relief to see her still alive and well, if a little pale and dishevelled. And in her dressing gown.

'Frannie, are you OK? What happened? What's the ambulance for?' The questions tumble out as I struggle to overcome the panic that had taken hold only a few minutes earlier.

'It's Mr Pearson, poor, poor man,' she utters, a sob catching in her throat. 'He just popped in for a cup of tea, and well, we got a bit carried away, you know, in the bedroom.' This last she proclaims in a loud stage whisper, behind her hand, discretion getting the better of her, although all the emergency personnel present clearly know the circumstances that have brought about Mr Pearson's collapse.

'It's his heart, you know,' she continues. 'There we were, going at it like a couple of rabbits,' I have to take time out here to compose myself. It's more information than my brain can handle. Good on her, though. I hope I still have the inclination and the energy at her age. As she explains what had happened, I consider the dazed expressions the paramedics were wearing when I arrived. No wonder they all look a bit shell-shocked. It's not every day you have to prise a pair of septuagenarian lovers apart because one of them has had a heart attack, pinning the other to the bed.

Fortunately for Frannie, her phone had been on the bedside table and she had been able to reach across and call for help.

Poor Mr Pearson is now in the back of the ambulance, his departure to hospital imminent, and I ask Frannie if she would like me to take her into town, so she can be at his bedside when he wakes up.

'No, dear, it's very kind of you to offer, but actually I don't think his wife would be too pleased, do you?' Despite everything, she can't help letting out a giggle at the thought of this, and she puts her hand up to her mouth to stifle her ill-timed mirth. The elderly wife and mistress, standing by the bedside, waiting for their husband/lover to wake up. What a thought. It could be enough to give the poor man another attack if he sees the two of them hovering over him. He'd probably think he'd died and gone to hell, to face his come-uppance for eternity, with the two of them fighting over him. I'd assumed, wrongly now it would seem, that Mr Pearson is a lonely old widower, seeking solace and a bit of company with Frannie. Not that she has been having an affair with a man who still has a living wife! She is amazing. I just hope everything turns out OK for Mr Pearson, and I wonder how he will explain it all to the current Mrs Pearson. That's village life for you, never a dull moment.

Eleven

Several weeks later Frannie is hovering in her garden as I arrive home from work, obviously waiting to catch me.

'I want you to be the first to know dear, I'm getting married!' Well, knock me over with a feather, I hadn't seen that one coming.

'So, who is the lucky man?' I venture. I know it's unlikely to be Mr Pearson, unless he has managed to recover from a minor heart attack, and bury or divorce his wife within the space of a few weeks.

'Do you remember those lovely young men who came in the ambulance when poor Mr Pearson was taken bad? Well, one of them was a real stunner, I could tell he liked me the moment he set eyes on me. Which is something as I was hardly dressed for courting that day, was I?' she laughs. She goes on to fill me in on the details. It turns out there was an older member of the recovery team that I hadn't spotted in all the confusion, a sixty-five year old man called Gerald, who was about to retire from the emergency services. He is the dashing 'young man'. Well, he is a good decade younger than she is so I suppose that makes him young in her eyes. It had been love at first sight, apparently. He had come back to visit her the next day to make sure she was alright in the aftermath of Mr Pearson's heart attack, and it had all gone from there. Amazing really. I'd not seen him coming or going, but then I had been wrapped up in my own busy little world recently.

'Marriage at last, then, Frannie,' I comment. She has always managed to avoid tying the knot in the past, in the avoidance of being stuck with someone who would become a burden to her later in life.

'Well, I think it's about time, you know,' she goes on, 'and with him being younger than me, I'm more likely to lose my marbles before he does. But he says that's fine, he's utterly devoted to me. At this rate, it'll be me having a heart attack on the job. He's a very sexy man, he says he wants to make love to me every time he sets eyes on me.'

Too much information again. Frannie cracks me up. She is always so full of the joy of life (and the Joy of Sex, too, by the sound of it).

'I'm so pleased for you Frannie, it's fantastic news.'

Just as I lean across to plant a congratulatory kiss on Frannie's papery cheek, a small, red car pulls up outside her house, and out springs a rather fit looking man of around retirement age.

'I presume this is your intended?' I ask Frannie, smiling at Gerald as he approaches the two of us. He is clutching a large bunch of pink roses, which he presents to Frannie with a flourish. I do believe I see her blush, and she comes over as coy as a schoolgirl at her first prom.

'Oh Gerald, you are a darling,' she drools. 'Meet my dear

neighbour, Grace.'

He really is charming, and incredibly good looking for his age, too. I can see what Frannie sees in him; she has done very well for herself there, but so has he. He is acquiring all the wealth she has tucked away over the years; she is from a very well-to-do background after all. And as she is childless it will all go to him eventually, I presume. Although judging by the look in his eye, that thought has barely crossed his mind; the man is absolutely smitten. She is acquiring a kind and gentle man who will look after her in her dotage, love, honour and worship her, and give her the experience of marriage and sharing a home that she has missed out on until now.

'I am so pleased for you both,' I smile. 'May I be the first to congratulate you,' I add, kissing Gerald on the cheek, as he stands there beaming like a teenager on his first date, and gazing at Frannie with big doey Labrador eyes.

I leave them to it and head into the house. It cheers me to the heart to see two people in the twilight of their years, embarking on a relationship that has more passion and commitment than many younger people would ever experience in their lifetimes. I have always been a great believer in Fate, and this is obviously what the higher powers have mapped out for them. I am so thrilled for them both.

Twelve

Spring half term is coming up and Mark and I have booked a week's holiday. God knows we need it. Things have not been easy at home recently; Mark threw himself back into work in the wake of the crisis a few weeks earlier. He had to work all hours to bring the client back on board, and succeeded too, much to his credit. But that meant our home life suffered, and not only because of his work. Things are far from good between us at the moment. We both recognise the fact but neither of us seems to know how to take things forward, or even what the true cause of our dissatisfaction is.

Surely a holiday will help us? A bit of time out from the daily grind, spend some quality time together, have proper conversations and rekindle the physical side of our relationship, which has dwindled seriously in the past few weeks. Mark has always had a very high libido, and I am generally more than obliging, even if I do need a little coaxing sometimes. But just lately there has been a clear demarcation between us in bed, with little touching, let alone love-making. It's like the Berlin Wall has sprung up between us. I am a firm believer that if the physical side of a relationship trails off, then the emotional side does too. How can you achieve the level of closeness there should be between a couple if you are afraid to touch each other? It immediately puts up a barrier, and once it's there it's very hard to demolish. All couples have their lean patches, we can't all be 'at it like rabbits' the whole time, *à la Frannie*, but as long as there is some sort of physical connection, even if it is only hugging or kissing, or doing 'spoons' in bed then there is still something holding them together.

In a way I am relieved that Mark and I aren't having sex; to fall pregnant now, with things as they are, would be disastrous. We are hardly in the right place to become parents at the moment. I haven't dared broach the subject of me going back on the pill and deferring our baby plans, even though it would be the most sensible option, as it seems to be an out-and-out admission that things aren't good and I'm not sure I am quite ready to admit that. Both of us seem to be very adept at burying our heads in the sand right now, both assuming, and hoping, that this will all go away in its own time. I know it's a very bad thing that we aren't physically close and that it is going to take some effort from both of us to get back to where we were.

So we leave for our holiday with our suitcases packed not only with clothes, cossies and creams, but with a vast pile of expectations that our time away will be an instant fix for an ailing relationship. The hotel is gorgeous, an old 'Palazzo' on the Amalfi coast; you can't really ask for a more romantic location. Reassuringly expensive, it really is first class and worth every penny. The views over the bay are fabulous, the sun shining and the May sky unblemished by cloud; not too hot but warm enough to lie on a lounger with a good book and get the basis of a reasonable tan. Quite perfect, really. And normally Mark and I would lap up a place like this; enjoying the luxury of being waited on hand and foot, eating gourmet food night after night, planning our days to visit the local attractions, or hiring a car to escape the tourist trail and explore the surrounding countryside.

This time, though, it takes us a while to settle in. Largely I think due to the fact that we aren't entirely comfortable in each other's company. We haven't spent much time recently being properly together. At home we manage to live our own lives, and the house is big enough for us to do that, our paths only converging at meal times and bed time. Somehow we have been living fairly solitary existences under the same roof. Now suddenly, here we are, sharing one room, with nowhere to escape to. Usually we would spend the first couple of days of a holiday doing practically nothing, glued to our loungers whilst we caught up with sleep and chat, learning to relax, away from our hectic lives. This time, within an hour or two of our arrival, Mark has read all the guide books in our room from cover to cover and has already planned out a long list of places he wants to visit. Not an ounce of consultation with me; he has chosen what he wants to do and his decision is final.

'It sounds lovely, Mark, but I'd just like to chill out here today really,' I comment as he explains his itinerary for the day over our first breakfast on our private terrace. We only arrived yesterday afternoon, and I am still at the unwinding stage, not ready to be whisked off to see all the sights. It looks to me like the hotel has plenty to offer for at least the first twenty four hours of our break; a beautiful terrace with amazing views and waiter service, luxury pool-side loungers with enticingly squishy cream cushions. The pool itself, heated too, which is unusual for Italy, but means that we can swim this early in the season. I don't feel the need to move too far from that, and I feel a huge pang of disappointment that Mark doesn't want to as well. We usually have similar ideas about how we want to spend our time on holiday, and high levels of activity this early on don't normally feature.

'OK then Grace, you stay here and 'chill out' as you put it,' he says pointedly. 'I'll go and see what Positano has to offer. I'll see you at dinner, if I'm not back before.' His tone is cool and detached. He doesn't seem to appreciate how it cuts me to the quick.

'I thought the whole idea was for us to spend some time together on this holiday, Mark?' I try not to sound pleading, but at the same time hope to appeal to his conscience. 'We're not going to fix 'us' if we don't talk to each other, are we?'

'Yes, but you could come with me, and you don't want to, so we can't talk, can we, if you're holed up here alone?' He isn't going to compromise. But then I am sticking to my guns too, so maybe I'm just as bad as he is.

'We wouldn't get much chance to talk amongst the heaving crowds, would we?' I say. 'This place is perfect for us to have a relaxing time together and catch up a bit. We could go for a walk later, if you want to?'

'We can talk at dinner. I need to get ready for my trip. The shuttle bus goes at ten thirty.' So that's that. No room for manoeuvre, he's off.

And the next couple of days of the holiday continue in much the same vein. We seem to have transposed our way of life at home to our holiday location; he goes off exploring, sometimes meeting me for lunch if he runs out of churches, monuments or other interesting historical relics to visit, otherwise staying out all day and coming back to the hotel for dinner. Mostly I dine alone at lunchtime, and I find myself enjoying the solitude, rather than resenting Mark's absence. I usually take a book to the outdoor restaurant with me, order a large glass of Pinot Grigio and a bowl of the pasta of the day, and read until my meal arrives, sometimes barely looking up to register what is going on around me.

Mark and I do talk at dinner in the evenings, but it's not easy going. There is no hand holding across the table, no playing footsie under the crisp white table cloth which would be long enough to hide our antics from other diners. It is as though a light has gone out in our relationship and neither of us can find the switch to turn it back on again. We talk about what he has visited that day; he recounts amusing anecdotes about places and people he has seen, and I tell him about the latest book I'm reading, or hotel gossip from around the pool. He is pleasant enough company, but we are more like just good friends than lovers.

On the third evening I decide to bite the bullet with the physical side of our relationship. I will seduce Mark, force him to make love to me, and make him realise what he has been missing over the past few weeks. After all, it isn't really that long ago that we last made love, weeks rather than months, surely we must be able to rekindle some passion, it just needs a spark to ignite it. We finish our meal with a glass of the local Limoncello, a gorgeously crisp citrus liqueur which slips down all too easily. So we order another, and then another. I reach for Mark's hand across the table and begin to stroke it. He gives me a strange look which I interpret as surprise. He doesn't pull away, but neither does he reciprocate. I am left there, stroking his hand which lays motionless on the table, and feeling a bit of a fool. I don't know how to interpret him.

'Shall we call it a night before we drink them out of Limoncello? They'll think we are a right pair of old sots,' I make an attempt at a joke to lighten things up a bit. Mark duly follows and within minutes we are back in our room, ripping the clothes off each other. Not much seduction required after all, then, so why the cold fish act downstairs? There is a focussed look in Mark's eye that I haven't seen since that night after the meal at Alex's house. I hope to goodness we're not in for a repeat performance of that. There is nowhere here I can go to get away from him, short of locking myself in the bathroom, and that isn't something I've ever envisaged myself doing. I'm not some downtrodden abused woman. But in the end his lovemaking is surprisingly tender; no strange behaviour, just gentle, normal, unreconstructed sex, and it's lovely. I have missed his touch so much, and lying naked next to him is more arousing than anything else he has done to me all evening.

'That was lovely, I've missed you,' I venture afterwards, as we lay sated and still entwined.

'I didn't think you were interested any more,' he replies. 'You're always busy when we're at home, you always seem so distant. Sometimes I'm afraid to touch you in case you push me away.' Funny, that's the way I've been feeling about him as well. Why hadn't we just talked about this so much earlier? It would have saved an awful lot of heartache.

'In any case, I thought Tom was the one you fancied now, not me,' he goes on. I sit up in shock, pulling a sheet around me and suddenly feeling uncomfortable in my nakedness. That's a bolt out of the blue. 'You talk about him all the time, sometimes I feel like a bit of a spare part.'

I'm not aware that I do talk about Tom as much as Mark says. I try to play it down.

'He's my boss. Of course he's going to come up in conversation.'

'Yes, but it's not so much in conversation as you coming over all dreamy-eyed and telling me what a great bloke he is, even if it's not in those words.'

I gulp, feeling sick. This isn't the post-coital relaxed talk I had planned. So far I hadn't considered my friendship with Tom, and that is all it is, to be a threat to my relationship with Mark. But it appears he views it as more of a threat than I do. Nor had I realised that I speak about Tom quite as much. Or that I look dreamy-eyed when I do. Maybe Mark is just being a jealous partner and over-reacting at the mention of another man's name? I don't talk about him that much, do I? I try to think back over our conversations of the past few weeks; to be honest I didn't think we'd had that many discussions about work, we'd been skirting around each other most of the time. And I wouldn't talk about him for any other reason, would I? I begin to doubt myself.

'And he texts you too, doesn't he? I hear you giggling at your messages. They're from him, aren't they?' Mark knows I spend a lot of time texting my friends, and I get the feeling he is trying to trick me into an admission, that he wants to find something concrete to put on me. The texts could have been from anyone and he would have no way of knowing.

'And at weekends too? That's hardly work related, is it?' Now he really is trying to put me on the spot. By now there is a gap as big as the Berlin Wall between us again. He is as far away from me on the bed as he could possibly get, running his hands through his hair in exasperation.

'You know what it's like, Mark. The girls text me all the time, that's how we sort out our social life, you know that.' I sound like I'm pleading, desperately. Actually Tom has been texting me more and more, but I'm not going to admit that to Mark. But his aren't always the messages that make me giggle; usually the amusing ones are from the girls, having a moan about their other halves or forwarding on something funny or rude. I feel cornered, like a rabbit in the headlights, but despite all that, I still feel I have a relationship worth saving, and I'm not admitting to anything. Besides which, I don't feel I have done anything wrong, but the evidence for the prosecution seems stronger, whichever way Mark looks at it.

Weeks had passed since that night at Alex's when Tom and I had sat side by side, and really nothing has changed. I still find him dangerously attractive, but it's like when you learn a fact, you can't then un-learn it. Now I have noticed just how gorgeous he is, I'm not going to suddenly find him unattractive, am I? Unless he turns into a psychopathic axe-murderer or something, and that doesn't seem too likely. Our friendship has moved on a certain degree, I suppose, in that we are now firm friends, in and out of school (although our paths don't cross that often outside school, despite his close friendship with James. Am I sorry about that? – Yes, I suppose I am). We spend a lot of time chatting in the staffroom and in his office, and I feel a good deal more comfortable in his presence than I did in the early weeks after the 'Big Flirt', as I call that night at Alex's. We have to work closely together; we are a small, tight knit unit at the school, we have no choice.

Tom has texted me on holiday, but I don't admit that to Mark. I haven't done anything wrong, but I can see that if I do confess to receiving (and sending) messages (every day in fact), then he will blow the whole thing out of the water and I am immediately *'having an affair'*. I don't need to give him any more ammunition. Actually Tom's texts have been quite ordinary, but then they usually are. They tend to be along the lines of a friendly checking-up; finding out where I am, what I'm doing, what have I got planned for the day, that sort of thing. Two friends keeping in touch, nothing more than that. No flirtatious messages full of innuendo and sexual connotation. Far from it. In fact we haven't moved on from adding the few 'x's' I had been so paranoid about only a few weeks earlier. We are in quite constant contact, I suppose, with at least four or five messages winging in each direction on most days, so I suppose Mark could misinterpret that as something going on, but they are all so innocuous I wouldn't have any hesitation about letting Mark see them, and I tell him so. Perhaps I secretly know he wouldn't dream of looking at them, and I am proved right.

'Don't be silly, of course I don't want to see your messages. If you tell me there's nothing going on, then I believe you. What exactly are your feelings for him though?'

'Feelings?' I say, sounding a little baffled. 'He's a good friend, nothing more.' A little bit of a white lie? Not many of my friends are male, for one thing, and none of them have Tom's hot body and gorgeous blue eyes. Who am I deceiving here, myself or Mark? Yes, I do fancy Tom. There, I have admitted it, if only to myself. Well, I can't go and tell Mark that, can I? 'By the way, Mark, that gorgeous head teacher of mine is an absolute God. I'd like to rip his clothes off and do unspeakable things on my desk with him.' I feel myself blush as this latest thought enters my head and hope Mark can't read my mind. I imagine I have 'LUST' written in large letters across my forehead for the world to see. I decide the best option right now, before I give myself away, is to nip this conversation in the bud and get some sleep.

'Come on Mark, stop being so silly and paranoid,' I say. 'Let's get to sleep, we're both shattered. Can we please have a day together tomorrow?' I plead.

'OK, in that case, why don't you come out with me in the morning?' I might have known it would be on his terms, but this time I decide to go along with it. Otherwise we will end up spending the whole week apart. We have a relationship to fix here; one of us has to give in, and it looks like it's going to be me. Again.

By ten-thirty the following morning Mark and I are bumping down the hill into the town, at quite a laborious pace, on the hotel's little shuttle bus, which despite the opulence of the hotel, is barely more than a cattle truck.

'This place is amazing,' I drool, open-mouthed. I'm not so much admiring the picturesque bougainvillea-covered dwellings which seemed to tumble down the cliffs as though they will drop into the sea at any minute. No, true to my usual form wherever I roam, I have spotted the shops. And these aren't just your average tourist shops packed with tacky souvenirs, useless ornaments or cheap jewellery which will turn your skin green on the first wear. No these are QUALITY retail establishments, all virgin and new and waiting to be discovered. By me, retail queen of the Midlands. Already we have chugged past the most fabulous shoe shop, with a sign outside proclaiming that they can make you a pair of soft leather sandals while you wait. I can smell the leather from the minibus, and close my eyes to inhale its intoxicating aroma.

Then there are jewellery shops, all of the highest quality, the windows crammed with unusual rings, necklaces and bracelets, set with beautiful highly-coloured stones. They are as bright and colourful as the town, and it seems almost as though the gems have been hewn from the surroundings themselves. There are clothes shops too, floral dresses, shirts and scarves oozing from the little shop fronts, inviting passers-by to come and look, touch, try and buy. I feel like flinging myself off that bus there and then and diving head first into this paradise of merchandise. It would be an experience for all the senses, not just the wallet. The textures, smells, sounds of a foreign town, with the promise of unearthing a real gem; an unusual piece of jewellery, a beautiful hand-crafted bag or a meltingly soft silk dress. I can't wait to get stuck in.

'Why didn't you tell me about the shops?' I turn to Mark, realising now what I have been missing over the past couple of days.

'Well, you seemed so determined to stay behind and 'relax", he says pointedly. 'Besides which, I haven't been shopping, I've been sightseeing, doing all the cultural stuff that you appear to be not so keen on.' He can't seem to speak to me without that edge in his voice. Actually I love the cultural stuff too, and I begin to wonder if maybe I have been a little over-stubborn in my refusal to join Mark on his daily excursions. But then again he has shown no willingness to stay behind with me either. We are both as bad as each other, neither wanting to acquiesce.

Suddenly there is a screeching of brakes, and horns sounding in all directions. I had forgotten what it's like to be in the middle of an Italian traffic jam, if it could even be classified as anything as civilised as a traffic jam. There appears to be a bit of a blockage a few cars up front, and in true Italian style, no one is prepared to wait. Just to our right a middle aged man, his face tanned to leather from the sun, is leaning out of the window of his tiny, beaten-up Fiat, both hands gesticulating madly in the air, wildly insulting the parentage of the driver in front. I can just about understand enough to grasp the colourful nature of his outburst. Not a happy chap. We seem to be surrounded by cars now; no one believes in queuing for anything here, and they don't do it in their cars either. Traffic jams become a mêlée of vehicles converging from all directions. Mark and I decide it might be prudent to disembark here, and leave our driver to find a way through the congestion. Besides which, we are outside all those gorgeous shops and wasting precious shopping time.

I begin to wonder how I am going to fit all my purchases in my suitcase when it comes to packing at the end of the week. I lay everything out on the bed to admire it and gloat over it all. It had been a fabulous day's shopping and I am on a retail high like no other. Mark hadn't been bitten by the same bug, and was out on our private terrace, on a lounger, reading a copy of *The Times* that he'd managed to pick up in town. I am busily getting things out of bags and boxes, stroking silken clothes, smelling the new leather on shoes and a bag I've bought, trying on jewellery and parading in front of the mirror, happy as a little girl with a new string of beads. None of it had cost a fortune, either. It's all quality, but not designer, and all original and different to anything you can buy at home. I am thrilled to bits. I select a softly draping cream silk dress which I will wear tonight, and some coordinating jewellery, and set about packing the rest back into bags and boxes, carefully folding clothes and trying as best I can to wrap them in their original tissue paper. I will probably have to ditch all the packaging in the name of fitting it into my suitcase, but for now I am happy to see all my purchases lined up in their smart paper bags, in a rainbow of colours and shapes, a trophy to my day's success.

Mark comes strolling through into the room. 'I've been thinking, Grace, and I reckon it would be best if you hand in your notice next Monday,' he utters, totally out of the blue. My head is still in the shopping zone and I look at him aghast.

Thirteen

I set foot back on home soil with a cracking tan and a suitcase full of new clothes, but without the feel-good factor that normally follows me home after a great holiday. Probably because it hadn't been a great holiday. Things hadn't really got any easier between Mark and me, in fact they were probably worse. We'd had a couple of day-trips out together, which were fine as long as there were some shops for me and some sights for Mark, but it felt at times like we were on different holidays, just sharing the same room.

I am gutted really. I'd had such high hopes that Positano and its sun and atmosphere would fix our relationship. Silly, but there you are. If we can't fix it at home, then what is the likelihood of it being repairable anywhere? I'm not really sure where we go from here. Although things are bad, neither of us has dared broach what happens next. Do we stay together, keep plugging away at it, hoping some spark will rekindle itself somehow, or do we call it a day and agree to go our own separate ways? Scary and unpleasant whichever way you look at it.

Mark's comment about me giving up work had been the

icing on the cake. I know he'd vaguely mentioned it when he first threw the idea of starting a family at me, and I'd tried to pretend I hadn't heard it. But he was deadly serious. For God's sake, I didn't want to have a baby with him at this point in time or even let him near enough to me to be able to father one, let alone give up the lifeline which is my career. I would have to be mad even to consider it.

Despite the way things are between us, bizarrely Mark does still talk about us having a child together. Come on, if a holiday can't fix our relationship, then all the stresses and strains of parenthood aren't going to make one iota of difference to the way we are with each other, are they? Isn't early parenthood supposed to be really stressful and hard work, neither parent having time for the other whilst caught up in the demands of the newborn? Plus if things really are on the rocks, I have no ambition to be a single mother, left on my own to face nappies and broken nights whilst Mark goes off and builds a new life with someone else, as undoubtedly he would. A child deserves parents who are happy and together, not ones who are using it as a means to test whether their own relationship will succeed or fail. That's far too much to put on narrow shoulders.

I had really exploded when Mark brought up the giving up work idea again. I was still away with the shopping fairies on my fluffy retail cloud, and being a house-bound expectant mother was the furthest thing from my mind. And why would he see my being stuck at home as a fix to our a) bad relationship and b) failure to fall pregnant as yet. (Wouldn't he need to be home too for that to happen?) I don't have much recollection of what I actually said to him in reply, but I do remember a lot of arm waving and gesticulating – must have been the Italian influence on me, I was going native. We had left things completely up in the air, neither of us with a solution to the way forward, both expressing our opinions, which it would seem, were poles apart.

I can't wait to get back to school today. I need to escape the house and Mark, and return to some sort of normality, whatever that might be. I get the feeling Mark is chomping at the bit to get back to work too. He spent most of yesterday in his study, reviewing client files, as though he had been away for six weeks, not one, and had forgotten what was going on. That suited me fine; I was able to prepare myself emotionally and practically for today. I would be seeing Tom again, for one thing, plus I had a lot of unfinished prep that I'd left until after the holiday, as I hadn't really been in a state of mind to concentrate on it before. I am probably no more in that state of mind now, yet I somehow feel more focussed; now that I know I am wasting my time trying to improve things with Mark at the moment, I can concentrate on work as it is something I know I can get right and do well, and it gives my life the direction that it's lacking in other areas.

So it is with great relief that I finally leave the house on Monday morning for the short drive into school. Just getting into my own car, on my own, with just me and my own pleasant company, feels like a release. No one to worry about upsetting or saying the wrong thing to. No catty comments or undercurrents. Just me. For ten minutes, at least, and then I will be at school. Where Tom will be too.

And how do I feel about that? Excited, actually, I have to admit. Not in that heart-racing, lust-inducing way of a few weeks ago, but in a much warmer and more comforting way, as though he is my refuge in stormy seas. I can't wait just to see him, have a good chat, catch up on news, hear what he's been up to, all that sort of thing. We continued to text throughout the holiday – it was all fairly innocuous stuff, but it had been nice to know he was thinking of me. I hope we manage to find some time on our busy first day back. And what I really crave is a hug. Tom and I haven't ever hugged – in some friendships you do, and in others you just don't, and we are of the 'don't' variety at the moment. I suppose I am missing closeness generally, as there is no physicality on any level between myself and Mark right now.

'Hi, Grace, good to see you,' he says, sounding genuinely pleased to see me, as our paths cross for the first time in the corridor. He squeezes my arm and plants a kiss on my cheek. 'How are you, how was the hols?' As the questions tumble out he bends down slightly so that he is more at my level and his eyes are desperately meeting mine, searching for the truth in them beyond what the words will say.

'I'm good thanks,' I say, but he probably sees it differently. 'Nice to get some sunshine, but great to be back,' I grin, trying not to let him see that there is anything wrong. It's eight thirty in the morning; we don't have time to get into the intricacies of my holiday at this point in the day. Maybe later. I hope.

'How 'bout you? Do anything nice?' I ask, and I find myself wanting to know what he did day by day, hour by hour, whilst he was away from this place. And from me. He reels off a couple of things, but then I find I'm not paying attention. Because what I really want to do is climb inside those big strong arms and have a huge hug, lay my head against his chest and smell him, wrap my arms around his back, touch the smooth expanse of him, feel warm, and safe, and protected. I have to pull myself together quickly, and I shudder with the effort of it.

'I'll see you later, we'll catch up then,' he says, sensing my distraction, probably assuming I am preoccupied with the day to come, and bringing things to an end so that we can both get on with it. He squeezes my arm again and gives it a little rub, then he pauses, his fingers come up to my cheek and he strokes it a couple of times with the back of his hand. It's such a small gesture, but so intimate and gentle, and I want to grab hold of those fingers with both hands and pull them to me. I can't, so I make do with a quick smile and another glance at him, before I head off to my classroom.

Well that had been an unnerving start to my day. I hadn't been sure how I would react when I first saw Tom; we'd had no contact for over a week other than the texts we'd exchanged, and I hadn't known what to expect. What does he want from me, and more to the point, what am I expecting from him? I am worried about using him as an emotional crutch – it always seems fine to lean on your girlfriends in times of trouble, but is it the right thing to do to turn to another man with all my problems? Oh God, so much turmoil in my head, I'm not used to all this.

There are two men in my life, and I am not entirely sure how I feel about either of them. Tom is a lovely friend, but I have to be so careful here to make sure I concentrate on getting things back on track with Mark; he has to be my priority, that's only right. But I find myself thinking about Tom more and more. Maybe it is because he is the one who comes without all the emotional trauma attached – it's less complicated to think nice thoughts about him than burdening my brain with all the Mark issues.

Tom and I don't see much of each other throughout the course of the day – probably a blessing, as I need all my concentration to get me through it. It's a bit of a shock being back at work after a week of not doing very much. We are having another rehearsal for *Joseph* after school, so it's going to be a long day. Tom grabs me whilst I'm in the playground at the end of school, seeing off those not staying behind for the practise.

'I'll probably still be here later – pop by and see me, won't you?' he asks.

'Course,' I say, trying to sound non-committal, but knowing that I will be there like a shot as soon as the rehearsal is over.

The kids have me in stitches for the next hour and a half with their singing and dancing antics, and that's a great diversion. Somehow we seem to have managed to put our own comedy spin on *Joseph*, by virtue of the kids we've cast in the leading roles, who seem to be largely made up of the class clowns. I think the parents will love it – I know they will. I'm not going to change a thing, let it roll as they want to play it and just polish up the parts so that they are singing to perfection, and there are no slips other than the inevitable ones that always happen on the night when you are staging a production that's fully staffed with kids. No school show would be the same without those endearing little faux pas.

Tom is still in his office when I arrive back from the village hall after the practice. Nothing new there, he is always in with the lark and hardly ever leaves before six. So it wasn't like he was waiting for me specially or anything... I dump my stuff back in my classroom and tidy up a bit, clean the whiteboard and pin up the next day's lesson plan; I don't want to look too keen. Even if I am desperate to see him and have been waiting all day for this.

'Hi,' I breeze into his office, without knocking, feeling a bit breathless and full of anticipation – but of what I'm not really sure. Gone are all the formalities of the day, he has taken off his tie and unbuttoned his shirt, and his hair looks even more unkempt and wild than usual, as though he has been running his hands through it. Oh no, more glimpses of that smooth chest, how will I cope? He looks good enough to eat, and it's as much as I can do not to go straight over to him, perch on his lap and throw myself into his arms. Instead I throw myself into one of the squishy chairs in front of his desk. Some furniture between us is probably a good thing right now.

'I've missed you, Grace,' he says. He stands up and walks round to my side of the desk. I'm not safe here after all, but I'm not sure I want to be safe. Give me danger any day, if it feels like this. My heart is pounding, and I can hardly breathe. Tom pulls me up in one swift movement, and I am in his arms. Finally. It feels so good here, it feels right. His huge body dwarfs mine and I feel so safe, so comforted. I don't want it to stop. He nuzzles into my neck, and I am happy to stay like that, melting against his huge chest. I can feel his heart pounding beneath the firm muscle and bone.

He turns his head and his hair brushes against my face as his mouth seeks mine. It's just the briefest of kisses, gentle and fleeting. A kiss full of promise of more to come, but not so intense as to scare me off at the first embrace. He moves his head back so that he can look at my face, his arms still around me.

'Grace,' he says, his voice crackling, and there is so much depth in that one word. His hands unwrap from my body and he brushes my hair away, tucking it carefully behind my ears, and cupping my face in his hands. He kisses me again gently, then pulls me down onto one of the chairs and turns to face me on the other.

Wow. I am blown away. I am breathless and unable to speak, and I sit there, staring at Tom, trying to take it all in, his hand clasped in mine. I would be happy to be struck dumb forever if I could feel like that just from a hug and a couple of small kisses.

There is a knock at the door and I pull away quickly, feeling my cheeks blush scarlet. Thankfully other members of staff have the courtesy to knock before they come barging in, unlike me. It's Ginny, the Class One teacher, just clocking off for the night and popping in to say goodbye to

Tom. She looks at each of us in turn as we sit there side by side – fortunately there are now several inches between us – makes a brusque little 'hmmm' noise which could mean anything, says goodnight, and leaves. God knows what she thinks, but then she has no reason to think anything, I am often in Tom's office, during and after school. We're not always together on the comfy chairs, I suppose, so it does look a little more intimate than usual, but so what, everyone knows we have become good friends, don't they? I find myself not actually caring what she thinks; we have done nothing wrong and therefore have nothing to hide.

'Sorry about that,' Tom says, turning back to me once Ginny has left. I assume he is apologising for kissing me, not for the interruption. He takes hold of my hand again in both of his, rubbing the top of it with his thumbs. 'I've wanted to do that for so long. I can't stop thinking about you, Grace. Half-term seemed endless, I just wanted to get back here and see you. Knowing you were away with Mark was killing me.'

'Don't be sorry,' I reply, 'it was lovely. A bit unexpected, but then in a way it wasn't really. I don't know what's going on in my head at the moment. I spent all my holiday thinking about you, when I should have been trying to make things work with Mark. It was what kept me sane. I was terrified about seeing you today, because I knew it might make me realise that what I feel for you is more than just friendship. And it is. And it didn't take you kissing me to make me realise that. I knew it as soon as I saw you this morning. I makes it all a bit more scary to know you feel the same way, because suddenly it's not just in my head any more, it's real.'

'I'm not a home-wrecker though, Grace, I know you are with Mark, but I have such strong feelings for you, I don't know what to do with myself sometimes. It sounds corny but I'd like to whisk you away from all this and disappear into the sunset, leave all our problems behind,' he says, his voice full of frustration.

'What about Alicia?' I ask. He'd told me a bit about the new woman he had been seeing, but hadn't mentioned her recently.

'It all finished just before half-term,' he replies. 'She could tell my heart wasn't really in it. In fact she asked me if there was someone else. I said 'no' of course, what was I supposed to say? I didn't know what to do about you, but over half-term, I realised I had to do something, had to let you know how I feel. Even if it meant you shooting me down in flames, I had to at least try.'

'So what do we do now?' I ask. 'I've never done anything like this before. I don't do cheating.'

'I'm sorry Grace, I've made you break your high moral standards.' Actually he doesn't look too gutted about this; there is a smile playing at the corner of his lips. He's secretly pleased to be the one to lead me astray, I think.

'I owe it to Mark to try to patch things up, we have so much history together,' I say, knowing I am saying the morally right thing, even if it's not really what I feel. I would like to dive headlong into Tom's arms right now and forget all about my loyalties towards Mark, even if only for a few moments. 'You and I need to try to be 'just friends' and I need to get things in order at home,' I say, knowing I sound much stronger than I actually feel. 'I have to know where I stand with Mark, this is all too much otherwise. I can't just give into this and have an affair with you, it's not what I do. Even if I want to,' I add, looking up at him. And I do want to, and he knows that.

'Mark's a great bloke, he's lucky to have you,' Tom says, which is pretty noble of him in the circumstances. Given that I could go straight back to Mark and patch things up and today's kiss would be a mere blip on the horizon of a rocky patch, and Tom would still be on his own. 'But I don't want to have just an affair with you. That's way too sordid. I want all of you, Grace, for keeps, not just for a quick fling behind another man's back.'

'I can wait, though,' he goes on. 'If you need time to sort yourself out and work out if you and Mark have a future together, that's fine,' he says. 'I'll still be here.' But he could be the one to end up with no one. My decision is between two men; I won't be the one to end up alone in all this.

Fourteen

Evie's car is on my drive when I get home. It's not like her to call round unannounced – she's usually too busy just to pop by and say hi – so my suspicions are instantly aroused. It sounds selfish, but after the intensely emotional experience I've just been through, I'd quite like to let myself in and sit alone in a darkened room for a while, and go over the conversation and sensations of the past hour with a large glass of wine in hand. I don't really remember the drive home; my head and heart were whirring for competition, but my brain in cruise control got me back safely without putting the car in a ditch.

'Evie, hi, are you OK?' I ask as she gets out of the car. She looks awful, not her usual perfect self at all. She collapses onto me and dissolves into floods of tears. This has to be a record afternoon for emotional outpourings. On any other day I'm sure I'd cope fine, but I am drained and feel like a bad friend who would rather not get involved.

'It's James, I think he's having an affair,' she blurts out between sobs. 'I know he can be a pig sometimes but I love him,' she wails. 'He can't leave me, what will I do?' All this from my strong, brave, independent friend, who, faced with her perfect world crumbling beneath her feet, turns out to be as mortal and easily bruised as the rest of us.

'Are you sure, what makes you think that? He worships you,' I offer, desperately clutching at reality. It would seem affairs are the topic of the day, then. My sudden transition from realising how easy it could be to embark on one, to seeing what possibly being the victim of one can do to a friend, is shocking.

I really genuinely don't think James would be the sort. Despite his shortcomings, he has never had eyes for anyone but Evie since they met, and kisses the very ground she walks on. But I know now how easy it is to rock that boat, and my own choppy waters are bobbing around me, waiting for me to choose which path to navigate.

I take Evie inside and pour a glass of wine for us both. Uncharacteristically she pushes hers away and asks for a cup of tea instead. 'I have to pick the girls up in a minute,' she says. 'Where have you been, anyway, you're late home tonight, I waited for you for ages,' she adds, slightly accusingly. Suddenly in the face of her own security being shattered she has turned into my mother, chiding me for coming home late. But I'm not about to embark on an explanation for that right now – I think Evie has enough to deal with without adding my problems to her own, and it wouldn't really be appropriate subject matter in the circumstances – so I quickly turn the conversation back to her, and ask her why she thinks James might be cheating on her.

'He's always on the phone, making secret calls, then

hanging up when I come in the room. To his PA of all things, out of hours, too. She only works nine till four so what reason would he have to call her in the evening if there wasn't something going on? I've started checking his phone, looking in his pockets, all those things people do in films. It's horrible, Grace, I'm so scared. How could he? I wouldn't mind if she was ten years younger and a bimbo… Well I would mind just as much, but you know what I mean. But she's well into her forties and a bit mumsy, if you get my drift.'

'Have you talked to him about it, confronted him?' I ask.

'No, I'm too scared. He doesn't even know I'm upset about anything,' she replies. 'As far as he's concerned there's nothing wrong. It's so hard keeping up this act.' We are so similar, us girls, both of us letting situations get on top of us and not confronting our partners and talking them through, instead playing along with things just to keep the peace.

'Right, here's a plan,' I say, more boldly than I'm feeling, but wanting her to go so that I can get back to my own issues. What a terrible friend I am today. I will make it up to her at some point, to appease my conscience more than anything else. Fortunately she's too wrapped up in her own dilemma to notice my abruptness. 'Drink your tea and calm yourself down, and go and fetch your girls. Then when they are out of the way tonight, sit down with James and ask him what is going on. Tell him what you think is happening, and what you've seen and heard. Don't settle for being fobbed off, you need to know the truth. Look at the effect it's having on you, you can't keep hiding that from him. You have to get this cleared up, and know where you stand one way or the other.'

I pack Evie off with sensible suggestions and reassurances that it will all be OK, and I hope I have given her enough confidence to face James. My gut instinct tells me somehow that it *will* be OK; hopefully Evie has just got the wrong end of the stick about something or other. She has no tangible evidence to go on, after all. I hope it's not just wishful thinking on my part. I had always thought Evie and James' marriage was so good; I don't want anything shattering the illusion that married life *can* be perfect. I still need to be able to worship at the altar of someone's flawless life.

Mark has texted me to say he won't be home till late tonight. That's good; I am planning a long soak in the bath, with scented candles and a glass of wine on the side. I don't need interruptions, and I certainly don't need bad feeling, uneasy silences and repressed anger. I could do with a night off from all those tonight. As I run the bath, I mull over the few minutes I spent with Tom this afternoon. It really was only a few minutes, although it felt like we packed a lifetime of emotion into them. Being held by him was the most gorgeous feeling; I haven't felt like that since I first met Mark, I realise guiltily. I know there's always a bit of extra excitement due to the newness of things, and although I know it's wrong whilst I'm with Mark, I can't help the rightness of how it felt.

Suddenly, I don't want to dwell on it all any more, my

brain is aching with the effort, and a soak in the bath, with time to contemplate my lot, is the last thing I fancy. No, what I need right now is to run. I turn off the taps and instead get on the phone to Alex. She's usually my running buddy, childcare permitting. Fortunately her nanny hasn't left for the day yet, and leaving Josie up to her eyes in kiddie tea-time, she is able to slip out for a while and join me.

Alex and I pound the paths, roads and fields around the village together, and it feels so good. It always seems to clear my head; I'm in danger of emotional overload at the moment, but doing something physical helps to dispel it all. Alex is one of those annoyingly fit women who seem to be able to string together full sentences and run at the same time. I'm far from unfit, but I usually struggle to manage more than a few grunts, or a puffy 'yes' or 'no' in response to Alex's questions. At least it means I can't go into any detail about today. I'll just speak when I'm spoken to, pleading breathlessness if she wants to know any more. I don't want to tell Alex about Tom; great friend that she is, I just want to hold it all in for a bit longer, keep it special and safe. It's not for public consumption yet, it's just for me.

'How are things with you and Mark?' Alex ventures, sounding nothing like she has just run a mile and a half over bumpy ground.

'Yeah... not great... you know...' I pant, glad the lack of air in my lungs won't allow me to expand on it.

'He popped in the other night,' Alex says. That floors me, and I almost come to a standing halt so I can grill Alex about it. Instead I manage to keep my cool and keep running. He'd not mentioned it. But then he doesn't say much about anything at the moment.

'What... did... he... want?' I manage to puff out, feeling increasingly suspicious. I don't know why I should be, we're all great mates, but somehow it just seems odd when one member of our gang seeks out another member of the opposite sex, alone, without their other half in tow. Get real, Grace, Alex isn't some predatory widow, pouncing on my man whilst he's going through a bit of a rocky patch. She'd never do that to me. To anyone. I recognise what I'm feeling as possessiveness. I'm not sure yet if I still want him for myself or not, but I don't want any other woman, friend or otherwise, getting in there either.

'Oh, just to talk. I think he's found a new sounding board in me,' she says, smiling, trying to make light of it and sensing my panic. 'He is quite mixed up at the moment, but then you know that.'

I still find it odd, and a bit sad too, that the man I live with, and love – theoretically – would prefer to call in on one of my friends for solace, rather than coming home to me, and sitting down and talking things through. I don't know what he hopes to achieve by such behaviour.

I pick up speed, and Alex follows suit. I'd hoped coming out for a run was going to be a way to escape the dramas in my life, but it looks like I've just walked – or rather run – into another one.

I work myself harder than ever, knowing that if I'm absolutely shattered later, I will just collapse into my bed and sleep like the dead, rather than toss and turn and mull everything over in my head.

It becomes clear to me at this point that I couldn't possibly tell Alex about Tom. That is, if I could speak enough to say anything, which I can't. I'd trust her implicitly not to say anything to Mark, I'm quite sure she wouldn't. What would she have to gain from doing that? But I know it's not what she needs to hear. She likes to feel she's helping us, I think, by hearing Mark out, and trying to advise him on what to do for the best.

If I were to mention my involvement with Tom, I'm not sure what she would think of me, and I suspect it might make her question my level of commitment to Mark. She could certainly never have imagined cheating on Peter. There's no doubt that his death has put him on something of a pedestal, made him more perfect than he probably was in reality. But he was her one and only love in life; she was loyal to him during his lifetime and she is still loyal to his memory now. Even though I'm sure he would not have wanted her to be alone after his death, she shows no sign of wanting or needing another man in her life.

We clock up about five kilometres and decide that's enough. Alex invites me back to her place for a drink, but I decline her offer. I really don't want to talk any more, and without the excuse of shortness of breath, I'd have no choice but to talk. And there's no doubt the conversation would head in that direction eventually.

As I jog towards home at a much gentler pace, hoping to ease my aching muscles, Frannie and Gerald are out in

Frannie's front garden. She has a perfectly serviceable back garden which would offer the pair of them a little more privacy, but I get the feeling she's still at the stage of wanting to show off her new beau to anyone who happens to pass by. The loved-up couple are pottering around her small plot arm in arm, as though it's a display garden at a National Trust property, examining the flowers and plants, and exclaiming over the latest blooms to burst into colour. I half expect them to be regaling each other with the Latin names for each one. 'Oh yes, that's *bloomus splendiferous*, a rare species that one, and much more robust than the *flora fabulosa*', or something along those lines.

'Grace, darling, yoo-hoo, over here,' she calls to me, waving her arm in the air. 'We've set a date for the wedding!' she announces proudly. 'Invitations are at the printers. You and the man of your choice are invited, of course, I'll leave it blank so you can decide who to bring,' she says, mischievously, with a naughty smile. She is so perceptive, Frannie. Nothing gets past her. She knows nothing about Tom and me: it's all so new and secret that no one does. I only just know myself, after all. She is aware, however, that Mark and I have been having problems, and it won't have escaped her that I haven't been looking that downcast for a woman whose relationship is potentially on the rocks. She also expected that we'd both be planning our weddings around the same time, and I haven't exactly been swapping dress and bouquet ideas with her, have I?

Given her history with relationships, she is never one to judge when it comes to the path of true love, but she has clearly put two and two together. And come out with the correct answer.

'July 18th,' she goes on. 'Little service here in the village, then off to Compton Hall for a slap-up lunch. Put the date in your diary, my dear!'

I make all the right noises and opt for a hasty departure, pleading sweatiness, exhaustion and hunger. They can both see I've been out running and wouldn't expect me to hang around and chat, I'm sure. Frannie looks so happy; it's great to see her so contented. She has always been the sort of woman to make the best out of any situation, she's incredibly strong, but I'm so pleased she's found someone to share the rest of her years with.

I can't help wishing it was me setting wedding dates, despite everything. Funnily enough, July 18th was one of the dates I'd been thinking about, in the early days after Mark finally agreed that we could get married, as it's the day after school breaks up for the summer. It just seemed like a good way to start the holidays, plus I wouldn't have needed to take extra time off school for my honeymoon.

So now I will be going to someone else's wedding that day instead. I wonder how that will make me feel, seeing another couple walk down the aisle and make those promises, another couple's 'till death do us part' speech.

I haven't been to a wedding for a few years, and really had thought that the next one I went to would be my own. Oh well, no point crying over it now.

I am so sad about the way things are with Mark and me, but so confused about whether I actually want him or not.

And now I have Tom to add into the equation too. Goodness knows who I will be taking to Frannie and Gerald's wedding. Nobody but my own good self at this rate.

Fifteen

The day of the long-awaited school production dawns. It's been a brilliant source of distraction for me; I've been so wrapped up in it all for the past couple of weeks, I've barely had time to think about the love-triangle that is my life, and to step back and look at how things stand at the moment. Everything has remained relatively quiet on the two sides of the triangle that I have any influence over, so far.

Mark and I have entered into a sort of stable, platonic phase, and we seem to be getting along OK. We are perfectly pleasant towards one another, but the major factor making everything *not* really OK is that we are more like housemates than lovers. It's a bit of a weird set-up really, but neither of us has yet been brave enough to take the leap and suggest that maybe, possibly, things are never going to get better and that, finally, our relationship is over.

I'm still wearing my engagement ring – until we know where we are heading I can't bring myself to take it off. I know there has to be finality at some point, and that we probably will end up separating, but it's so hard to move things forward to that next step.

My relationship with Tom, if you can call it that, is on an

even keel too. He has been fantastically supportive, in a lovely, friendly way, both towards my emotional needs, and with all the additional work I have on my plate at school at the moment. At no point has he tried to kiss me again; he has well and truly kept to his word about backing off and giving me time to think. The trouble is, I haven't really done much thinking, I've been so busy. Maybe once this week is over then I really should start to at least consider making some decisions on where my life is heading. I owe it to both the men in my life.

For the meantime, I have a production to stage. We have three performances of *Joseph* to knock out from Monday to Wednesday this week, so the children (and staff) involved will be doing relatively little else. Still, it's a great experience for them and I am very excited about it – I think it's going to be brilliant, if I say so myself. It's a complete sell-out, tickets have gone like hot cakes, and the children are wound up like coiled springs, desperate to bounce onto the stage.

Tom stands at the front of the hall, waiting to make his welcoming speech to the first heaving hall of parents, friends and fans who have turned out to watch their little darlings make their stage debut. Whilst hovering in the wings and nervously tweaking costumes and headdresses I spot Frannie and Gerald, cuddled up like a pair of lovebirds in the seats I reserved for them at the front, so they would have a good view. And Evie has brought her girls along to watch as well – they are currently fidgeting around near the back, Imogen and Anastasia catching up with some of the friends they left behind when they moved off to their new school. It hadn't even occurred to Mark to come and support me, and see what all my hard work has been for. Fat chance of that. At no point has he expressed any interest in buying a ticket and coming to see me in action. He just isn't bothered at all. Still at least I have my own mini fan-club in attendance in the form of Frannie and Evie, and I am really glad of their support, as my pre-production nerves kick in.

Finally the lights dim and the spotlight hones in on Tom. He looks particularly gorgeous tonight, I think, immaculately turned out in suit and tie, and with his wild hair slightly tamer than normal. But I don't have time to kick back on my laurels and admire, so I pull myself together quickly. He is a picture of confidence and self-assuredness as he waits there, thoroughly in his element, his staff and charges about to give off a performance which can only further his reputation as the best head teacher Cropley School has ever known. (And undoubtedly the sexiest, too, I can't help myself from remarking with an inward nervous giggle.)

'Ladies and Gentlemen, children, parents, staff and friends,' he begins, slowly and surely, making eye contact at various places all around the room, to ensure he has everyone's attention. The audience falls silent immediately, such is the spell he is capable of casting over them. Let's face it, you'd have to be mad or half blind not to sit and gawp. 'Welcome to our production.' The smile that he bestows after his simple opener out-dazzles the spotlight by about a zillion watts, and I can imagine that a significant proportion of the female population will be glued to their seats, and not just because of his stage presence. I half expect one of those flashes to appear on his teeth, like in the toothpaste adverts, where some hunk with an unnaturally white set of pearlies grins at the camera and 'Zing', up pops the flash of Colgate white.

Tom goes on to whip up his audience into an excited frenzy of anticipation, then thanks all the relevant people, but singles out one in particular – me. I gulp. I hadn't expected to be mentioned at this point. Maybe at the end of the run, after the final production, I'd expect a big thank you and possibly a bunch of flowers presented by one of the kids, the usual sort of thing. But Tom wants me out the front with him right now, sharing his glory, I realise in horror, as I'm not prepared for this.

'...my wonderfully talented director, Miss Grace Connery,' I hear him continue. The fingers on the end of the arm he extends towards me are beckoning for me to come forward, and I realise the spotlight is now coming my way, honing in on its target like a searchlight in the Blitz. I manage to get myself to the front of the hall, hoping my cheeks don't match the red of the stage curtains, and as I walk towards him he pulls me to his side, and we stand there together, with his arm protectively around my shoulder. I'm not sure what he actually says, I'm so shocked about being dragged to the front today, when I was least expecting it, and my legs have turned to goo. But the gooey legs are more to do with his arm around my shoulder, not nerves.

We haven't had any physical contact since that late afternoon in his office when we kissed for the first time, and I realise how much I have craved his touch. The whole lower half of my body feels like it's melting. Please can I stay here all evening, the prayers inside my head beseech. Make these people disappear and leave the two of us alone. I could stand here like this all night. Well, I might want him to kiss me too, eventually, but that's beside the point. And certainly not with all these people watching.

Speech over, I am released from Tom's clutches and head off back to my director's hideout, tucked just out of sight behind the curtain at the side of the stage. I manage to resuscitate myself from my state of Tom-induced lust and torpor and everything goes off brilliantly, as I knew it would. The kids display all their superstar qualities to the full, and the rapturous applause at the end makes all the hard work feel worthwhile.

I suddenly realise how shattered I am, now that it's over and the adrenaline rush has deserted me. Oh well, we only have to do all that twice more, should be a doddle – ha! I foresee a weekend of long lie-ins ahead of me to recover. At least I know what to expect tomorrow evening if Tom whisks me out to the front again, for a repeat of this evening's speech, which no doubt he will. I'll have to make sure I'm wearing my Bridget Jones-style reinforced and very unsexy industrial-strength pants, to be able to cope with that twice more in front of a big audience.

'I… am… knackered,' I manage to utter, as we stack the final chairs back in place in the village hall. There are only a few of us left now; just myself, Tom and the other two class teachers, plus a couple of parents whose commitment to costumes, make-up and props has been unwavering throughout the whole process. We couldn't have managed without them, and here they are still, helping us get cleared up. We had produced our final performance tonight and again it had gone without a hitch.

'Bye, Dawn, thank you so much,' I call, as one of these work-hard mums finally beats her retreat.

'It was worth it,' she smiles, as she pushes the door open. 'What a night! See you tomorrow. Enjoy the rest of your evening,' she adds, with a glance towards Tom and a knowing smile back at me. What *can* she mean? I wonder, but I feel that smile trying to play at my own lips too.

Everyone drifts away until finally it is just Tom and me, left together to lock up, turn off switches, and generally make sure we have left the hall as we found it. The secretary for the village hall committee is a dragon to rival the one slain by St George, and we don't want to risk her fiery breath for not leaving everything in a state of absolute immaculateness.

'So where's the after-party?' Tom asks cheekily, knowing it's safe to pose that question now that everyone has left, and the only potential partygoers are the two of us. 'Shall we go and get a drink somewhere?' he tries again, a little more of a realistic proposition this time, standing squarely in front of me with his hands on my arms. Here come those gooey legs again. 'You're not expected home yet a while, are you? Mark's bound to assume we'll all go off somewhere afterwards, isn't he?'

All these leading questions – does he really want to know the answer to them? 'Don't worry about Mark, he won't be home till late anyway, and he's unlikely to care whether I'm home or not,' I reply, realising how down I sound, and then adding more brusquely, 'Forget about him, let's go.' I amaze myself at how easily I have just shelved Mark and decided to go off with Tom tonight, despite all my earlier intentions of keeping a distance between us for the moment.

Suddenly he pulls me to him and there are those wonderful lips of his again, seeking out mine. I melt into the shape of his body; he seems to absorb the whole of me, like a sponge, and I can't tell where the sensations are coming from, every part of me is tingling with excitement. Suddenly a door bangs and we jump apart quickly.

'I thought everyone had gone,' he says. 'Let me just nip outside and check everything's OK.' But as he heads for the door, Ginny pops her head round.

'Sorry to startle you – forgot my coat,' she says. There's that look again, sizing us up, eyes going from one to the other and back again, trying to get the measure of us and work out what we are up to. Maybe she had stolen back in here on purpose, in the hope of catching us out.

'Damn, why did it have to be her again?' I groan to Tom, 'Do you think she knows what's going on?'

'Well what is going on?' Tom teases. 'I am only standing here kissing my gorgeous Grace, the most brilliant director... and teacher... and woman... ever. And as beautiful as any Hollywood superstar, I reckon.' He grabs me to him again and I find myself not caring what Ginny thinks, anyway.

'Let's go,' he says. 'We'll take my car, I'll run you back

here later so you can pick yours up.'

'So,' Tom says, as we fasten our seatbelts, 'where's it to be?' I make a stab at a couple of pubs in the neighbouring villages, then there is a pause before he says, somewhat gingerly, 'Or back to mine?' I glance at him as he's driving. I am not shocked; I don't want to go to a public place with him. Not because I don't want us to be seen together, although that could be awkward at this point in time, but because I want to be alone with him. I want him all to myself and I want him to make love to me. Now. Tonight. I'm not going be the one to suggest it; I am just going to go along with whatever he wants. I can't pretend any longer that I want to keep him at arm's length, because I don't. I've tried that, and it hasn't helped. I think I know finally in my head, and heart, that Mark and I are over, it's now just a matter of all the practicalities to be sorted out, and how we go about it. Being with Tom before I've drawn a final line under Mark and me was never what I intended, but it's killing me. I want to be his, emotionally and physically; I can't wait any longer.

'Yes,' is all I can muster.

He steals a quick glance in my direction and reaches his hand out to me. I grab it and hold it tight, tucking our joined hands between my knees. I never want to let go. His hands are large and warm and very soft. I need them on my body tonight. But I am going to let him take the lead; whatever he has in mind for this evening, however far we go, is fine by me. Well, more than fine, actually. I hope to God he isn't planning just to ply me with a coffee then drop me straight back here. But it's not coffee vibes that I'm picking up on right now.

During the twenty minute drive to Tom's flat, neither of us says very much. We are both exhausted from the events of the past couple of days, but I don't think our silence has anything to do with that. For my part, I am savouring the moment, enjoying the anticipation of what is to come. Tom sneaks the odd glance at me, when he can without compromising his driving. He looks like he needs to check I am still there and that he can't believe his luck that I am.

Tom pulls up outside his flat. Neither of us moves to start with, then he jumps out of the car and is round at my door in a flash, opening it for me and holding my hand as I climb out, as if to ensure I don't suddenly change my mind and make a bolt for home. But the only bolt that hits me is the lightning strike when he kisses me again. It's only a gentle peck on the cheek, but it's enough to send me sky high, completely away with the fairies. He puts his arm round my waist and together we go into his home. The whole thing feels as though it takes place in slow motion, like an out of body experience, frame by frame. Only once he has closed the door to his flat does he let me loose. *Don't worry, Tom, you don't have to lock me in and hold me prisoner here. It's exactly where I want to be.*

He skips off to the kitchen to pour some wine – which will later go un-drunk – and I look around his flat, liking what I see. Fortunately there is no sign of a woman's touch; it's all very tasteful and elegant, but there is nothing girly in the slightest, or at least nothing obvious, anyway, and I'm not about to go rifling through drawers looking for clues to ex-girlfriends. I can't imagine the extremes of jealousy I would suffer to see Sophie's or even Alicia's mark on his home, although Alicia probably wasn't around for long enough to have any influence on his interior décor.

Tom returns with a glass in each hand and sets them down on the low table in the centre of his living room. Then he turns slowly back to me, tilts his head to one side and just looks at me, before bringing his hands up to the back of my neck and cupping my head in his palms, his thumbs reaching up into my hair and sending spasms of excitement down my spine. I push my head back into his hands, enjoying the sensation and the touch of his electrically charged fingertips. He pulls me to him and we kiss again. This time it's a proper kiss, his tongue urgent and searching, as his arms move lower and hold me tight against his body. We seem to fit together so perfectly; there is so much of him, I feel lost in him, as though I melt and disappear and we both become one entity. I never want him to stop kissing me like that. All this passion; I can't remember ever feeling like this, although I suppose it must have been like that with Mark in the early days. Was it ever this good? I push Mark out of my head; I'm only feeling ever so slightly guilty about being here with Tom – and not enough to make me want to stop – but I don't want any bad thoughts clogging up the pure intensity of this moment. I want to savour every minute of it. I feel like I should be committing these sensations to memory, bottling them even, so that in my crusty old age I can get them out and relive the moments of passion from my youth. And know that I was loved and had experienced the heights of an emotion as strong as it could ever be.

Tom is leading me through to his bedroom. This time I don't stop to admire the soft furnishings on the way. He gently lays me down on the bed and starts to remove my clothing. He deftly flicks on his iPod speakers and the strains of James Blunt's 'You're Beautiful' fill the room. Well, that was good planning, if ever it was planned. No, surely not. Neither of us could have anticipated being here together, tonight, could we?

'She smiled at me on the subway, she was with another man.' Well, yes, right on that one.

'But I won't lose no sleep on that, 'cause I've got a plan.' Does he have a plan? Really? Had Tom known that I would come back here with him tonight?

At that point I stop taking notice of the lyrics and cross-questioning myself – I have been living with a lawyer for too long, it's rubbed off on me – as Tom is down to my underwear and playing very close attention to the inside of one of my thighs. He is lying beside me, stripped to his own underwear – when did that happen? Nice pants though, not those nasty little tight ones, I notice – and his fingers are stroking the soft skin of my thigh; I usually find this unbearably tickly but tonight there are no giggles bubbling up. This is so erotic and as his hands move up across my stomach, closely followed by his lips, and up to my breasts, his thumbs tweaking my nipples, I shiver and wonder how I can wait any longer to feel him inside me. I don't want to rush things, but I need him on top of me, crushing me with his weight, and bearing down on me with his kisses whilst I wrap my legs around him and pull him deep into me.

Sensing my urgency, Tom quickly divests both of us of any remaining garments and is inside me, filling me with his passion and we move together gently on the bed. His eyes are open and looking into mine, full of love and adoration and deep, deep lust, and we are so desperate to melt into each other that it's all over in a matter of seconds. We lay sated side by side, each gently caressing the other's skin, exhausted and panting.

'Wow,' Tom says when he finally gets his breath back. 'You are amazing.'

I feel the urge to giggle, something to do with all the love hormones kicking in, and the great speed of events, no doubt.

'We'll take our time next time,' I reply, half-apologetic. 'I just needed you.'

'Glad to hear there will be a next time, and a time after that and a time after that, too, I hope,' he says, teasing me, and tenderly tucking a stray strand of hair behind my ear. 'I needed you too. I've needed you forever, Grace.'

And there is a next time, pretty soon after – we don't have to wait very long. This time it is slow, and lovely, and languorous, and we take the time to explore each other's bodies properly, discovering sensitive spots, and ticklish bits, and we laugh and talk and roll and move together, before finally needing to seal the moment. This time I let him take the lead, and he is so, so gentle and slow, bringing me to the most amazing climax before giving into his own passion.

I wake with a start some time later to see Tom's bedside clock flashing a bright blue 02.17 at me. Oh God, how did I manage to fall asleep, I am supposed to be going back to collect my car and get home, for at least a few hours' sleep in my own bed and a pretence at having just stayed out a bit too late at the supposed 'after-party'. Tom is flat-out beside me; he looks so beautiful and peaceful, his arms flung wide in total abandon, it seems a shame to have to wake him. How I would love to lie here with him all night, snuggle up to that huge, smooth chest, wake up together in the morning, make love again… Yes, well, time to knock those thoughts on the head for now, my practical and sensible side is taking over and I know I have to get home, so I give him a gentle nudge.

'Tom, wake up, its twenty past two, I have to get back.' He mutters and grunts in his sleep, then rolls over and carries on doing what he is doing. Good job I stirred or we would both still be here in the morning, and my all-night absence would certainly take some explaining. It wouldn't be the done thing to turn up at school later this morning in the clothes I had been wearing at the show. Oh no. I give him a harder shove this time; I have to get back. He wakes with a start and leaps out of bed, stares at me with a bemused expression, then as his mind wakes up, he seems to suddenly remember where we are and what happened and tries to pull me back under the duvet with him. Oh, such temptation, and so hard to resist, he's warm and smells so good, but I have to.

We both dress quickly; there's no time for me even to grab a quick shower, I will just have to make sure I am up before Mark in the morning. That could be tricky on so little sleep. We don't speak until we are in the car and then Tom says, 'I'm sorry, Grace.'

'What for, it was lovely,' I reply. 'Perfect. I just wish I didn't have to leave…'

'I've said before, I'm not a home-wrecker,' he says. 'But I want you Grace. I want all of you. Not for it to be like this.' He reaches out and holds my hand, and looks so sad, despite everything that has happened tonight and the gloriously ecstatic emotions of earlier.

'I know,' I say, then taking a deep breath: 'I know what I need to do, Tom,' I am sure I sound braver than I feel. I know I have to end things with Mark, and soon. It's not fair to either of them not to know where they stand, although I have to keep any evidence of my involvement with Tom out of the picture until I have sorted out the end of my relationship with Mark. He doesn't deserve, after all the mostly happy years we have spent together, for me to leave him to go directly into the arms of another man. I have to be leaving him because that in itself is the right thing to do and because our relationship has run its course, not because I have had what I consider to be a better offer. I don't do and have never done affairs; one man at a time is enough and I need to play fair now, too. OK so I have cheated on Mark already, but he doesn't need to know that. He deserves a reasoned explanation for the end of 'us'. I owe it to him to do that. I am pretty sure he is expecting it; so much so that I'm surprised he hasn't been the first one to make the move towards the beginning of the end.

I slip quietly into the house and between the sheets of mine and Mark's bed, feeling slightly treacherous, but still glowing from my love-making with Tom. There, that's it, I am a true adulteress. That horrible word now applies to me. A bed-hopper, fresh out of one man's bed and into another, with the smell of the first one still on me. But that's what I am. I won't be one for long, though. My very onerous task for this weekend is to end my relationship with Mark. I'm not chickening out of doing it tomorrow, or rather today, as of course it's already the next day. But I know Mark has a really important couple of days coming up at work and a big deal to finalise, and I don't want to cause him problems by throwing his home life upside down as well. No, let things tick over as they have been, and we will talk at the weekend. I don't plan to spend this weekend as Mark's partner; by Saturday morning we will have this all sorted out and we can both be on the path to the rest of our lives.

I can't help going over the events of the evening in my head. I am doomed on the sleep front, I know that. Those couple of hours I snatched in Tom's bed, plus the passionate parting kiss he gave me as we went our separate ways just now, have ruined sleep for me for the remainder of the night. I know I am going to be shattered tomorrow, but then everyone will be expecting me to be sporting bags the size of suitcases under my eyes, from all the hard work of the past three days. The children will be tired, too, so hopefully

I will slip under the radar relatively unnoticed.

Tom had dropped me back at my car, then followed me home to make sure I got back safely. I could see his face in the moonlight as I turned the key in the lock, and the little kiss he blew me. His expression was very melancholy; he must be wondering what the outcome will be from this situation he has embroiled himself in. Had we just been a one-off, a gorgeous but never-to-be-repeated event, or was I about to embark on a steamy affair with him, safe in the knowledge that I still had Mark at home as fall-back, should I decide I didn't want him after all? Covering my options? He had no way of knowing whether I really would end things with Mark and be with him instead. Poor man, caught up in all this complicated relationship stuff. All he wants is me, and I have so much baggage to unpack and tidy away first.

But I will deal with it; I am resolved to do what I have to. I want to be with Tom. I don't love Mark any more. There, I said it. I look at the man lying next to me and feel such sadness. Mark and I have been together for so long and been through so much together. What happens to all that history, all those shared moments and memories when a couple part? The stories that couples recount together, and that are so much fun to recall *à deux*, but mean practically nothing to a third party, tales of funny moments, special holidays, that sort of stuff. They are unlikely to ever get an airing again — a memory is pretty hollow unless it can be shared with the person who experienced it too. It's like losing the best part of a decade from my life, boxed up and put into storage the instant I tell Mark I am leaving him. But a relationship cannot survive on the memories of happier times; if we are not constantly creating more happy memories for the future each day we are together, then what is the point of us being together now? I feel no love for him as I lie there. Instead I feel sad, and a little sorry for him. I know he will be fine, though. He must know things are over between us, so hopefully it won't come as too much of a shock. Will it?

Sixteen

I'm going to need some matchsticks this morning to keep my eyelids open, I reckon, as I shuffle to the bathroom, barely upright, like Neanderthal woman after a particularly rough day of being dragged round by her hair. Oh God, look at those ugly bags under my eyes, enough compartments to pack for a family holiday for a week. My skin looks all grey and sallow, and I ache all over. Although not in a bad way, I realise with a tingle. The insides of my thighs twinge with that lovely 'had-lots-of-sex-last-night' sensation, and my chin feels a bit rough and scratchy from Tom's stubble. Mmmmm. The physical reminders get me thinking about what happened and put a smile on my face which does something to shore up the bags a little. We did kiss a lot, and it was so lovely. We hardly stopped, really. No wonder my chin feels like it's been given a close shave with a blunt lawnmower.

But there is the hint of a twinkle in my eye, despite the greyness of my complexion, which I hope will carry me through the day ahead, until I can come back home and sleep. Sleep is all I want to do tonight; the thought of crawling between my crisp white sheets, (alone – no man there to complicate things) with a good book, and reading a couple of pages before nodding off into the deepest of sleeps. Bliss. My memories of last night and the total high I am feeling from being so loved and wanted and lusted after, will keep me going until I can come home and collapse. I hope.

Mark was up and out of the house before I even stirred. Just as well, really. I'd planned to get up and have a shower before him, but it hadn't happened. There was no way I was responding to an alarm clock that went off at anything beginning with a six this morning. I had only just managed to drag myself out of bed at seven thirty and that was cutting it as fine as I possibly could for getting to school on time. I hadn't wanted to still feel Tom's handprints all over me, and the smell of his body, in Mark's company (despite the fact that I had just spent the night sleeping next to Mark and doing just that). I'd wanted to get up and shower away all that invisible evidence, just to assuage, not my guilt, as I didn't have any, I'd reconciled myself to that, but my awareness of a sense that I could still do the right thing by Mark. All part of that adulteress versus one-man-at-a-time battle going on in my head, I suppose.

Anyway, that was by the by, and no longer relevant, as Mark had already gone off to work. But amazingly, and quite touchingly I thought, he had left me a note:

'Hi, you! Didn't hear you come in last night.' Thank God for that, no need to explain my extreme lateness. *'Hope show went off well, you deserve the accolades after all your hard work! Will be back late tonight but will text later, Love Mark xxx PS Hope the*

after-party was fun! x'

Oh God, there is a real physical pain in my stomach and a sinking feeling which this time I do recognise as guilt. I thought I was past feeling guilty, that Mark and I were over love and all that, and that my clean break plan for the weekend was going to be easy to administer. But then Mark goes and shows me that he can be a kind and caring person, and that he is still thinking about me after all. I wobble for a bit, feeling bad about what Mark said about the party – if only he knew what I had really been up to. There I was in another man's bed, in another man's arms, letting him make love to me like the past eight years had never happened, and Mark thought I was innocently grabbing a few celebratory drinks with the production team in the local pub.

I am wobbling, but at no point does it make me consider that what happened with Tom was wrong, or that I want it to end. No, the strange feelings in the pit of my stomach mean that I am not cut out to cheat, and I know that Mark and I are definitely over, despite his kind gesture this morning – so I have to be strong and do what I intend to do and end our relationship. Maybe if he can be as nice as he was in his note, if we can be civil with each other and behave like adults, it won't be so hard, and he will understand that us separating is for the best.

'Hi, gorgeous,' Tom mimes to me as I pass him in the corridor. 'Morning, Miss Connery,' is his formal, audible greeting, as we are engulfed by a speedy swarm of children, all heading for their classrooms. He gives me the most delicious, cheesy grin, and his eyes twinkle mischievously.

'Morning, Mr Parry,' I reply breezily, my smile wide, making strong, engaging eye contact with him and wishing I could touch him. I will have to find a moment at some point in this school day to grab him and hold him tight and have him kiss me again, or I will go mad. I don't feel like a responsible member of staff today, but a love-struck teenager trying to keep the boy she snogged behind the bike sheds under wraps. Oh, today is going to be so hard! But the warm fuzzy glow in the pit of my stomach makes the thrill of it worth every moment of pain.

My class look like they have been drugged. If I thought the bags under my eyes were bad, then my classroom is like the luggage department in John Lewis. And they are supposed to be young, energetic kids with tonnes of energy. Oh well, we will all muddle along somehow, today, I'm sure. I don't expect anything too remarkable from them and hopefully the feeling is mutual.

My classroom assistant, Mrs Woods, is the only one looking even slightly perky, but then she probably isn't the sort to have spent the night in another man's bed, having illicit, passionate sex for hours on end. But then who knows, eh? I'd never have put myself down as being the type either, so you never can tell. But that's too much information for my sleep-deprived queasy stomach to process; her rather rotund frame and sensible twin-set don't exactly lend themselves to fantasies of nights of passion. Let's not even go there. I shake myself down with a 'Brrrrrrr' and face my class.

PE. That's what we all need today. Forget the scheduled classes, what we all need is some fresh air and exercise, me included.

At break time I head towards the staff room to grab a much needed coffee. As I pass Tom's office, there is a loud 'Pssssst', and I see his hand round the door, beckoning me to come in. He must have been waiting there for me to go past, peeping through the gap between the door and the frame, so no other member of staff could hijack him and mar his opportunity.

Like an opportunistic thief checking they are not being watched before striking, I throw a furtive glance over one shoulder to check for stray adults, and dive in. No sooner am I inside the door, than he slams it shut and turns the key, and the two of us are up against it, our tongues in each other's mouths, our hands desperately searching for flesh under clothing. Before I can protest – and why would I do that other than the danger of being found out, but I notice Tom's blinds are conveniently down, good planning Mr Parry – he has my skirt up around my waist and is inside me, and we are moving together, desperate not to make a sound, but urgently needing to be together.

The door to his office is one of those cheap, hollow plywood things, and I realise that each movement we make together is echoing through the wood and with a stifled giggle, I gently manoeuvre his hips to one side, so that we are against the solid wall instead, without losing our intimate bodily contact.

When it's all over, I collapse against Tom in a heap. 'I can't believe we just had sex in a school,' I gasp, 'It's so naughty! Do you think we'll get expelled if the headmaster finds out?' This I say amid a fit of the giggles, my hand over my mouth for volume control. I can't quite believe what we have just done. I start sorting out my clothing, straightening everything down, and combing my fingers through my hair.

'I couldn't wait Grace, sorry,' he says.

'Stop apologising, will you,' I reply. 'Do I look like I am here under duress? You'll have to stop dragging me off to the headmaster's study, though, Sir. Your ideas of corporal punishment just aren't in line with twenty-first century Ofsted requirements, you know,' I am giggling again, wagging my finger at him in mock chastisement.

Somehow we both manage to calm ourselves down. In all seriousness, we can't do that again, I resolve, despite all the hilarity, and I tell Tom. Just imagine if we were seen or overhead, there would be an absolute outcry amongst staff and parents. I can imagine the lurid headlines in the local papers and beyond – 'Respected head teacher dismissed for break-time antics' – the consequences don't bear thinking about. No, we are both professional people; it was fun, and so, so erotic, but that is it. No more school hanky-panky. Still, I can see the funny side of it for the moment; we would definitely win any 'Most-dangerous-place-you-have-ever-had-sex' competition. Mile High Club members eat your hearts out.

The following day we have a whole-school trip planned.

After the hard work of the week, and with the end of term fast approaching, we thought it would be perfect timing for the annual school outing. And yes, the kids will have a blast and heaps more fun than on a normal day in school; they need the emotional outlet today. But I can imagine that the staff stress-levels will be just a little higher, as we try to reign in eighty-five energetic kids, outside, around a wildlife park, with children wanting to go in all directions, and the hazards of ice-cream-hungry wasps and hay fever outbreaks to add to it. We have co-opted a few parents to come along and help supervise small groups, and Ginny, in her usual efficient manner, has planned everything to the n'th degree, so hopefully it won't be too bad. The real downside for me will be trying to keep my distance from Tom. I wish I could stroll round the park, hand in hand with him, but instead I will have to be ultra-conscious of my behaviour towards him – try not to make too much eye contact, maintain a professional distance, no secret smiles, all that sort of stuff. It's going to be impossible!

I can't even sit next to Tom on the coach now; before the events of the past few weeks I wouldn't have given any more thought to parking myself next to him as to any other member of staff. He is a couple of rows in front of me; I can see his blond curls bobbing as he chats to Louise, the class two teacher. They are deep in conversation and I can't help myself from feeling just a little bit jealous of her. She'll have him all to herself for the next forty-five minutes, lucky thing, although I'm sure she's not sitting there contemplating what a lucky woman she is, like I would be. In any case they are hardly each other's type – she is mid-fifties, well maintained but exceedingly plain – and I suspect Tom won't be using any of his wayward charms on her today. At least I know he is safe in her clutches, and I have no real reason to feel jealous. Even though I am. Had either of us been unfortunate enough to have Ginny as our travelling companion, we would have felt slightly more uncomfortable, I'm sure, knowing that she is probably – for the moment – the only member of staff to suspect that there may be a relationship evolving between Tom and me. She'd have been watching us both like a hawk.

We arrive at the Wildlife Park and are duly split into our groups. I am lucky enough to find myself assigned to the year five girls, so they shouldn't be too much trouble, and the plus side is that they are unlikely to want to see the bats and invertebrates, which give me the heebie-jeebies. So a pleasantly easy morning, strolling round the more aesthetically pleasing animals, and hopefully grabbing a half-decent coffee later whilst they let off some steam in the park – should be a doddle. Tom, I notice, has the year two boys. Ha – a morning of stress-inducing high-speed chasing around the park, pulling them down from the enclosure walls and ensuring they don't feed each other to the lions. Oh well, never mind! Ginny hands us all our instructions – where to go, when to meet, what to see, she really is far too organised, she has planned this outing like a military operation – and I grab Tom for a quick second before we head off with our respective groups. I just need to say *something* to him, *anything*, no matter how mundane, just to have him to myself for a few brief moments. But I have to do it under the guise of discussing our plans for the day.

'Hi,' I say, strolling over to him as he gives me one of his huge knee-melting, discombobulating smiles.

'Hi, are you all set?' he asks.

'Yes, I just need to check something with you, though,' I ask, keeping a wary eye on Ginny who is just out of my line of vision, and pretending to consult my clip-board.

'*Mr Parry and Miss Connery, sitting in a tree, K...I...S...S...I...N...G,*' comes the chant from behind us – it's Tom's year two boys. Oh God. I am so glad the other groups have already moved off to start exploring the park.

'Mr Parry loves Miss Connery,' I hear someone whisper. I try so hard not to blush – they might only be kids but they are pretty astute at picking up on any signs which might give us away and prove their whisperings to be true. Tom turns round and fixes them with the sort of stare I didn't think he was capable of. Eat your heart out Medusa, half of Cropley school's pupils have just been turned to stone in one fell swoop.

Once his stony expression has faded, Tom handles it very well, and very delicately; to tell them off too strongly would just give them cause to think they had hit on the right note, and then they'd never let up. For all we know, they may simply have chanced on it as they saw us standing together, and any other female member of staff standing where I am might just as easily have been dropped into their little rhyme. Let's hope so. Tom and I are still such a big secret, we've only just realised ourselves that we are having an affair (there, I said the A word), so the chances of anyone else knowing, or even hazarding a guess, especially children, are pretty slim. It's just a bit of innocent stirring from a bunch of cheeky kids. God knows why we came here in search of monkeys today – we have enough of them of our own.

Seventeen

By the end of the day, I am shattered, not least because of the week we have had, plus the trip and the responsibility that goes with taking a party of kids out of their safe school environment and into the big wide, dangerous world.

No, it's more to do with what I know is imminent, the demise of my relationship with Mark. I am still resolved that it's the right thing to do. Nothing has changed my mind, and certainly not the events of the past couple of days. Even if Tom and I hadn't properly kicked off our relationship this week, then ending things with Mark would still have been very high on my list of priorities – maybe not necessarily right now, but very soon.

I can't stand this kind of limbo state Mark and I seem to have drifted into. It doesn't allow either of us to draw a line under things and move on with the rest of our lives. I'm not expecting too much in the way of protest from Mark tomorrow, but at the same time it's not a nice thing to have to do, and I feel very sad and melancholy on the coach on the way back to school, knowing that the week is coming to an end and I have a daunting task ahead of me.

As I arrive home the phone is ringing. It's Evie. She

wants to pop round for a chat. 'Everything OK?' I enquire, hoping this isn't about to be Episode Two in the 'James is Having an Affair' saga. Nice to have some notice this time, though, so I can get myself into the good, supportive friend state of mind that I owe to her to be in, putting aside my own troubles for a while. She's always so good to me, especially when I need a shoulder to cry on, so I know I have to be there for her too when she needs me.

'Tell you in a mo,' she says. She doesn't sound even mildly suicidal, so hopefully things have resolved themselves.

No more than ten minutes later and she is in my kitchen, glass of wine in hand, not refusing it this time. There is a glow to her cheeks which I haven't seen for a couple of weeks; clearly her suspicions had really dragged her down, and it's only now she has sorted everything out (which clearly she has, given her general state of euphoric bounciness) that I realise how awful it was making her feel and look.

'Guess what,' she says, as gleefully as a small child in a toy shop, 'We're off to Florence!'

'Great!' I reply, trying to muster some of her enthusiasm and wondering where all the suspicion and unhappiness have vanished to. I wait for her to expand further, as clearly she is about to, she looks fit to burst.

'James was sorting out a surprise trip for my birthday. You know I'd always wanted to go to Florence? Well, my sister Lydia's studying art there, she's always raving about the place, loves it, and I've never been. Well, James' PA was helping him sort it all out, doing the hotel bookings and all that sort of stuff. That's all it was, can you believe it?'

She looks so excited and so happy. 'So did you confront him, then? How did it all come out?' I ask, wanting to know the details of how she'd managed to set her perfect marriage back on track.

'I just came out and asked him if he was having an affair, told him how unhappy I'd been. He hadn't even realised it'd looked dodgy. He was so shocked when I told him what I'd suspected, he almost cried, poor thing. Said he'd never wanted anyone but me, swore undying love to me and all that, and he was so sorry for giving me a reason to think those things,' she explains. 'Anyway, we made up big time, if you get my drift,' she adds with a naughty giggle, as her eyebrows waggle up and down conspiratorially.

'I'm so pleased for you Evie,' I say, giving her a hug, and I mean it. If the two of them can't make it work, then there's no hope for the rest of us.

'Anyway, can you come out shopping tomorrow?' Evie asks. 'Now I've got a trip to plan for, I need some new clothes! I thought we could go up to the Bull Ring.'

'Hang on a minute, you're telling me you're off to Italy, the home of fashion and style and all things gorgeous, and you need to buy clothes *before* you go?' I pretend to protest, then add quickly after, 'Of course I'll come. But not tomorrow, there's something I need to do…'

'Next Saturday, then,' she goes on, barely noticing the shadow that passes across my face. I don't want to have to tell her what I am doing tomorrow; she is on such a happy cloud that I wouldn't want to clip her wings and send her spiralling back down to earth in sympathy. No, I will tell all to her and Alex when the time is right. We'll have a lovely girly day next weekend and I'll pour my heart out, if the timing feels right. I think I should be ready for it by then.

'Anyway, you're looking pretty perky, Grace, things on the mend with Mark?' she doesn't wait for a reply but continues 'Tom was very complimentary about you the other night, wasn't he? Seems to think very highly of you.' I don't know if she is digging, or just saying it as she sees it. In any case, she has no reason to suspect there is anything going on between Tom and me.

I feel a huge blush spreading up from my chest, via my neck, to my face, and I head for the fridge and the wine bottle, to top Evie up, and cool myself down. I think I'd need to climb right inside it to do that, my face is so glaringly puce.

'We're sorting stuff out,' is all I say, avoiding eye contact with her. I think Mark should be the first one to hear what I have to say, not Evie, and I don't really want to go into it all this afternoon. And I'm *certainly* not letting on about Tom, not until my relationship with Mark has been properly brought to an end.

'Tom's a nice bloke. He's great to work for,' is all I say, trying to be casual. I feel a bit bad, as Evie, Alex and I have always shared everything up until now. But for some reason I want to keep this close to my chest. I quickly change the subject, asking Evie about the details of the Florence trip, and as excited as she is, the diversion works and she is off and running, whisking me through the ins and outs of her itinerary like a tour guide on speed. My friend is happy again.

Eighteen

'Mark, we need to talk.' How I hate those words. That doom-laden phrase which so often presages the end of a relationship. A conversation about the weather, our plans for the day, work, booking a holiday, or a multitude of other stuff would never be kick-started with that awful phrase. It's up there with 'It's not you, it's me,' as the expression no one wants to hear. No one in a relationship that means anything to them, at least.

But once said, there is no going back. I think Mark realises what is coming, and as we sit together at the kitchen table, in the beautiful home we share and have made our own, I am swallowed up by the immensity of what I am doing, and how profoundly it is going to change the rest of our lives. Since that moment when I first met Mark, and I knew he would be someone to matter to me, there has not been a bigger event in my life. Meeting Tom, and everything that has happened with him so far, is small-fry in comparison. Not to belittle what I feel for Tom or anything, but Mark and I have History. Tom and I have yet to make our history; we are both so new to each other. I know we will make a go of it, and a good go at that, but I'm in the here and now of Mark and me for the time being. We have spent more than eight years together, and here I am, putting the lid on the box that contains our relationship, relegating it to a memory on a dusty shelf.

I have been rehearsing what to say, but when it comes down to it, what I'd prepared seems wrong and way too formal. I tell Mark simply that I want us to separate. I tell him there has been no love between us for a long time, and that we both need to move on in our lives. I tell him it's not fair to either of us to carry on the way we are as we both have different expectations. He sits quietly and listens to me speak. I realise I have tears rolling down my cheeks, and before he says anything in response, he passes me a tissue.

'I loved you so much Grace. I think we both just want different things in life, that's all. We've grown up and grown apart. It's very sad.' He is calm and collected, but there is a faraway look in his eyes, and although I don't see any hatred for me in them, gone is that heart-spinning mix of adoration and worship that they used to glow with every time he looked at me. 'I don't think there's a way back for us though, I think you are right.' Ever the pragmatic lawyer, but at least he is agreeing with me, and not begging me to try again or pleading on bended knee, declaring his undying love. I think we've been through all those conversations just once too often of late and now we both know our relationship is well and truly over.

'I'll go and stay at Evie's, I'll call her later. I'm sure she won't mind. It'll give us time to sort out the house and all our stuff. It's not long till the end of term, and then I'll have time to find somewhere more permanent to live. We might even have the house on the market by then.'

I realise I am nervously ranting, pouring out all the things I've been going over in my head these past few days, trying to deal with the emotional side of a forthcoming break-up, but also being practical and attempting to work out where I will live, what I will do. There is so much involved when a relationship ends, but the practicalities will help detract from mourning the end of Mark and me. And I will mourn. Even though I have Tom, Mark is the man I thought I would spend my life with, and it's still a harsh reality to swallow that he won't be. We'd expected and planned to grow old together, and I need time to get my head around that, adjust my expectations of what my future holds. Tom and I are so new, I don't know if we will still be together in a week, a month, a year, a decade. We haven't reached the stage of discussing our futures yet. We've no track record, so I have no evidence on which to place my bets.

The rest of my day passes in a blur. Mark disappears off, I don't know where, presumably to give me some space to get my things together and make any plans I need to for the next few days. We'd agreed that I'd be the one to go; now that it's a done deal, I can't imagine having to share the house with Mark for one minute longer, and I need to be gone by the time he gets back. It's not that I hate him or anything; I don't, far from it. I may not want to spend my life with him anymore, but I have no animosity towards him whatsoever.

My feelings for him are so much more subdued than they have been now that he is officially my 'ex'. But it would just be too weird. We're no longer a couple, so to continue to share a house, bed, living space or whatever else with Mark would just be wrong, and really hard. Having made the decision to move on, we have to do just that and follow it through. He'd suggested that he be the one to move out, but to be honest I feel like I need the change of scene to reinforce the sense of moving on in my head. To stay here would feel too similar to before, and even to contemplate bringing Tom back here at some point (in the future, not now) would seem inappropriate. No, new life, new home is what it has to be for me. I know the latter is going to take a bit of time to sort out, but a clean break now can only be the right thing to do.

I put in a quick call to Evie and explain what has happened. She's a bit shocked, but supportive none the less, and I don't have to ask for somewhere to stay, she offers me her spare room almost immediately.

'When you said you were sorting things out yesterday, I thought you meant getting back together,' she says, sounding sad, and I feel bad for putting all this on her, particularly as she has only just pulled her own relationship back from the brink of what she believed to be disaster.

'No, sorting things out as in ending it,' I reply. 'I didn't want to tell you yesterday, Evie, you were so happy. I won't impose on you for long, I promise, just until we can decide what's happening with the house and work out who's going where and all that sort of stuff.'

'You can stay as long as you like, you know you are welcome. Anyway, we're off to Florence the week after next, then Mallorca with the girls just after that, so we'll hardly be here. You take your time, get things sorted out. You'll have the place to yourself. In fact you'd be doing us a favour, house-sitting for us. Save me getting James' mum round every day to water the plants, feed the cat and all that stuff. Stay, Grace, don't rush off, take all the time you need.'

She is so generous, so kind, I am overwhelmed and I feel myself welling up.

'Get some stuff together and get yourself round here,' she says, sensing my imminent collapse, and her bossiness is just what I need to kick me into action. I pack a few bags, enough clothes to get me through the week, and very carefully choose some shoes to go with them. My lovely wardrobe and the rest of my footwear collection will have to manage without me for a while, and I gaze at it all wistfully as I close the zips on my suitcases. Still, I can always pop back when Mark is at work and get more stuff, it's not like he's going to change the locks or anything. I hope.

Evie and James are just wonderful, so welcoming and comforting. I feel cosseted and looked after, and it's just what I need. It feels a bit like running home to my parents, only with more champagne. Honestly, these two need no excuse to crack open a bottle. This time it is to celebrate 'New Beginnings' for me, and it's slowly giving me a warm and fuzzy feeling, making me feel a lot better. It's a very long time since I've been through this kind of thing but I have fabulous friends, and lots to look forward to, and I know I will be alright. Eventually. The three of us have taken up residence on the Brookes' decking area, admiring the stunning views across the hill, soaking up a bit of sun and putting the world to rights. The girls are off at their usual Saturday afternoon activities, and it feels very calm, and civilised, and adult. James is discreetly coming and going, giving Evie and me a bit of girl-time when we need it, topping up our glasses, and generally keeping an eye on us, only joining us for the conversation when it veers away from relationships and onto safer topics. I'm so glad there was nothing bad going on between the two of them after all; they always have been and still are the perfect couple. And even such a perfect couple are allowed to have the odd glitch from time to time, I realise that now.

Loosening up under the influence of alcohol, I wonder if I should tell Evie about Tom, but decide not to for the time being. She has been generous enough to put a roof over my head, and I don't want to make her think I've left one good man just to run into the arms of another. It sounds too shallow and clichéd. And a bit sordid too, even though it's far from that. I *will* tell her about him soon, I don't see how I can avoid it, but not today, and when I do I need to make it quite clear that the growing love between Tom and me has had nothing whatsoever to do with the end of my relationship with Mark. All it has done is act as a catalyst to make me finish with Mark, and I would have done that eventually, Tom or no Tom.

By Sunday morning I am nursing a bit of a champagne head, but feeling much better in my mind about everything. Evie and I had talked last night until our lips were numb, although some of that numbness could undoubtedly be attributed to the alcohol as well as the conversation. She had listened whilst I spouted, and been a real rock, a shoulder to cry on, and a good, non-judgemental friend. We'd sat outside till the small hours, until the patio heater was no longer enough to entice us to stay out there, then I'd somehow managed to get myself up to bed in her sumptuous guest room, but that part was all a bit of a blur.

Yesterday had been exactly what I'd needed and I have woken up feeling much more on top of things this morning. I have resolved not to impinge on the Brookes' family Sunday too much, having monopolised half their weekend already. Instead I plan to keep myself to myself today; I have a bit of prep to do for work tomorrow, and might even go into school to do it. It would just be easier than hanging around here, making them feel like they need to entertain me or keep me occupied. They need their family time today – the girls are around for the whole day, which only happens on a Sunday, and it's important I don't get in the way of that.

So by eleven in the morning I am in school. It's a bit weird as I hardly ever go in at weekends, but also quite cathartic too; familiar, but different enough not to feel like a normal working day. Fortunately there are no other cars in the car park, so I will be alone. I haven't heard from Tom this weekend. Normally we text fairly regularly, but I know he is giving me some space to do what I have to do. I hadn't actually come out and said to him that I was finishing with Mark, but had implied as much, and although it would be easy to drop him a quick line saying 'I've done it!' or 'That's it!' or something similar, somehow it doesn't seem appropriate, and I feel I don't want to devalue what I've been through by turning it into a triumphant, short and sweet, exclamation-marked proclamation. I'd rather wait and tell him face to face, and impart the news with a little more gravitas, give it the status it deserves. He's just as unlikely to text me for similar reasons. It's all just better left for when we next meet, and when the new week comes, we can start to move on and see what the future holds for us both.

A couple of hours later I am engrossed in my work, and feeling really good about how far I have got with my planning, when I hear the main door to the school swing shut with a bang. I know I should go and investigate, and in the corridor come face to face with Tom. It's a bit of a shock as I hadn't expected to see him until tomorrow, and haven't really yet thought through what to say to him, or what I want to happen or not happen between us, so soon after breaking up with Mark.

'Grace, what a lovely surprise!' he says, kissing me quickly on the lips and holding onto both of my hands. 'Are you OK?' he asks, probably wanting to avoid having to ask me directly if my plans had been put into effect.

'Good thanks, didn't expect to see you here either. I'm staying at Evie's so I thought I'd give them all a bit of space today and get some work done.'

'So, if you're staying at Evie's does that mean…?' he begins gingerly, and I can't really blame him for not wanting to come out and say it. Nor can I blame him for the brief flash of pure joy that passes over his face. He quickly tries to hide it; he's a good person and he knows he needs to hear me out, let me explain everything in due course. But it's no surprise that he would feel elated that there is now, in theory, no impediment to the relationship between the two of us ploughing ahead at full speed.

He leads me to his office and sits me down. 'Tell me about it all, Grace. That's if you want to, of course.'

'There's not much to say really, other than it's over between Mark and me. Eight years of "us", consigned to the dustbin.' I try not to sound too down, as it's not actually how I feel. Today I have a great sense of release and relief, but when prompted to talk about it again, it's easy to slip back into the momentousness of the act and get dragged back down into the mire.

Tom pulls me to him and we just sit there, my head on his shoulder, feeling the warmth from his body. He doesn't make a move to kiss me, and I feel sure it's because he must be terrified of frightening me off at a fragile moment. It must have occurred to him how easy that could be; newly split from a long-term partner, not every woman would necessarily want to jump into the arms of a new man, even if he is one she has tested the waters with a little beforehand. His position is still in jeopardy to some degree, I can see that, and no doubt he can too – I could mutate at any moment into a crazy, mixed up person, not wanting involvement with any man until she has well and truly got over her ex.

'What are you doing here on a Sunday, anyway?' I ask,

moving back from him and changing the subject in an attempt to dispel the mood from the air.

'Oh, I was at a loose end. Couldn't stop thinking about you actually, and wondering what was happening,' he runs his fingers through his hair, 'and work is a good distraction, so, well, here I am. Added bonus to find you here, though,' he grins.

Suddenly I am really glad he *is* here. We would have had limited time to talk tomorrow, and he would have been bursting to hear the news I was bursting to impart. At least we have been given that opportunity today. Neither of us would have been the first to make contact this weekend so if it weren't for this chance encounter we would both still be wondering about a lot of things.

'Come for some lunch with me,' he proposes. 'No pressure, just lunch in a pub somewhere. We can chat, relax, and do something normal with our day off, rather than be stuck here working.'

'Yes but look what happened last time we tried to make it to a pub,' I laugh, 'and haven't you got work to do?'

'Nothing that won't keep,' he replies. 'I'm only here because I couldn't think what else to do to pass the time till I saw you again.'

Then he does kiss me properly. Just gently, tenderly. It's luscious and bolts of lightning-lust sear up through my body. I still feel it's not quite right though, too soon, and I don't want to rush things. I want us as a couple to work and I want us to get the order of things correct, not be too hasty to rush into a full-on relationship. I know we have already slept together, but that was before I was single, and it feels different now, somehow. We no longer have the restrictive boundaries that we had before the weekend, but that doesn't mean that now the fences are down we need to make a bolt for it. Also I am still in mourning for Mark to some degree, and I need to give myself time to grieve for the relationship that was.

'Just lunch, then,' I accede, pulling away from him, but keeping hold of his hand so that he doesn't think he is being entirely rebuffed.

And we have a thoroughly lovely time. We spend the afternoon in the village pub garden, eating, chatting and laughing. The day is warm and balmy, the Pimms flows, and we are both totally relaxed with each other. We don't talk about anything heavy or serious, we don't mention Mark and I, or where Tom and I are heading. We spend the time starting to get to know one another properly, which is something we haven't really done yet, and it has all the feel of a first date. We make each other laugh with stories of our youth, tell tales of our families and all their idiosyncrasies, and discover more about each other than we have had the opportunity to do until now. It's perfect and lovely, and the afternoon flies by.

It's early evening before we finally agree, with a huge chunk of reluctance, that it's about time we went our separate ways. Tom is only just within the legal limit for driving, I should imagine, and thankfully I left my own car in the school car park, but it'll only be a short walk to work from Evie's in the morning. Tom offers to run me back to her house, but I decline. I don't think it would be a good thing for my friendship with her to arrive back, clearly somewhat tipsy, chaperoned by Tom. They might not even spot him dropping me off, but for now I don't want to take that chance. Not until I've had an opportunity to speak to Evie properly about this new man in my life. I don't want to get 'sprung' at this stage and have to make excuses for my behaviour. I know in reality Evie has no entitlement to an explanation for anything I have chosen to do, but all the same I feel I owe it to her, and to our friendship.

'Will you come to Frannie's wedding with me in a couple of weeks?' I ask Tom drunkenly as I walk with him to his car.

'I'd be honoured,' he replies, smiling. 'Are you sure, though? Will you be ready to be seen with me in public places by then?'

'I'm at the pub, with you now, aren't I? You know, that pub in the village we both work in and where no doubt someone will have seen us together on a Sunday afternoon and put two and two together. How more public can you get than a pub?'

'Well, they might think we're having a planning meeting?' he jokes.

'Yeah, right, we always do that on a Sunday afternoon over a jug of Pimms,' I reply, then add, 'Now there's an idea. Maybe we should put that one to the rest of the team. Alcohol always helps, I find.'

'I think you're a bit pissed, Grace,' he laughs, stroking my face affectionately. 'Go back to Evie's and have a relaxing evening and I'll see you tomorrow. Thanks for today, it's been lovely, and I'm glad you're OK,' and here he leans in a bit closer and whispers, 'And I'm glad you're mine.' He kisses me one last time, and climbs into his car. 'You are, aren't you?' he adds, looking up at me, the confidence of his previous comment suddenly gone.

'I am,' I reply.

I practically skip back up the hill to Evie's, a combination of the alcohol pumping through my veins and a wonderful sense of being at the beginning of something very big and exciting.

Evie's car is not on the drive, so presumably they have gone off somewhere for the afternoon. Can't blame them for wanting to avoid the lodger, in case she should return home full of woe and want to talk about her break-up all over again. No, I'm sure they don't think like that about me really, but all the same it is nice to have some space, in a neutral environment, to get my head together and think things over. I really am still genuinely sad about Mark and me, but I know I have so much to look forward to with Tom, and the sense of expectancy and excitement is overwhelming.

I grab my book and head for the patio and one of the lovely, comfy loungers. I'm still there, snoring away, when Evie and James arrive back with the girls. I wake up and shiver, feeling the chill as the gentle evening sun has now taken over from the full-on heat of the day. Sober, at least, after a long nap, which is something.

'Hi Grace, how was your day?' Evie asks.

'Yeah, good thanks, got lots of work done.' I leave it at that.

'We met up with Alex and the kids, she was asking how you are. Surprised to hear you are our new resident!'

I bet she is. I haven't really spoken to Alex much about my relationship with Mark, since she revealed that the two of them had become good friends. It just seemed disloyal, somehow. But I know I will have to. Whatever my friend's reaction is going to be, I owe it to her to tell her everything that's going on, not because I feel I need to justify my actions, but because she is one of my best friends and we normally share everything.

'She said she'd grab you at school tomorrow, but she's coming next Saturday, too, so we'll have a good catch-up.'

'Great,' I say, trying to sound more enthusiastic than I feel. It's going to be tough explaining my complicated and newly adulterous love life to my two best friends.

Nineteen

'Round One' of shopping completed, two intense hours of retail therapy under our belts and our credit cards have taken a substantial hit. Three pairs of well-laden, aching arms are ready for a trip back to the car to dump the bags before we head off to find somewhere for lunch. This is a source of dispute at the moment, and my two friends are scrapping like a pair of teenagers. Evie fancies the revolving sushi bar in Selfridges, Alex says she gets motion sickness watching it all go round and in any case doesn't see the point of raw tuna and rice – it's not real food. I would just be happy with a glass of water and somewhere to sit down for five minutes. I seem to be living on air since last weekend; I haven't fancied food in the slightest all week. Probably down to 'new relationship euphoria', the reason why so many women newly *in lurve* shed the pounds like they're on some kind of magical diet. It's an oft-proven theory, and here I am, a walking casebook for the phenomenon.

Finally, and after some well-timed refereeing from me to stop world war three breaking out in the ranks, we settle on an Italian restaurant with a terrace overlooking the shops. We can eat, *and* people-watch, wear our designer sunglasses and look like proper 'ladies who lunch'. Perfect.

In our devotion to retail therapy, no one has yet mentioned my, or anyone else's love life, but I sense the moment could be fast approaching. More than anything, I am unsure of what Alex's reaction is going to be, especially when I tell them about Tom. I don't know why I feel like I need her approval quite so much. I can't get my head round this strange feeling I have that she might actually take Mark's side in the whole debacle, instead of mine. I think I just want my friends to be able to respect my decisions, and still love me and accept what I've chosen to do. After all these are the friends with whom I have shared so much, they are hardly going to judge me, are they? But then Evie's own marriage is so rock solid and perfect, and Alex still has her deceased husband on a pedestal of perfection, so I am the only one to have officially failed, not only to get a ring on my finger, but to be able to make my relationship work and last. And here I am, newly split from a long term partner, jumping into the bed of a new man, and that man no less than my boss! Whatever will they think of me?

They are on their second glass of wine each (fortunately for them I am today's designated driver), before Alex asks me, 'So, Grace, how are you? How's it all going?'

'It's been a funny old week,' I reply, trying to break the subject in gently. I tell them (well, Alex, really, Evie has heard it all before) about the break-up, recounting the conversation that Mark and I had had, what happened, and how I came to be Evie's new lodger. She listens sympathetically, and doesn't at any point venture to make a stand for Mark's case.

She doesn't mention if she has seen him this week, and I'm not really sure I want to know, in any case. I'm sure he is suffering too, but I have no desire to hear about it – we both have to manage to survive this in our own ways, and we will. 'I'm OK though,' I add, 'I'm getting there.'

I consider this is a good juncture at which to mention Tom, and take a deep breath before launching in. 'There's something I have to tell you both.' I have their undivided attention instantly. 'There's someone else. But before I tell you who, you have to believe me that he's had *nothing* to do with Mark and me splitting up. That would have happened regardless. We grew apart and that's that.'

'Grace, you sly old thing!' Evie snorts with a giggle, looking astonished, but the huge smile she beams out indicates that she is at least pleased for me. 'How did you manage to keep it so quiet?'

'It's Tom, isn't it?' Alex asks, her face a picture of disapproval, and my silence just affirms her suspicions. She looks far from enthusiastic about the whole idea, and her gaze wanders outwards towards the passing shoppers, instead of inwards into our conversation, as though she can't bear to look at me.

'No way!' Evie giggles, still in her high-pitched, excited squawk. 'I knew he liked you, but I was only teasing you the other day,' she goes on. 'He *is* gorgeous, though, can't say I blame you! That hair, those muscles, mmmm. So have you…?'

'Evie, how can you?' Alex butts in, cutting Evie's enthusiasm dead. 'Grace, I can't believe you'd do that to poor Mark, he doesn't deserve that,' she goes on.

'I thought you'd find it hard, Alex, that's why I made it quite clear first that it has absolutely nothing to do with Mark and me splitting up.'

'Don't be so silly, how can it not? Can you honestly say you would still have left Mark by now if you didn't have Tom lined up and waiting?' she asks.

I hate arguing with my friends, but it's as I'd feared. I knew Alex would jump to Mark's defence, seeing him as the wronged, cuckolded partner in all this, even though she's *my* friend first and foremost, not his. And nor is she usually so quick to judge, she can be a lot more open-minded when she wants to be. But I'd had a bad feeling about telling her, and I'd been right.

'Yes I would, and I can say that in all honesty,' I try to explain. 'I've tried so hard in my head to keep the two things separate. I've never done anything like this before, you know that, but I knew Mark and I were over well before I realised I was in love with Tom. I've tried to do the right thing, Alex, really I have. You can't say Mark and I haven't tried time and time again to get things back on track. And I know it's kind of clichéd, but you can't help who you fall in love with. You know, ideally I'd like to be completely on my own right now, to get over Mark properly, and all that. But Tom is there, he's waiting for me. He's not going to rush me into anything, but I'm very, very glad I've got him. And it's not a rebound thing, either. I just love him, simple as that. He makes me feel wonderful, and beautiful, and happy. That's how it is.'

Despite Alex's negativity, I can't help the glow that spreads across my face, and I feel myself blush. 'Please be happy for me, Alex. I didn't do any of this on purpose, and I definitely didn't set out to hurt Mark. We made the decision together that we should go our separate ways. It's been coming for a while now. It's hard for both of us.'

'I'm sorry, Grace,' Alex says. 'It's just that I've seen quite a lot of Mark lately and he's so cut up about it all. He's so sad, poor thing, and when I saw you happy and full of this new love it seemed wrong, somehow. Unfair.'

'I'm sorry too, Alex,' I reply. 'I know you two have become quite close, and you must think I've moved on and forgotten him already, but I haven't. We spent eight years together, for goodness sake. He'll always be a massive part of my life, you can't just forget all that. Just because I've had the opportunity to move on sooner than he has, don't resent me for it, please.'

She pulls me into a big hug across the table, and we whisper our 'Sorrys' into each other's shoulders. I think we will be OK. It's understandable that she should feel for Mark, he's probably talked to her more about our problems than I ever did, so no wonder, really.

'So,' Evie persists with her earlier line of questioning, 'Have you...?' Her eyebrows wiggle up and down naughtily.

'Yes,' I squeak, pulling a face like an excited child on Christmas morning, and bouncing up and down in my seat, unable to contain myself any longer. 'Yes, we have!'

'And?' she continues.

'And... it was lovely,' I reply, with a smug, self-contained expression that lets Evie know not to ask for any more detail. I don't want to embellish; it's all just for Tom and me for the moment. 'It was before Mark and I split up though, but please, please, please don't judge me!' I plead quickly. I glance at Alex to check her reaction, but she is fine this time. She smiles at me, and I sense in that smile that at last I have her blessing. Thank God. I can't bear the thought of losing one of my best friends as a result of all this. I think I have managed to convince her to be happy for me, and that I'm not some kind of wild, voracious man-eater.

Lunch over, we still have more shopping to do. Evie is on the look-out for the perfect outfit to travel in next week. Only Evie could be so concerned about how she will look when she's on a plane. The rest of us are happy to go in our comfy jeans, but Evie is up there with the celebs in the fashion stakes, she needs to cut a dash at Florence airport and show those Italians that style isn't only home-grown.

So we help her hunt down a gorgeous little dress which looks so lovely on her, plus some shoes and a bag to go with it. She has to be the only woman I know to buy new leather goods *before* going to Italy. I am still revelling in the fruits of my shopping in Positano, back in May. I have tonnes of new bags and shoes in my… wardrobe.

I suddenly have a pang of longing for my dressing room and all the clothes and accessories I have left behind. I feel a sneaky trip back to the house coming on this week. Well, it's not really that sneaky, is it? It's still half my house, after all. Perhaps I shouldn't be out spending all this cash, I might need it over the next few months, as I don't know what the future holds for me financially. I can't imagine for one minute that Mark would leave me with nothing, but at the same time, I only have my salary to fall back on now, not our joint income. Maybe I should be sensible, so I decide against any more purchases today. My role will be purely as personal shopping consultant to Alex and Evie for the rest of the day.

'Excuse me madam. Do you have a few minutes?' Oh God, it's one of those annoying survey women that are the scourge of our high streets and shopping centres these days. Usually I am pretty adept at adopting aggressively off-putting body language as I walk past so they daren't risk their lives asking me to stop and tick their boxes. This time though I am caught unawares, my head up and away with the fairies in the clouds, and I don't have time to prepare my defence. In any case, she looks quite nice, this one. Not too cringe-worthy, no cloying 'How are you today?' and no hand on my arm. I can't abide being physically grabbed by a total stranger. Being verbally grabbed is bad enough.

'Do you mind if I ask you a couple of quick questions?' she asks. I notice from her badge that her name is Fenella. I bet her Home Counties parents never expected her to have a dead-end job like this when she grew up. With a name like that she ought to be a doctor or a lawyer. She's clearly far too middle-class for all this. 'It won't take too long, I promise.'

I clock out of the corner of my eye that Evie and Alex have disappeared into another shop, no doubt to avoid the same fate as me. They throw a sly smile over their shoulders as they abandon me to Fenella and her clipboard. Thanks girls.

'What's it about?' I ask, hoping that it's something completely irrelevant that I won't be able to contribute to, such as a nappy-effectiveness survey, or a Horse Rider Monthly subscription.

'Oh, just your shopping habits, that kind of thing. I'm not selling anything, I promise.'

'OK then, fire away,' I acquiesce.

'Firstly, can I ask which age bracket you fall into?' I point to the 26-35 box and she ticks.

'Are you married, single, co-habiting, divorced, or other?' she asks. Suddenly that seems a difficult question to answer.

Er, single, I suppose,' I reply. I'm not about to explain my circumstances to a complete stranger. I'm not single either, really, but Tom and I are so new I don't really feel I can quite call him my boyfriend yet, even though he is. This is hard – I didn't expect to find a street survey so challenging.

'And your household salary bracket, if you don't mind me asking?' I look at her clipboard, and my eyes are instantly drawn to the £125,000+ line, right at the bottom. That would have been true up to a week ago, when our combined salaries were well in excess of that figure. But then I do a double take and realise that most of that is Mark's salary. Of course it is. Mine is only a lowly teacher's salary, I can't include Mark's paycheque with mine any more, so I meekly point to the '£25,000 - £35,000' box and she ticks again. How depressing. Not that Mark's salary prospects would have been sufficient to keep me with him, of course they wouldn't, I'm not that shallow, but I have just been knocked from highest to second to lowest, as far as this survey is concerned. Depressing thought, and I resolve yet again that I am done with spending for today. Time to be sensible, Grace. After all I have a huge wardrobe back at mine and Mark's house (I no longer want to use the word *home*, as it isn't any more), I don't need any more clothes, shoes, bags and make-up. I need to be grateful for what I have and curb my materialistic streak from now on. Grace, Queen of Shoppers, has just been demoted. Dowager Queen now, at most. I've had it too easy, I realise.

Time for a reality check.

Twenty

Frannie is radiant in her cream silk dress and she looks a picture. Well done to her for being brave enough to wear a wedding gown; women of a certain age and above almost always seem to get married in a sensible trouser suit, and it does seem such a waste of a great opportunity for dressing up in a posh frock of some sort. OK so she hasn't gone for the great big meringue – that would have looked more than a little inappropriate – but instead she has chosen a simple, long, straight dress, with full-length sleeves and a scooped neck, and a small veil too. She's never done this before, so I can't blame her for wanting to do it in style, and she looks beautiful and just right for the occasion.

Gerald's son has the honour of walking her up the aisle to meet her future husband, and he carries it off with such aplomb, proudly delivering her to his father's side before taking his own seat at the front of the church. Gerald himself is resplendent in his morning suit, looking quite dashing. His son is a carbon copy of himself, only a couple of decades younger. He must be reassured, looking at his father, that he is likely to retain his good looks well into his old age. What a handsome family they make.

Tom and I stand side by side in our pew, near the front, on the side of the bride. Gerald had given strict instructions to his ushers to ensure we had good seats, and a very nice young man, one of Gerald's colleagues, I think, escorted us to our places and made sure we were properly installed. There aren't that many people here; Gerald does have family, and those that can be here, are, but Frannie is effectively alone in the world now, apart from her friends and the family she is about to acquire via marriage. So as one of her closest and truest friends, I have pride of place on her side of the church, almost like an honorary daughter.

I'd wondered how I would feel about today. After all it was one of the days I had originally earmarked for my marriage to Mark. A wedding that never actually made it to the planning stage. Probably just as well, given how quickly things between us deteriorated. At least we hadn't got as far as booking the church, the reception, the honeymoon and all that, so there were no cancellations to be made when we broke up, to add to the pain and the sense of failure.

Actually, I feel fine. There is no longing, no aching wish that I was the bride standing there with Mark by my side. No, definitely not, despite how I had longed to be married for so long. I sneak a look up at the handsome man standing beside me and know I have made the right decision. Tom looks gorgeous in his smart morning suit, a tall and commanding presence, and I slip my hand into his as the vicar starts on his 'Dearly Beloved…' Tom looks down at me and smiles, and squeezes my hand.

'…I pronounce you man and wife. You may kiss the

bride.' There is a cheer from the small congregation as Gerald pulls his new wife into his arms and kisses her hard on the lips. Frannie really has been swept off her feet, and I am so pleased for her. Her smile is enough to light up the whole church, as the service ends and the pair of them practically skip down the aisle together, in an elderly person sort of way, to the strains of Handel's Music for Royal Fireworks. No 'Here Comes the Bride, La Da De Da' for Frannie; it had to be a lot classier for her. And no doubt there will be a few fireworks tonight for Frannie and her new husband, given her track record. Let age be no barrier, and all that…

We all trundle off to Compton Hall for the wedding breakfast, and are thoroughly spoilt from the moment we arrive. Frannie may never have seen herself as the marrying type before, but now that she has crossed that boundary, it's obvious that she has planned everything to the tiniest degree, from the delicious canapés and crisp champagne awaiting us, to the little wedding favours on the table, the coordinating flowers and balloons, all tastefully done of course, but all indicative of the fact that she has probably spent hours and hours poring over brochures and getting things just the way she wants them. She has done herself proud.

The champagne flows and the evening wears on. No loud and booming disco for our Frannie and Gerald; instead a swing band moves onto the stage to take the place of the string quartet from earlier, and the music picks up pace. The newlyweds take to the floor for their first dance, and Gerald handles Frannie like a professional, whizzing her round and twirling her under his arm. He doesn't go as far as any lifts or leaps, even though she must be as light as a feather – we don't want his paramedic colleagues to have to don their working gear tonight – but the two of them put on a real show before they beckon to the onlookers to come and join them.

'Are you dancin'?' Tom asks me.

'Are you askin'?' I smile in reply as he pulls me to the dance floor. To the strains of 'Great Balls of Fire' we whizz around the floor, wondering how these older folk manage to keep up with the pace of it, but amazingly enough, they do. After a couple of tracks my head is spinning and I make for our table for some water. As I go to sit down I feel the ground come up to meet me, and Tom catches me in time before I collapse into a heap on the floor.

'Grace, are you OK. What is it?' Tom asks worriedly.

'I don't know, I came over all dizzy for a bit there. Must have been all that spinning round.'

'Do you want me to take you home?' he asks.

'No, no, I can't do that, I'll be fine. I'm OK now,' I reply. I can't abandon Frannie in her moment of glory. I feel pretty lousy but I keep that to myself. A few quiet minutes sitting here and I'm sure I'll be fine.

'I'll go and get you some more water,' Tom offers. As he goes off in search of a jug, I rest my head on my hands at the table and try to work out what just happened. I'm not predisposed to fainting, it's not normally my thing. I suppose I haven't eaten much today; somehow I just didn't fancy the smoked salmon starter, even though it looked gorgeous, and only managed a little bit of the main course, too. The pudding though, that went down a treat. Me and my sweet tooth. Yes, that must be it, too much alcohol and sugar and not enough proper food to soak it up. And it's really warm in here as well.

By the time Tom comes back, looking white and concerned, I am much recovered, and make a move to stand up.

'Stay there, Grace, sit down for a bit longer,' he says. 'Are you sure you don't want to go home?'

'I'm fine, really,' I protest. And I am, now. I don't know where it all came from. As quickly as it hit me, it's over. I jump up quickly and pull him onto the dance floor as it seems the only way to convince him that I am fine.

Tom and I have taxis booked to take him home and me back to Evie's house later.

'Cancel your cab, come home with me tonight,' he whispers in my ear as we dance a 'slowie' together. 'I can keep an eye on you, make sure you're OK,' he goes on. 'With the added bonus of being able to make passionate love to you, too,' he adds with a twinkle in his eye, and I feel the hairs stand on end on the back of my neck. 'If you're feeling up to it, of course,' he jokes.

I giggle and nuzzle closer to him, my face against his shoulder, breathing in his fabulous smell. I know I hadn't wanted to rush into things straight after the break-up with Mark, but I have to say the idea of being looked after, when I *am* feeling a little delicate, has a huge appeal. Not to mention that it would be just gorgeous to spend the night in his arms. All night, with no guilt attached, and no one to rush back to in the morning, for the sake of keeping up appearances. And Evie is away, so I have no explanation to give there either, even though I'm sure she wouldn't have expected one, had she been home. I'm a big girl now, quite capable of making my own decisions, thank you very much. A night in Tom's arms, even if I'm not up to much in the passion stakes – I am still feeling a little drained after the earlier dizzy episode – is just what I need. The thought of it sets my senses all a-tingle. What better cure.

'You're on,' I say, trying to sound casual, but knowing that it is what I want, one hundred and fifty percent. How on earth are we going to take this relationship slowly, I wonder, if I'm already agreeing to spend the night at his place, only a fortnight or so after splitting from Mark? Slow quite obviously just isn't the way to go, as I'd thought it would be. But as long as whatever I do feels right to me, then it can't be the wrong thing, can it?

I wake up to the smell of fresh coffee and bacon. My stomach growls in anticipation and I remember just how little I'd eaten yesterday. Tom comes into the bedroom in just his boxers, bearing a tray with coffee and said bacon in a couple of large, crusty baps, and I could fall on him with gratitude. How anyone could turn vegetarian and miss the pure, unadulterated culinary bliss of a bacon sarnie I will never comprehend. It has to be the most fabulously mouth-watering smell on the planet.

'Thank you,' I say, through a mouthful of sandwich, as he pulls back the covers and climbs back into bed beside me.

'Well, isn't this nice,' he giggles, snuggling up and tucking into his own breakfast. 'What's for dessert?' he sniggers, putting one hand under the covers and rubbing it electrifyingly along the outer edge of my thigh.

'You'll have to wait and see. No one comes between me and a bacon sarnie,' I reply.

With that as a challenge, Tom finishes his breakfast and dives under the duvet whilst I'm still chewing on mine, his salty lips and tongue reaching down and seeking me out under the covers, pushing my legs apart. The only thing that comes between me and my bacon sarnie at that point is me. Ha ha.

'What shall we do today, then, my lovely?' Tom asks when he has emerged from the darkness of duvet-land. 'Shall I keep you here all day as my sex-slave, or would you like to take me out somewhere nice and show me off?' He nibbles at my ear and sets the nerves in my nose a-tingling.

'Both options sound very appealing, I have to say,' I reply, 'but I do have to get back and feed Evie's menagerie. Why don't you pop over later and we could go for a walk or something? Grab a bite to eat in the pub?'

We agree on a venue – I don't really feel right about inviting him back to Evie's, even though I know she wouldn't mind – and I make an attempt at getting up and showered. This takes three goes, as each time Tom pulls me back to bed and it's such a wrench trying to get back up again when he is covering me in kisses and caresses.

'Let me go, you sex-crazed maniac,' I plead, jokingly. He does, but then follows me into the bathroom, turns me around, and in one deft movement, lifts me up onto the vanity unit and makes love to me again. At this rate I won't be able to stand, sit, or do anything involving the lower half of my body for at least a week. I'm not complaining, though, as he works his magic on me yet again before finally yielding to the fact that I do actually need to go, and letting me get into the shower – unaccompanied.

'See you later, gorgeous,' he says as I eventually make it to the door, fully clothed and without him attached to me at some contact-point. The taxi he has called for me has been honking its horn outside for the past fifteen minutes, and it feels like an advertisement to the world at large that I have just spent the night making wild passionate love with the man in flat number 53.

'Not if I see you first,' I joke, planting a big sloppy kiss on his cheek as I finally leave.

Twenty-One

What a blissful thought, six weeks of holiday yawning like a vast chasm ahead of me. Well, five weeks, really I suppose, if you take out the final week – I will be in school for most of it, sorting stuff out ready for the new academic year, plus there's usually a bit of training to be had, too. But that's fine.

And for the first time in I don't know how long, I have absolutely nothing planned, and that's a surprisingly refreshing feeling. I used to be pretty quick off the mark at getting holidays booked, arranging time to see family and friends, and organising Mark's diary and annual leave around all those. But this time, all I have to worry about is me, I can take each day as it comes, go away if and when I feel like it, and generally just please myself. Plus of course see lots of Tom as well, although he does still have some work commitments over the holidays, being the Head and the chief responsible person and all that. We haven't discussed a holiday together; it seems too soon and a bit too scary to be entering into a joint venture like that just yet, but we will have lots of days together and generally see plenty of each other. We've both said we want to invest lots of time really getting to know one other, and we're lucky that we share the enviably long summer break in which to do just that.

I wake up on the first Monday morning, and yawn languorously. Oh, what to do today, the first day of what feels like an infinitely long break? Over a solitary breakfast in the sunshine on Evie's decking, I decide on a bit of shopping in town first, then a surprise visit to Tom's. I'll land on his doorstep bearing food and wow him with the prospect of a home-cooked meal – it'll be our first proper night in together. I'm not going to call him and pre-warn him – that would spoil the surprise. He told me he had some paperwork to catch up on today so he would be in all day. And how could he not be pleased to see me, the love of his life (so he told me yesterday) arriving on his threshold with all the ingredients to knock up a gourmet meal for two. He can pour me a large glass of something cold and crisp and sit and watch me cook, and we can chat and... well, we'll just see, but if previous experience is anything to go by, I'll still be there tomorrow morning. Lovely. Better make sure I have a toothbrush and an emergency set of spare undies in my bag...

My phone beeps, and it's a text from Evie. They're all in Mallorca now, for three weeks, lucky things, which works out well for me staying here and getting my life in order for just a bit longer. Mark and I have put our house on the market, and there has already been some interest, so we should be able to sort things out financially before too long. Evie is still insistent that I stay here for as long as I need to, but I think I may well look into renting somewhere if the house sale drags on – it's not really fair to them all otherwise.

But in the meantime I am enjoying her gorgeous house and garden, and acting as house-sitter, so everybody is happy.

'Having a great time here, weather fab, girls brown as berries & getting webbed feet. Forgot to send you this pic of me, Lydia & our new mate David in Florence,' it reads. 'He reminds me of your Tom, but only U can know how much!!! Hope all OK at home xxx' I scroll down to see a photo of the sisters standing in front of the copy of Michelangelo's *David* in the Piazza della Signoria, smiling away and pointing to the more obviously male attributes of *David*'s. Trust Evie, cheeky as ever... But I can see where she's coming from. With his curly hair and muscular body there is some resemblance, although thankfully I can say that Tom is significantly better endowed than his sculpted counterpart. I giggle at that thought and tap out a reply to Evie:

'Yes can see the likeness – in some places more than others!!! x' Let her make of that what she will!

Animals fed and watered, and all my house-keeping responsibilities dealt with, it's just before noon when I finally head off into town, for a bit of a leisurely browse round the shops –I am meant to be keeping my spending on a tight leash, remember – followed by a trip to the supermarket to stock up on ingredients. I'd raided Evie's collection of cookery books this morning, and settled on grilled swordfish, green beans and tomato salsa, followed by crème brûlée, but then changed my mind on the pudding when it occurred to me that Tom's kitchen implements just might not include a cook's blowtorch. So far it gives me the impression of a warmer-upper's kitchen rather than a cook's, but as yet I've had no opportunity to discover how extensive or otherwise Tom's culinary skills are, other than I know he makes a cracking bacon sandwich. When I lived with Mark, I'd got used to having every possible kitchen appliance known to man at my disposal. So instead I settle on chocolate pots, adding the ingredients to my list, although on second thoughts I might actually cheat and buy pudding, just in case we get carried away and decide we have better things to do…

A couple of hours later and I am sitting in the window of Costa, poring over today's paper and nursing a half-cold cappuccino. It hadn't occurred to me how hard it would be to go shopping but not *actually* go shopping – abstaining from spending is torture, and I just don't have the commitment to it that I possess when my credit cards are ready, willing and able to be flexed. So I have parked myself here to pass some time before I head off on my food-buying mission. And it's great, don't get me wrong. I love watching the world go by, in all its multi-coloured, multi-racial glory, and am enjoying catching up with what's going on around the globe, as I so rarely get a chance to read a paper. Slowing down to the pace of the holidays just takes a bit of getting used to, that's all.

Something catches my eye – a man that looks a lot like Tom. Hang on a minute, it *is* Tom. My hand goes up to wave, to beckon him over to come and join me but then I see that he is not alone. He is not looking my way at all, but is totally engrossed in the company of the tall, slim blonde, around whose shoulder his arm is draped.

I feel sick. Completely and utterly sick to the pit of my stomach. I don't know whether to run out of the coffee shop, chase after him and demand to know who she is and what right she has to be parading in front of the world with *my* boyfriend, or to crawl into a hole and wail until my heart breaks. I have a physical pain in my chest, and want to double up with it and howl, give full vent to my rage and jealousy. Either way I have to get out of here and I stagger out of the coffee shop in a blind panic, no longer sure of where I am going or what I am supposed to be doing.

Somehow I manage to make my way back to my car. I open the door, climb inside, clasp the steering wheel tightly in both hands and cry and cry and cry. I feel like my heart is broken in two, I feel totally crushed, and confused too. Who is she? What right does he have to do that to me? None whatsoever is my verdict. He's only just declared to me that I am the love of his life, and look how long he's waited for me to be free! Is that what the problem is? Now that I am no longer a challenge, suddenly it's all too easy and he's off to make the next conquest? Somehow it just doesn't fit with the Tom that I thought I knew and loved.

Eventually I find enough energy to start the car up and drive away. I don't know where to, though, as suddenly my plans for the day are in tatters. Completely decimated, more like. You can forget the surprise visit and home-cooked meal, Tom; in any case you'll probably still be out with the blonde and not safely tucked away in your flat, tackling your paperwork like you told me you would be. Liar! How dare he! No wonder he'd been non-committal about his plans for today, probably trying to put me off seeing him, in case I interrupted his liaison with this woman, whoever she is. And who is she, anyway? Some ex-girlfriend or other, or the latest challenge to add to the notches on the bedpost, now that I am too readily available and not exciting enough?

I don't recall much of the drive back to Evie's house; somehow my own personal in-built sat-nav gets me there safely, and I pull onto Evie's drive, absolutely shattered. I am totally knocked for six and don't know which way to turn. Suddenly I revert to a childlike form and all I want is my Mum. I want to run home crying and screaming, and have Mum rub my back and say comforting things, make me some homemade soup and tuck me into bed. I don't feel I can cope with facing up to this – I want to go off and hide, so that is exactly what I decide to do.

'Mum, can I come and stay for a few days?' I wail into the phone a few minutes later. Mum senses the desperation in my voice, but doesn't ask what's wrong.

'Of course you can, sweetheart, come now. Text me the train time once you're on it and I'll send Dad to come and pick you up. You can tell me all about it then. We haven't seen you for ages, it'll be lovely.' Lovely, yeah, right. She doesn't know what she's in for, poor thing. Her heartbroken youngest daughter is about to arrive on her doorstep, in desperate need of some major TLC and serious love-life counselling. I haven't even told my parents about Tom. It seemed too soon to have to explain it all to them. They wouldn't have understood how I could move on so quickly

– it didn't happen like that in their day. Couples worked at it then and made more of an effort to get their relationship back on track. Although in those days I would have had a ring on my finger by now, so the break-up would have been a lot harder, from an organisational perspective. Thank God Mark and I weren't married – I am grateful for that now – as I have been able to just walk away from our life together, and the only thing still binding us is our house full of joint possessions. And most of those I could live without.

Mum will no doubt assume my heart is breaking over Mark. I'll have to tell them about Tom, of course. Eventually. Somehow. I can't go to them for help and then not be entirely truthful with them. I just hope they can see it in their hearts to understand why my love-life became so complicated, and how I could fall in love with another man when I was already in a supposedly secure relationship with another.

I put in a quick call to Evie's mother to tell her I am going to be away for a few days, and to ask if she can take over responsibility for pet feeding and house sitting. She accepts graciously and can quite clearly sense that I am not entirely right in myself. She tells me kindly to 'Take care, dear, and don't worry about the house,' and promises to come over that evening to make sure everything is OK.

Absolved of my responsibilities to Evie, I pack a quick bag and ring for a cab. Three and a half hours later I am hanging out of the train window and have already spotted my dad, standing on the platform, waiting for my train to pull in. I feel myself well up when I first set eyes on him –

something to do with the normal-ness of him. He looks so unchanged from the last time I saw him, maybe just a teensy bit older, but otherwise just my plain old regular old Dad, lovely and comforting and my rock in stormy seas, a bit of normality amid the current chaos of my life.

I hurl myself off the train as soon as it stops and into Dad's hug. And then the tears start to flow.

'Come on, sweetheart, your Mum's made chicken soup,' is all he says, and it's all that's needed.

Twenty-Two

'Oh, Muuuuummmm,' I wail into her shoulder the minute I walk through the door. She grabs me and pulls me into a big hug, whilst Dad quietly fetches my bags from the car and makes himself useful putting the kettle on.

'Oh, my poor baby girl,' Mum says, and she rocks me from side to side as we stand together in the hall. 'I never thought he'd treat you like this, not in a million years. He always seemed so reliable.' She sounds so indignant – how dare anyone do this to her precious daughter? Just as I thought, and because they have no reason to think otherwise, my parents *do* believe my tears are for Mark, and I don't have the heart, or the soul, at the moment to tell them otherwise, so I go along with it for now. I'm not deliberately misleading them, of course I'm not. It's just that at this point in time I don't think they'd be ready to hear the real reason for my anguish. I suppose I am terrified of being thought of as a foolish girl, which is exactly what I feel I am at the moment.

'Come and sit down, dear, tell us all about it,' she goes on. Yikes, that's just what I don't want to do. So I decide to stick to generalisations and soak up their sympathy for a while longer, as I have a feeling their reactions may be a little less compassionate if I tell them about Tom and my life since my relationship with Mark came to an end.

'It was horrid, Mum,' I say, 'But I don't think I really want to talk about it just yet. What I really need is some time away from there to get my head straight. Is that OK?'

Mum makes promises of staying as long as I like and, seeing that she won't be needed just yet as chief shoulder-to-cry-on and all-round relationship counsellor, reverts to her usual busy-bee mode, buzzing around the kitchen, warming up the soup, setting the table, and doing what she does best and has given her life to – looking after her offspring.

I can hear my mobile ringing from my bag in the hall but decide to let it ring out. Whoever it is can leave me a message, after all. I don't want to speak to anyone, particularly if that someone turns out to be Tom. I haven't spoken to him at all yet today, so the likelihood is that it's him. Well, he can go hang, for all I care.

But I'm such a techno-addict and rubbish at being parted from my mobile for too long – I try to leave it but then can't resist popping out to the hall to check my call history. *Missed call – Tom* the display reads. Thought so. Phoning up to tell me it's all over then, were you, Tom? Were you going to tell me all about the new blonde in your life and how you and I were a lovely little fling, and how sorry you are, but that's it? Yeah, I bet you were. Either that or you are planning to have your cake and eat it, stringing us both along at the same time. Well, I don't want to hear it. It's the biggest mistake I ever made, thinking you were someone special and that I could trust you and be happy with you. How could I have been so wrong? Bravely I switch the thing off. No more than two points braver and I would flush it down the loo. I have better things to do with my time than listen to feeble excuses.

Mum spends the rest of the evening consoling me with beautiful food, and I stuff my face as though I haven't eaten for weeks – which I haven't properly, I suppose. Falling out of love with Tom bizarrely has given me my appetite back and I astonish my parents with the amount of food I manage to tuck away. *But then I haven't fallen out of love with you*, my heart wails to my head inside my body, via a rumble in my stomach, and it's as much as I can do not to cry out loud, mid-mouthful of Mum's gorgeous apple pie, with sheer broken-heartedness and physical pain as I remember the last few times we were together, and how special it was. There may only have been a few times, but each one was perfect. No, I haven't fallen out of love with him, I love him more than anything, and that just makes it so much worse. If I could switch off the emotions and hate him, then it would all be a lot easier to swallow, I feel sure.

Mum puts me to bed and tucks me in with a hot water bottle, back in the room that I used to share with my sister, Alice, in that comfortable, homely semi-detached house where I spent my childhood years. It's all so familiar, yet so different; our once pink ballerina'd walls are now tastefully painted in cream, and there is a double bed and duvet where our twin pink candlewick bedspreads used to sit. Mum has let go of the past and redecorated her daughter's bedrooms to accommodate her now adult offspring, their partners and in some cases, children, when they come to stay, instead of leaving the rooms untouched as a shrine to their childhoods. I am glad of it as I lie on the bed, trying to sleep. This feels like neutral territory now, only with the added bonus of the familiar and comforting presence of my parents.

The next morning I wake to the noisy rabble of children in the kitchen. I glance at the clock and see that it's 11.08 – I have slept for over twelve hours. Total exhaustion had taken control of my body, and I feel so much better, physically, at least, than I did last night. But then I remember, and a pang of pain shoots up through my body, along the same tracks where only so recently the thoughts of Tom sent pangs of lust. How things have turned about in such a short space of time…

I check my phone and there are nine messages from him, varying from cheeky little texts, sent yesterday, saying the naughty but lovely things that he usually does, gradually migrating into very concerned voice messages this morning, wondering where I am and asking me to contact him as he's so worried about me. Which I'm not going to, of course.

I realise my presence must be expected downstairs – no doubt Mum has rallied the troops round in an effort to keep me occupied and cheer me up, so I quickly shower and attempt to scrub the 'victim' stamp from my forehead. I plaster on a smile and head for the kitchen. Sarah, my eldest sister, is there, with her brood; Charlie, who is ten, and, shockingly, nearly as tall as me, and the girls, Amy and Lulu, Louise really, but no one has ever called her that, as far as I know. They are eight and six, if my Good Auntie vibes are working correctly. I haven't seen them for ages and they charge at me like a small herd of wild buffalo, planting sticky kisses (Mum's latest round of baking – brownie this time?) all over my face. The reception they give me is totally natural and unprompted and it cheers me up no end.

'Look at you all, you've grown so much,' I say, with genuine surprise and affection, but hating that I'm trolling out the same comments that my relatives used to inflict on me as a child. Why *do* grown-up relations do that to children? I used to really take offence at it when I was in my teens and those ageing aunties and uncles were *still* saying it – did they think I was getting fat or something?

'We're taking you to Chessington, Auntie Grace!' Lulu, exclaims. 'There are loads of rides and animals and a roller coaster and...' she nearly bursts with the excitement of it all, pogo-ing around the kitchen, her dark brown plaits flapping up and down, but her mother cuts in quick.

'Slow down, Lulu,' Sarah pleads. 'We haven't even asked Auntie Grace if she'd like to come yet,' but she looks at me imploringly as if to say, *Do come, please. Mum's arranged this to try to cheer you up but actually I'd really like you to come.* It's funny how an expression like that, cast quickly between two women, can say so much. She doesn't need to tell me about the amount of conniving that might have gone on between her and Mum, but Sarah being Sarah, she won't have minded one iota, and will love the fact that we sisters get to spend the day together, whether forced into it or not, as we see so little of each other these days.

Head Over Heels

Sarah and I were so close as children, well, all three of us were. Even though Alice is nearest to me in age at only eighteen months older, and we shared not just a room but so much more, Sarah is my Big Sister, at a whopping three whole years older than me, and that means a lot. She was the one we both used to look up to, and, poor thing, the one who had to furrow the paths which Alice and I would then follow so easily. Dad would always come down harder on her, being the eldest. She was never allowed to stay out as late as we were when we reached her age, never allowed to take boys to her room – we did, even though Mum would hover nervously at the foot of the stairs – and if there was so much as a whiff of alcohol on her breath when she came home, then she was summarily grounded for a week. I lost count of the number of times that Alice or I would stagger home after a night out, seriously worse for wear after a bottle of cheap cider or something equally noxious, and manage to convince Mum and Dad that we were perfectly sober. Poor thing, but I suppose it's the lot of any eldest child, especially when that child is a girl.

So Alice and I both admire her immensely, and have a lot to be thankful to her for. Our teenage years would have been a lot more challenging without her, but not only did she ease the way for us both, she was a fantastic friend too, and we always knew we could turn to her if we needed help. As in the sort of help you can't really ask your Mum about when you're fifteen or sixteen. Such as how we felt the first time we went to 'first base' with a boy, and when it would be appropriate to let him go 'downstairs' as well as 'upstairs'.

She was brilliant at all that; even now it brings me out in a cold sweat to imagine ever having to discuss those sorts of issues with Mum. I just don't think we would have done, so God knows how we'd have fared. But then poor Sarah must have got through it herself, somehow. She'd had no big sister to turn to when she was discovering boys and she certainly wouldn't have turned to her younger, completely innocent and inexperienced sisters.

'That sounds brilliant!' I reply to Lulu, bending down to her level and holding her hands, as much to tether her to the spot as anything else, and I really mean it too. Had someone asked me yesterday what I'd have liked to do today I'd probably have said mope in my room all day, play some old CD's and sit around in my PJ's. But actually, a day out with Sarah and the kids will be lovely. I can't remember when we last did that. And whenever we did, it would have been with the men in tow, too, and that always puts a completely different spin on the day. Having to keep the other half happy as well as do the whole family thing, and I'd never been sure that Mark and Nigel, Sarah's husband, actually liked each other, although they both managed to put a brave face on it. So there would have been all the politics of that to deal with too. No, Sarah and I will have a lovely day, focus on the kids one hundred percent, plus catch up on each other's lives and have a really good natter. Will I tell her about Tom? I don't know yet, haven't decided. Let's just see how things go.

'Bloody hell, Grace, you have been through it,' Sarah says,

sounding emotionally drained when I finish telling her about the whole Tom fiasco, whilst we sip our coffees on a bench in the outdoor play area. The kids had been amusing themselves quite self-sufficiently, so the timing had seemed right to be honest with her and just come out with it all. And I feel so much better for it, too. I needed someone to tell me I'm not behaving like a foolish schoolgirl, that these sort of 'adventures' can happen to normal, sane women like me, and to help me come to terms with the grief I feel, so deep, deep down in the pit of my stomach. It's not going to go away or even get a little bit better unless I tell someone about it; I can't tell Evie, she's not even in this country at the moment, and it would be wholly inappropriate to tell Alex, given her closeness to Mark, and Mum, well, that just goes without saying. Mum and I are very close, but there are boundaries…

'You have to talk to him, Grace,' Sarah pleads. 'What if you've completely misunderstood something totally innocent? She might just have been a friend or something?'

'Yeah and she looked really friendly from where I was sitting,' I reply sarcastically. 'The sort of intimate friendly like she either knows him really well, or doesn't know him at all but can't wait to drag him back to her lair and rip his pants off. Why should I talk to him when he's done that to me? I'm so angry with him I might just kill him.'

'No you won't,' she says, 'You love him. This is the Big One. You thought Mark was, but I could always see you came second fiddle to his career. If you didn't you'd have had a ring on your finger a long time ago. You put up with such a lot from him. Tosser.'

'Blimey Sarah, that's a bit strong. Did you really dislike him that much?' I say, amazed. No one has ever been quite so blunt in their opinion not just of Mark, but of our relationship. Then without waiting to hear her reply: 'I always thought I was happy and that it was just in these past few months, but happiness is all relative, isn't it? When I look back on it, he was a complete control freak. About everything, not just the wanting a baby stuff. I couldn't be completely 'me' with him. With Tom, that's all so different. We're grown up enough to know what we want from life and to feel we have a right to things being perfect, and if they're not, well, that's that, I suppose. Maybe it's just a maturity thing. But now he's gone and blown it, so he can't have been that mature, can he?'

'Have you heard from him?' Sarah asks.

'A load of worried-sounding messages, which I haven't replied to, of course. Let him stew for a bit,' I reply.

Sarah was a great one to use as a sounding board. She had vast and varied experience when it came to men. She'd travelled for a year after uni, spending time in Europe and further afield, and had come back with, not just some excellent knowledge of the various mother tongues and local cultures, but intimate knowledge of male tongues from most of the countries she had visited, too. There'd been Frédérique le Fantastique in France, Pedro the Pants in Spain, Giovanni the Gorgeous in Italy and Heinrich the Horny in Germany, to name but a few, and she had kept in touch with quite a few of them when she returned home, and maybe still does, who knows. But then when she fell in love properly, she really fell, hook line and sinker. Although God knows why she chose a man with a name like Nigel, when she'd had the pick of all the exotic names under the European sun. Not to knock Nigel, of course, he's a good man, just a little on the ordinary side, but maybe that had been just what she'd needed, after all that adventure. Maybe deep down inside she'd just been looking for a Nigel the Nice amongst all those Pedros and Giovannis.

We glance across at the kids – just a cursory glance to make sure they are (a) still there and haven't been abducted by dirty old men in flasher macs and (b) still in one piece on whichever activity they are currently climbing on. Fortunately they all seem to hunt in a pack, a bit like we three did when we were kids. They look out for each other, too, which is nice. And Charlie is so protective of his little sisters; not surprising really, given that he almost lost his Mum and his youngest sister when Sarah was giving birth to Lulu. I'm sure Sarah has put it all out of her mind now, in the way that mothers do with childbirth, or there'd only ever be one child per family. But the rest of us certainly haven't and I will never forget the looks on Mum and Dad's faces that day I visited Sarah in hospital. Basically, we'd all come to say goodbye to her, as none of us thought she would pull through. And it had been touch and go with Lulu for quite some time too. Sarah had had an emergency caesarean which had turned scary; they'd had difficulty getting Lulu out and she'd lost gallons of blood. I hate to imagine it but I can't help myself – I've watched too many hospital dramas where the blood is all over the floor and the medical staff keep slipping in it. Vile to think of my precious sister being that almost-dead body on the table, with the blood and gore everywhere, and the paddles on her chest to try and get her heart started again. She makes light of it, she says she never felt like she was going to die – she just had this massive urge to get better as she had a baby, plus two other children and a husband, to get back to. They needed her, so she pulled through. For her, it was as simple as that. But for the rest of us it's still a bad dream that won't completely go away, and it haunts me sometimes when I see her, thinking of how much we could all have lost.

Whilst I'm sitting there pensively with my sister, my phone rings again, and it's Tom. I have a really strong urge to answer it; I'm feeling confrontational, emboldened by the discussion with Sarah, but then at the last moment, with a sigh, I chicken out. I just can't face speaking to him. I don't know what I would say, really. A few seconds later there is the beep of a text message. Here he goes again. Persistent, isn't he? Has he finished entertaining Miss Blondey Locks Long Legs now and fancies getting his boring old teacher girlfriend round for some extra-curricular fun?

'Grace, where are you? Why are you ignoring me? Please let me know what's going on & if anything's wrong. Came to the house & you weren't there. Please PLEASE let me know UR OK. Love you & miss you, Tom xxx,' it reads.

I snort at it with derision and show it to Sarah. The expression on her face is the opposite of mine. She is taking sides with him, of all things! I don't believe it!

'You have to tell him where you are, Grace. Imagine if it was you, you'd be going out of your mind. At least send him a text and let him know you're still alive, even if you don't want to see him. Do it now,' she implores.

'OK then, I will, but only because you're my big sister and you know best,' I say, bowing to her superior knowledge on these matters.

'Am OK. At M&D's for a few days. Need some space. Grace,' I type.

'There you are,' I say, showing it to Sarah, 'are you satisfied now?'

'You normally add kisses to all your texts so you have to put one in otherwise what will he think?' she replies.

'Well, so he should be thinking,' I say indignantly. 'The man IS cheating on me, after all. He shouldn't be expecting kisses on the end of my texts.'

'You don't know that Grace,' she says, so calmly. 'Just do it,' she adds, exasperated, in little more than a whisper, so I do, and hit the *Send* button quickly before I can change my mind.

Several hours later we return to Mum and Dad's exhausted, but happy. Sarah and I have had a great time, and the kids even more so. They've worn us out and they are tired and suntanned, and full of all sorts of sugary treats which, given the fatigue, haven't (yet) sent them bouncing round the room like whirling dervishes. Sarah will probably reap the side-effects of that when she takes them all home for a bath later.

'You look better,' Mum says kindly as we struggle through the door with our empty picnic hamper.

'It was great, Mum,' I reply, smiling at her in an attempt to show that she need worry about me a little less today than she did yesterday.

'Cuppa?' Mum asks. 'Oh, by the way, Mark rang.'

'Mark?' I say, sounding surprised, but then realising that for Mum, he is the obvious person to be calling. He is, they still assume, as I have not yet corrected them, the source of my anguish at the moment.

'He's coming down to see you. Driving down now, in fact. He should be here in the next half an hour or so.'

Oh great, that's just fantastic. I thought I was through with sorting everything out with Mark, other than the house stuff once that all nears completion. What on earth is he coming down here to see me about? Surely he doesn't want a big reconciliation or anything daft like that? Mark and I are well and truly over, we both know that and I thought we'd both moved on.

Sarah decides to drag the kids off home and leave the house uncluttered for Mark's visit. Actually I think I'd prefer her to stay, for a bit of moral support, but I can see where she's coming from. I'm not really looking forward to seeing him, I just can't think what it is that's so important to bring him down here, but as he is making the effort to come, I do have to see him and hear him out.

Taking refuge in my room, I hear him arrive and greet Mum and Dad. To say they chat would be the wrong word to use, more like Dad grunts at him – he is the man who has broken his little girl's heart, after all – and Mum just tries to be polite and offers him a cup of tea, the solution to every problem.

He is already sitting with said cup of tea when I gingerly come downstairs and into the kitchen. Mum and Dad do an amazing disappearing act, something about vegetables needing weeding, or some such excuse, and once Dad cottons on to Mum's nudges and winks they are gone before I can make a bolt for it, back to my room, and Mark and I are alone together.

'Hi Grace, you're looking well. You took some tracking down!' he begins. 'Having a nice family visit, are you?'

Like he cares. Come on Mark, say what you have to say, then go.

He doesn't wait for my reply. 'I've been thinking.' Here we go. Another of Mark's prepared speeches, no doubt. I haven't said a word to him yet, but that doesn't seem to stop him launching into his diatribe.

'I still love you, Grace,' he says. Shock, horror on my face. 'Um... I want us to have another try. We had so much, it seems silly to throw it all away for nothing. Um... you're the love of my life, I've been missing you so much. Come home, please.' Not quite the usual eloquent Mark, but more a lonely and regretful Mark stumbling over his words, and not really knowing exactly how to say it. Nothing lawyer-like there at all.

He kneels on the floor in front of me and takes my hand, gazing up at me. For a brief moment I wonder if I really have done the right thing. Left a man I loved and with whom I expected to spend the rest of my life, for an affair which looks like it has fizzled out before it's barely started. Was I wooed by the excitement of the chase, in the same way that Tom clearly was with me? Am I just as shallow? I start to wobble a bit and suddenly I don't know what I'm doing any more. Before I can take charge of my senses, Mark has pulled me to him and is kissing me. But it's like it's not really me. It feels like another one of those weird out-of-body experiences, where I'm watching myself do something and have no control over it.

Suddenly a light bulb comes on in my head and I realise what is happening. I push Mark away and sit back down in my chair, looking at him as though he has just committed the vilest act. I can't help the horror spreading across my face, but his expression is one of total dismay, he looks utterly crushed.

'Did you really think that was all it would take?' I ask. 'You come down here and force yourself on me, remind me what I've been missing, and I'll follow you back home, meek as a lamb? We've been through all this so many times, Mark. I thought you were OK with it? There's nothing there any more, I'm sorry.'

'Come back home, Grace, and you could have what you want.' Hasn't he been listening to me? Not only now but all those times when we talked this through, over and over again. 'We can park the idea of a baby for now if you like. Leave it for a year or two. I don't even mind if you carry on working. We can do things your way for once.' Doesn't sound much like my way to me. More like the same old Mark, trying to control everything and expecting me to fall into line. I can't believe he is still so delusional about the starting a family thing, too. It's like our break-up never happened, like we never had all those conversations. The man is unbelievable.

'Go home Mark. It's over. Please try to understand that there is no 'you and me' and hasn't been for ages, and never will be again. I don't love you, and I certainly don't want to get back with you. I'll come and get my stuff from the house as soon as I get back from here, then we've only the house sale to wait for and it's all done and dusted. Go home,' I say again.

He looks dejected but what did he expect? That I would jump straight back into his arms with just one declaration of love, after everything we have been through?

'Your teacher friend consoling you now then, is he?' he asks bitterly, and suddenly his face is no longer dejected, but furious. It's like someone has pressed his big red rage button. I hadn't realised he knew about Tom and me, but then he did suspect for a while that we were more than friends, even at the stage when that was all we really were, so maybe he was just throwing a random comment, in the hope that it would strike true.

At that moment Dad comes into the kitchen to check everything is alright, and Mark turns to him. 'Don't suppose your precious daughter's told you about her lover, has she? How she left me for her boss? Left her fiancé of five years for a sordid fling. She's a tease, that one.'

By now Mark is puce and fuming. Dad isn't having any of it though, and despite all the years of boyfriend dramas he has been through with his three daughters, I have never seen him do quite what he does next. I see his Irish blood literally boil and rise to the surface and he seems to grow about six inches in stature (Mark is tall, and Dad obviously feels he has a height disadvantage). He pretty much picks Mark up by the scruff of his neck, ejecting him from the house within the space of a couple of seconds. He slams the door behind him, rubs his hands together with an 'Ahhhh' to show how pleased he is with himself, then calmly comes back into the kitchen.

Mum pops up from nowhere with a smile. 'So, have you two love-birds patched things up?' she asks me.

Twenty-Three

'So that's how it is,' I say to Mum and Dad, with a big sigh. I've told them my torrid tale; been through everything, the break-up with Mark, falling for Tom, the start of the affair, right through to spotting him with The Blonde and making a bolt for home. Obviously, for the sake of my parent's hearts, I left out the nitty-gritty of the finer detail – Dad has no need to know about his precious younger daughter's intimate love-life details. No, just a bare outline is more than enough to give them an idea of what's been going on in my life and my head over the past few months.

'Oh Grace, what a mess,' Mum says, and I feel guilty for putting them through all this, at their age. She slumps into her chair with a long sigh. But – and I am amazed at this – she doesn't embark on a long lecture on the wrongs I have done, and how I shouldn't have been with one man when I was already with another. It would have been unthinkable for her to do something like that in her day, I'm sure. But there you are, I've done it, and whatever they think of me, I owe it to them to tell them everything. Well, I'd had no choice after Mark's vitriolic outburst earlier, but actually now that it's all out in the open, I am quite relieved. I don't like having to keep secrets, and although I'd never really lied to them as such, I'd allowed them to assume something which wasn't entirely correct, and had been very economical with the truth.

Mum eventually pulls herself up out of her comfy chair and comes over to me with a big hug, so I deduce that I'm not in too much trouble. Funny how, even at my age, I still sort of expect to be told off by my parents for doing something 'naughty'. That parent/child relationship is so hard to break out of until, I suppose, it comes to that awful time later in life when our roles are reversed, with me becoming the carer, and they the cared-for. Let's hope we've got a few years yet, or even decades, before that happens, I just can't bear the thought of it.

'He sounds lovely, though, this Tom, despite everything,' Mum goes on, trying to sound cheery. Funny, Dad hasn't said a word yet, and I get the feeling he is battling with his emotions and therefore struggling to come to terms with my news more than Mum is. Mum just wants to get on and help me, forget anything I may have done that doesn't fit in with her strict moral code of conduct, and get me back on the road to happiness again. Dad, on the other hand, is either bothered about the cheating aspect of the whole thing, and therefore contemplating just how loose his daughter must be and where he went wrong, or brooding about how much hurt these two men have caused me. I don't feel I can ask him – he just needs to deal with it in his own time, too. Maybe he fancies a pop at the other man in my life, just like the earlier episode with Mark? His expression is dark and

Head Over Heels

brooding and hard to read, so I decide not to go there for the moment.

'Are you going to speak to him, Grace? You really should, you know,' Mum is on a roll now, on her mission to fix her daughter's love life, now that she has a few more of the details to play with. 'It might not be what you think. It sounds like he worships you, surely he wouldn't go and throw that all away so quickly?'

I tell them about his texts and the messages, and how Sarah made me send him a message, just to let him know I haven't fallen off a cliff or anything. I see a shadow of hurt pass across Mum's face when she realises Sarah knew about Tom before she did, but she disguises it quickly. Since that text, though, agonisingly, there have been no more messages from Tom, nothing at all. It feels to me like he doesn't care, can't be bothered, and doesn't want to explain anything to me. It's all too much effort for him. So why should I be bothered, if he's quite clearly not? He has obviously abandoned me. I explain this to my parents, but all they can see is my stubborn streak doing it's very best to wreck my life. They think I should just get on the phone to him and sort it out, once and for all. But it's not as easy as that. No, he needs to be the one to make the first move; I'm not going grovelling to him. If he has something to tell me – which he obviously does – then he can damn well do it, and get on with it.

'Grace, darling, time to get up,' Mum calls from the bottom of the stairs, and I wake up in the Eighties. I'm close to jumping out of bed and hunting around for my clean school uniform and last night's homework when I realise that it's actually 2009 and I don't have to go to school today. As the time-warp effect fades and I remember again the events of the past few days, I pull the duvet up over my head and try to ignore Mum's call. She's taking me with her to see one of her old friends today. Joy of joys, can't wait. But she seems to have this idea that (a) it will cheer me up to get out of the house and (b) she can't leave me alone as I might slip straight back into moroseness. Mum doesn't think I have anything to be morose about – she seems to think a quick call to Tom will sort it all out. Yeah, right.

My duvet dive is short-lived however, as a violent wave of nausea sweeps in from nowhere and thumps me in the pit of my stomach. I know that if I don't get to the bathroom THIS INSTANT I am going to decorate Mum and Dad's nice cream carpet with a map of the world, comprising the contents of last night's partially digested dinner. Fortunately the bathroom is empty (of course it is, no sisters living here anymore, spending hours over their black eye-liner and crimped hair in the mornings), and I stare into the white bowl, heaving my insides up like there's no tomorrow.

Mum's head appears round the door. 'You OK, Grace?'

'Nooooo,' I groan. 'Siiiiiiccccckkkkkkk,' I wail as another bout hits me. As I hold my hair back and puke for England I mentally try to work out what I might have eaten yesterday to cause such a violent reaction. I'd had some of Sarah's kids' sweets and candyfloss, but not enough to produce the effects I am experiencing right now, surely? And I hadn't touched a drop of alcohol last night; Mum had seemed reluctant to let me loose near their wine, for some reason. She said I looked like I needed to detoxify, which all sounded a bit twenty-first century for my Mum, but even so, I'd taken her advice and stuck to the soft stuff.

'Argggggg.' Another bout hits, and Mum is behind me, rubbing my back and making comforting sounds, just like she used to when I was sick as a child. When I think I'm all done, I make an attempt to clean myself up quickly, and turn to Mum.

'Don't think I'll be coming with you today, Mum, looks like I've picked up a bug or something,' I mumble, secretly relieved that I won't be subjected to being a voyeur in Mum's social life, after all.

'Oh, no, you'll be fine later,' Mum insists, sounding a lot more positive than I can. 'A cuppa and a piece of toast will sort you out, just you wait and see.' She leaves the room with a conspiratorial little knowing smile. What's she got to be so pleased with herself about?

But she's right, I'm not sick any more, and Mum's breakfast does sort me out, and suddenly I feel like a human being again. In fact I have bags of energy, tonnes of it, and I suggest to Mum that I might go out for a run instead of coming with her today. She turns to me and takes a deep breath before she speaks again.

'No, dear, no running for you, you should be taking it easy in your condition,' she says, enigmatically. I don't know what she's getting at.

'What do you mean, 'In my condition'?' I say sarcastically.

'Heartbroken? Jilted? Stupid? Gullible? A run is just what I need to blow all my troubles away.'

'Don't be silly, Grace,' she replies. 'Pregnant, of course. You're pregnant.'

I choke on my tea, and this starts a fit of coughing. Mum comes up behind me, and pats me on the back, for the second time this morning. When I can draw breath again she sits down beside me and looks directly at me. It's unnerving.

'You're pregnant, Grace. I spotted it the minute you walked in the door the other day. Your skin, your hair, you're positively glowing. These food fads of yours, and then, well, your performance this morning just confirms it, doesn't it?' When she has finished reeling off all the clues she's picked up, like some amateur sleuth on a fact-finding mission, she sits back in her chair with a contented sigh.

'Ahhh, another little Connery grandchild on the way, it's so exciting!' she clucks. I am still sitting with my mouth gaping wide, tea all over me, staring at her like she has just grown a second head.

'Don't be silly, Mum, of course I'm not pregnant. How can I be?'

'Well, if you need me to answer that one for you, dear, then no wonder your love-life is in a mess,' she chuckles. Her amusing quip sets her off and she giggles to herself whilst she clears the breakfast table, humming some nondescript little tune. I can't see the funny side in any of this.

I head back from the chemist in a blind panic. Mum sent me upstairs to get dressed, then packed me off to the local pharmacy clutching a twenty pound note. It felt a bit like being sent down the shops in the old days, with a list of groceries to buy for Mum, instructions not to talk to any strangers and to bring the change straight back to her. Only this time the stranger was potentially growing inside my stomach. Arghh! Scary. I can't be pregnant, can I? How can that have happened? But then the sinking feeling hits good and hard as I remember I'm no longer safely on the pill, and that I hadn't given a second thought to going back on it when Mark and I split up, or even before that when I started seeing Tom. I'd been too wrapped up in my new and exciting love-life to think about anything as mundane as contraception, I realise sadly.

How could I have been so stupid? Tom and I hadn't taken any precautions – there just hadn't been the time, or the right moment. To be honest, neither of us had given even a passing thought to it. Stupid, stupid girl. I still refuse to believe it, despite all Mum's old wives' tales about glowing skin and hair and that 'pregnant look'. No, the test will be negative, I know it. I just need to do it and show it to Mum, then this whole nightmare fiasco will be over. If I was pregnant I'd know, wouldn't I? Feel something different going on with my body, surely?

I am sitting on the floor in the bathroom, staring at this little white plastic stick, and the word that has appeared on it. 'Pregnant' it says, followed by '3-4' which according to the instructions is the number of weeks ago that I conceived. I have never used one of these things before, never been anywhere close to a scare in the past, never needed to worry if I might be pregnant and done a test just to make sure I wasn't. This is a whole new ball-game to me. And there is no doubt, either, looking at this thing. Gone are the little blue lines of the past that I remember friends saying were sometimes so thin and pale that you still weren't sure if you were really pregnant or not. No, mine quite clearly says that I AM PREGNANT. Shit. What now? A baby? OH MY GOD. All those feelings of fear and anxiety that I'd repressed since that day Mark had said he'd wanted to try for a family, come charging at me like a herd of bulls, knocking me over and trampling all over me. I can't move.

I am still sitting there with tears rolling down my cheeks when Mum comes looking for me. She doesn't say a word, just pulls me into her arms and we sit there together, while she rocks me from side to side and makes comforting noises. There are lots of 'Don't worry's' and 'There, there's' and 'It'll be alright's', but not a single 'I told you so.' But how can it be alright, I can't see a clear way through all this. All I see is me, with a baby, which I never really wanted in the first place, alone. And that is the crucial thing. ALONE. How ironic really, that my main bugbear with Mark about starting a family was that we weren't married. But here I am now, not only still with no husband, but without even a boyfriend to call my own. No, just me and a BABY. Arghhhhh… A single mother-to-be. What a complete disaster I have made of my lovely life. I don't even feel grown-up enough to look after a pet dog or cat, let alone a real-live human baby.

Despite my state as a fragile, emotional wreck, I am compos mentis enough to work out that at least the baby is Tom's, as it was conceived so recently. Mark and I hadn't slept together for some time before we split up, so at least there is no element of doubt whatsoever, and therefore one less dilemma to add to the whole scenario. Even though Tom hasn't been seen for dust since The Blonde incident, heaven forbid that the baby were Mark's, as he would be down here like a shot once more, wanting us to get back together and claiming his fatherly rights, and I can't be doing with any of that. No, better that it's Tom's, if anyone's, as I have no past with him and he hasn't accumulated any rights, as far as I see it, so at this point in time the baby is just mine, if I want it to be. Hang on a minute, for a baby I don't want, why am I suddenly calling it mine? My baby, or my problem? 'My' and 'baby' are two words I never imagined myself saying, but it's scary just how easily the possessive adjective slips in front of that baby word. I wrap my arms around my stomach; how weird to think that there is a new life growing inside me, so small, no bigger than the size of a pea, probably, but developing all the bits it will one day need to help it survive in the world outside my womb. Where did all these clucky baby thoughts come from? Hang on a minute, stop thinking about that little dot of humanity growing inside your body, Grace, and take a close look at your situation, will you? You are alone, with a baby on the way. A BABY, for goodness sake. That thought brings on a whole new bout of tears and I succumb to Mum's shoulder once again.

'Evie,' I wail, 'I'm pregnant.' I'd had no choice but to phone my friend. I hadn't wanted to disturb her holiday and burden her with my problems, but sometimes in life there are moments when only a best friend will do. A friend who has travelled the long and winding road of your life with you and understands exactly where you are coming from. I can tell Evie anything and everything and I know she will be one hundred percent on my side. Not that my parents aren't on my side, of course, but they have a vested interest in the embryonic grandchild that has taken root in my body. And my sisters each have a brood of their own, as well as being Family, so they are hardly impartial. No, I need to speak to someone to whom I'm not related, someone who can really understand how I'm feeling.

So I have dragged Evie away from her poolside paradise in Mallorca for a bit of friend-to-friend counselling. She is welcome of the interruption, so she says. She needed a break from the sun for a few minutes. Poor thing. And it's hardly like the Germans or Scandinavians are going to pinch her lounger and put their towels on it. No, Evie and James and the girls have the exclusive use of a six-bedroomed villa for the fortnight, complete with chef and staff, so the most that can happen in her absence is that one of her serfs will put out a fresh towel for her, top up her cocktail and move the umbrella into a better position for her on her return. Lucky thing. If only all life's problems could be dealt with so easily.

'Evie, I'm having a baby,' I wail again, in case she didn't quite get the message, across the miles, the first time. There is a stunned silence on the other end of the phone. Or is it the satellite time delay? Difficult to tell.

'Oh Grace, that's wonderful news!' she exclaims. 'Although you don't sound too thrilled?' I realise then that of course she knows nothing about The Blonde. I haven't spoken to her since before she went away, and our last texts had been when she'd sent me the photo of the *David* statue. At that time, things had been going really well with Tom and it all looked rosy for the future.

So I fill Evie in on all the details. Such a lot has happened, I don't really know where to start, and it all comes out in a bit of a jumble.

'So are you saying Tom is cheating on you?' she says, as I finish my outpouring.

'Well, she was draped all over him and they looked pretty cosy together,' I say. I realise then that I *don't* know if he is actually cheating on me, but all the signs seem to point in the direction of Cheatsville.

'Have you spoken to him?' she asks. Oh, not her as well. Why are all my family and friends so obsessed with me speaking to him, when it's he who's broken my heart and done the dirty on me? HE should be the one to speak to ME.

'No I haven't, he's cheating on me!' I scream down the phone, then apologise to Evie for my outburst. 'I don't want to see him, ever, ever again!'

'Don't be silly, Grace, of course you do. If you didn't love him so much, you wouldn't be in this mess. Not the pregnant bit, that's another matter entirely, but if you didn't want him back, you'd be over him, wouldn't you? You just wouldn't care so much. You're quite clearly still madly in love with him, so do what you need to do, and for goodness sake call him. AND tell him about the baby.'

'But I don't want a bundle of excuses. I want him to want me, and even if there was something going on with THAT WOMAN, I don't want him to feel a sense of responsibility to me just because I'm pregnant. It has to be me he comes back for, not the baby.'

'Just call him, Grace, you won't know anything until you do.' I know she is right, but I can't do it. He obviously doesn't want me any more. I've not heard a thing from him since I texted him to tell him I was still alive. If he cares that much, he'd have tried to find out what was wrong, wouldn't he? No, clearly I was just a conquest, a nice little interlude in his love-life, and nothing more. Why should I make the effort, it would be too humiliating to call him up, only to have him reject me. I can't face that. He doesn't want me, and I'll just have to come to terms with it.

I retreat to my parents' garden with a coffee (should I be cutting back on the caffeine now? I realise I know nothing whatsoever about pregnancy and what I'm supposed to do – or not) and a squishy cushion and park myself on a lounger. No pool and poolside attendants here for me, like lucky Evie in Mallorca, and not much sun either, come to that, but it is late July in England, what do you expect? I just need to get out of the house and out from under Mum's worried gaze, and sit here on my own to think things through for a while. I ran away from Evie's house to get some space between Tom and me, but now that my parents know so much about my personal life – and now the baby too – suddenly it doesn't feel so spacious here anymore. I need wide open spaces to clear my head and give me time to think. Although my parents' garden could never really be called a wide open space – there are houses on all sides and the garden is about the size of a packet of frozen peas. But it's all that's available to me for the moment so I shouldn't complain. I have bigger issues to contemplate.

All too late I realise Dad has quietly followed me outside. He hasn't yet broken his reticence from yesterday, and now that he has a further piece of news to digest, I dread to think what is going through his poor, addled brain. I'd managed to convince Mum it would be fine for her to carry on with her plans and go and visit her friend, making it quite clear that there was no way I was coming with here.

Dad perches himself on the edge of my lounger and clears his throat. 'It'll be alright, Grace, it's only a baby. And you're a coper, you always have been. Whatever happens, don't worry about it. And remember we're always here for you if you need us.' I dissolve into rivers of tears again; Dad's words are so simple, and his love so uncomplicated and unconditional. I throw myself into his hug and the two of us sit there for a while, not saying anything. I don't think I've ever felt as close to him as I do at this moment. Mum always wants to help, bless her, which sometimes means her getting more embroiled than I'm comfortable with, but Dad is made of the more non-interfering variety, and his presence and few kind words are enough to reassure me that maybe things will be OK, after all.

I wake up a couple of hours later to feel the sun beating down on me. Good old unpredictable English summertime. I had fallen asleep under a chilly cloud but wake up in the sauna effect of the midday sun. I am hot and sweaty and… pregnant. That word again, followed by another somersault in my stomach as I revisit the events of this morning. Way too early for it to be the baby kicking, tiny little dot that it is, but I imagine that must be a bit what it will feel like, a fluttery butterfly-like sort of sensation. This feeling is only nerves, though, or more like terror, as I contemplate my near future as a single mother. What will the baby look like? Will it be a boy or a girl? I find myself imagining a toddler-sized version of Tom, a little boy wobbling around on Bambi legs with a head full of Tom's blond, springy curls, and feel myself smiling, even though I don't want to. Or a little girl that looks like me. I'll have to get my own baby photos out later, see what I'm in for.

And then I pull myself together again. No more cooing over this new life that's growing inside me. No, I have to be pragmatic. I'll have to take time off work, heaven forbid, and in any case, how can I go back and face Tom at school after all this? Maybe I should just walk away from it, cut my losses and move back down here, away from him and my life as it was, be near to Mum and Dad. The thought of cutting loose from my home and my friends fills me with a fresh bout of anguish and I feel the tears springing in the corner of my eyes again. What am I going to do? How will I cope with all this? IT'S A BABY! HELP!

Dad comes into the garden with a large glass of juice for me and sets it down on the table. 'You look better now, love,' he says, sitting down beside me again. 'You're still my baby girl, you know,' he adds, tenderly tucking a stray strand of hair behind my ear. I can tell he is choked up, but he moves off again quickly, hoping I haven't noticed his emotions bubbling to the surface.

I am going to do this on my own and I'm going to do it well, I resolve. After all, women have babies every day, don't they, and some of them are in a lot less fortunate situations that me. At least I have a salary (for the moment, anyway) and a loving family who will help. It's not like I'm some poor, knocked-up teenager whose life is in tatters now that there's a baby on the way. I will find a way through this, and it will make me a stronger person. Yep. I can do it. 'BUT IT'S A BABY, YOU KNOW NOTHING ABOUT BABIES!' the other half of my brain shrieks, and I dissolve into a ball of jelly all over again. My brain is aching from trying so hard to get my head round all this. Ouch.

And then I make a pretty radical decision. I'm not going back. I'll email my resignation to Tom; I know I'm supposed to give a half term's notice, but it's extenuating circumstances and all that, and if he's quick he can get some temporary cover in time for September. No, I wouldn't be leaving the school in the lurch; if I do it now then I won't feel too guilty about it. No one need know about the baby, least of all Tom. I don't want him having anything to do with it; as far as I'm concerned, he's just the sperm donor. I have to be strong, I have responsibilities now. The baby has to come first, and I will stay down here, find somewhere to live close by to my parents, and let Mark sort out the house and all the financials that go with it at that end. I should be able to get myself a nice little place here, and I can build a new life, get a part time teaching job eventually, and get along just fine. I amaze myself at the speed of my decision, and how quickly I manage to plot out the rest of my life, but it seems the only logical thing to do. I'll put it to my parents later; after all, they said they wanted to help, and this is probably the best way for all of us.

Then the emotional side of my brain fights back once more and the tears start rolling down my cheeks, yet again. No chance of a drought this summer, with all the rainfall from my eyes over the past few days. I don't think I've ever cried as much as I have recently; not even in my teenage angst years of one broken 'romance' after another. I will miss my friends, no doubt about it, but they will only be at the end of the phone, won't they? And they can come and visit, can't they? I take a deep breath to confirm my decision. Despite everything, I know it's the right thing to do, for both of us. For my baby and me.

Twenty-Four

'Dear Tom,'

'Please accept this email as my resignation from my position at Cropley Village Junior School,' I begin.

I can't find my mobile – I wanted to give Mum a call and let her know my decision, but I seem to have mislaid it. Maybe I threw it somewhere the other day, in a fit of pique when I was annoyed with Tom for his continual pestering. Anyway, it's nowhere to be seen, so I will just get this off to him, and then I can present Mum and Dad with my decision as a done deal when they get back. I'm sure they'll be pleased. I know it's the right thing to do, so how can they feel otherwise? Dad has popped out to the garden centre or something, so I have the house to myself, and I can focus on my plans for my new life. Just need to finish this email to Tom before they get back. Funny, they both seem so concerned about me, yet they've both deserted me in my hour of need, haven't they? So I will just get on and do this and…

Suddenly the door to the tiny room that serves as a study in my parents' home flies open, and Mum is standing there, with Sarah beside her.

'What are you doing?' Mum asks.

'Writing my resignation letter,' I reply, adding a big smile to show that it's what I want, and that they should all be happy for me.

'Don't,' Sarah butts in. 'Don't do anything rash, Grace.' I notice she is holding my mobile. 'Here you are,' she says, guiltily, handing it back to me, 'you might need this.'

'Thanks, where did you find it?' I ask, mystified.

'Well actually...' she begins, but she doesn't get a chance to finish her sentence.

The door opens again and in comes Dad followed by... Tom. I don't believe it. What on earth is he doing here? I can't ask him, because I'm struck dumb by what seems to be this conspiracy unfolding before my eyes. Dad is jingling his car keys, and Tom is standing there like an extra in a B movie, looking like he wished the ground would open up and swallow him. Now it all makes sense. Sarah and Mum must have 'borrowed' my phone to get hold of Tom's number, asking him to come down, and Dad hasn't been anywhere near the garden centre, he's been to the bloody station to collect Tom, hasn't he? That's what they've all been up to whilst I've been trying to sort my life out on my own.

'How could you!' I yell at my parents and sister. 'What right have you got to interfere in my personal life! You did this, didn't you! You stole my phone and rang him and... well... how could you!' The accusations fly and I feel like I've been completely railroaded. There I am, quietly trying to get my head round it all, one issue a time, but in the meantime my own family, my nearest and dearest flesh and blood have been conspiring behind my back, making all sorts of decisions without even consulting me. The cheek of it! How dare they? I've been completely cornered, and now I'm stuck in this box of a room with them all in the doorway and I can't even run away from them.

Just as I'm about to let rip with a further explosion, suddenly my parents and Sarah pull off another of their amazing disappearing acts, and the study door closes, leaving just Tom and me, looking awkwardly at one another. I hadn't in any way forgotten just how gorgeous he is, but I am still floored by his sheer presence, the size of him, the sexiness oozing from his every pore, and just the fact of him being there in the flesh. I'm rooted to my chair.

Neither of us knows who should go first, so I try really hard to give him another of my withering looks, folding my arms across my chest in a defensive stance. 'You're not going to hurt me again,' my body language reads.

'Grace, I'm so sorry,' he begins, finally. He pulls up a chair alongside me and reaches out for my hand. I pull away quickly and his expression is one of hurt and surprise. What did he expect? One lame 'sorry' and everything would be OK again? Suddenly I'm hit by a sense of déjà vu and this starts to feel like a re-enactment of the episode with Mark the other day. The only, and major, difference being, that when I look at this man, I know I love him, despite everything. But even though he has love on his side, he still has a lot to explain and a lot to answer for, but now he's here I know I have to give him that opportunity.

I have to presume at this point that Mum and Sarah have filled him in on my reasons for running away. 'So, who is she, then?' I ask, trying to keep the poison from my voice, but knowing that I sound bitter. I can't help it.

'She's my sister,' Tom begins. I let out a 'huh', as if to say 'you're not trolling out that old excuse, are you?' He sounds like some dirty old man talking about his 'niece' to disguise the fact that he's playing away with a much younger woman.

'Come on, Tom, I've seen pictures of your sister, and no offence to her or anything, but you have to admit, she's not a patch on that woman I saw you with,' I say, clutching at the flaws in his argument.

'I swear to you, Grace, it's my sister, Lucy. I have to say I got a bit of a shock, too, when she turned up. I knew she'd just come back for the summer, she's studying at UCLA, and when she called me up and asked to meet in town, I barely recognised her. I walked right past her! There was this blonde beach-babe, utterly gorgeous. She's been California-d,' he laughs, 'all long blonde hair and fit and toned, nothing like the plain-Jane, blue-stockinged sister that we all waved off at Heathrow two years ago. That's what a couple of years on the west coast does to you, obviously!'

I don't know whether to laugh or cry, and to start with I'm stuck in that no-man's land of not knowing whether to believe him or not, but why would he lie? It's such a bizarre story that it just has to be true – why on earth would he contrive to make up something like that?

'Ohhhhhhhhhhhh,' I let out a huge sigh and look at Tom,

and then my hand goes to my mouth and I laugh. And laugh and laugh and laugh. Tom joins in and the two of us are laughing fit to split our sides, when he suddenly stops and pulls me to him and kisses me. He hasn't lost his touch and I feel all my bitter resentments floating away on a cloud of love and lust.

'I've missed you, Grace,' he says, pulling back a little and becoming serious again, but keeping hold of my hand this time. 'I thought I'd lost you, and it was killing me. When you disappeared and I didn't hear from you, I assumed you must have had second thoughts about us and resented me for splitting you and Mark up. Then I heard on the local grapevine that Mark had been down here to see you, and I assumed, well, that's it, they're getting back together. So I thought it would be best for everyone if I kept my distance. You and Mark were together for so long, after all.'

'Mark did come,' I explain. 'And he did want us to try again, but I don't. When I saw him I knew straight away it wasn't him I wanted to be with. My Dad threw him out, he was brilliant!' Tom looks relieved at this news, and the tension seems to disappear from his face. 'It was you I wanted all along, but I just couldn't get past seeing you with another woman.'

'If only I'd known you'd seen me that day, or you'd chased after us, or even if we'd just bumped into you on the street,' Tom goes on. 'None of this would have happened. I could have just introduced you to my Barbie-esque sister. I've told her all about you, by the way, she can't wait to meet you. The poor girl will be mortified that she's caused all this trouble between us. She's staying at my flat for a couple of days so you'll get to meet her when you come back.'

'Poor girl. Look at me, feeling sorry for 'The Blonde' now,' I laugh, 'when I've hated her so much since I set eyes on her. I'm sure she's lovely really and I'd love to meet her… when I come back.' I smile at Tom and he pulls me to him again. I can't begin to describe the relief I feel, just to be back in his arms. All that silly talk of running away… and then I realise with a jolt, I haven't told him.

'What were you up to in here, anyway, tapping away at that computer?' he asks.

'Sending you my resignation letter,' I reply. The colour seems to drain from his face. 'I was going to run away forever and stay down here.'

'That was a bit extreme,' he replies. 'Looks like I got here in the nick of time.' He smiles and those gorgeous dimples and little creases round his eyes bring tears to mine.

'What's with the tears, Grace?' he asks.

'I haven't told you everything.' I gaze round the room and sigh, wondering what the next piece of news will do to our newly reinstated relationship. Probably make him run a mile.

A few seconds elapse before I can pluck up the courage to say, 'I'm pregnant.'

Twenty-Five

The ultra-sound technician rubs my stomach with that nasty sticky goo and hits me with the cold probe. I flinch as it runs across the sensitive, very ticklish part of my stomach that no one is ever allowed to touch, as it always sends me into convulsions of giggles. This time I'm not giggling, though. I'm waiting nervously to see my baby on the screen, or 'the blob' as I've taken to calling it. I can't think of it as a baby until I've seen it looking like one. I need to reassure myself that it has all the bits and pieces it should have, before I can relax and enjoy this and really give in to the fact that I AM GOING TO HAVE A BABY!

Tom sits beside me, absolutely glowing, a smile like a Cheshire cat stretching from ear to ear and quite clearly, but unwittingly, charming the pants off the young technician, who keeps glancing in his direction. *Come on girl, take your eyes off my man and concentrate on my baby. I know he's gorgeous, but he's MINE ALL MINE and I'm having his baby.*

I needn't have worried about breaking the news to Tom. Although I'd been almost prepared to see him make a bolt for the door, leaving me alone once more, that couldn't be further from how things had actually panned out.

'I'm pregnant,' I'd said, then closed my eyes, wincing behind them, and trying to make myself invisible, expecting to see an empty space when I opened them again. But he didn't make a bolt for the door, and the look on his face when I'd finally dared to open one eye and have a little peek was so far removed from the reaction I'd braced myself for. I'd expected to see shock, horror, dismay, panic, all those things shoot across his face, before he located the nearest exit and stole my dad's car keys on his way out. Instead he'd looked serene and calm and proud, and, well, overjoyed, really, and there was a small tear trying to escape from the corner of each of his eyes. When I finally opened both my eyes, I cried too, and we hugged each other so hard I thought we might mould together for good.

'Grace, it's wonderful,' he finally managed to gasp, breathlessly and quietly. 'We're having a baby! Can you believe it! Us! We're going to be parents!' He was speaking in one exclamation mark after another, his eyes brimming with tears but with excitement too.

'So you don't mind, then?' I'd asked, tentatively.

'Mind? Why would I mind? It's the best news I've ever had! A baby! With you! Ahhhhhh!' the exclamation marks carried on until he dissolved into hysterical, happy laughter, and I had no choice but to join in. Again we sat there together, clinging to one another, our bodies shaking with mirth.

So any doubts I'd had about Tom wanting nothing to do with me were banished instantly. Why *had* I ever doubted him? I would never have fallen for a man who wasn't so gorgeously kind and caring, would I? But then even the happiest and strongest of relationships can be rocked by the news that there is a baby on the way. So many times one partner or the other cannot come to terms with the changes to their lives that are inevitable. But not my Tom. My gorgeous, gorgeously lovely Tom. We are going to be a family, and he is pleased and I am… well… suddenly I'm not as adverse to it as I've always been. It seems right, somehow. We will be a perfect little family with our perfect baby and all live happily ever after, won't we?

But as the twelve week scan day has been drawing nearer, I've been getting a bit twitchy and going through the entire pregnant woman trauma thing about the baby *not* being OK. What if there's something wrong with it? Will Tom still want me – and it – then? What I'm feeling is all perfectly normal, apparently, according to my new best friends and full-time companions, the Mother and Baby magazines and manuals. I am single-handedly keeping the publishing industry afloat with my recent purchases. Tom thinks it's hilarious. Me, a so-called 'non-baby' person, knee deep in all this literature. I can't get enough of it. The trouble is, though, that it points out all the things that *can* go wrong. I'd never realised being pregnant and giving birth was as complicated, and to say I am a walking medical dictionary of pregnancy related illnesses and complications is an understatement. I'm like a baby-info website on legs. Everyone keeps telling me to stop worrying, and that if I'm feeling fine then chances are the baby is fine, and growing normally and all that stuff. I just need to relax, and chill, apparently. Easier said than done.

Tom holds tightly onto my hand as the technician waves the scanner around a bit more and we are both riveted to the screen. Then she stops moving it and makes a bit of a 'Hmmmppp' noise.

'What's wrong? Is there something wrong?' I ask, panic rising in me and my heart starting to race inside my chest. Tom's palm goes clammy in mine and I know he is feeling it too.

'No, far from it,' the technician replies, cryptically. 'Do you have a history of twins in your family?' she asks.

'Twins?' I gulp. 'Er, no, not that I know of. Why? I'm not having twins, am I?'

'I'm delighted to tell you that you are!' she announces with a flourish, and a broad smile that encompasses us both. 'There are two very strong heartbeats, look, you can see both here.' This time when we look at the screen we can quite clearly distinguish the outlines of two baby shapes, two tiny bean-like things. Funny how we hadn't noticed that just now, but then we hadn't been looking for two, I suppose. There are definitely two small things in there, not one, and definitely two little flashing bits, which she points out as their hearts.

'Bloody hell, we're having twins!' I yell. I look round at Tom and he is open-mouthed, staring in shock at the screen.

'Fuck!' he says quietly, sitting back in his seat. I don't think I've ever heard him swear before. But I don't need to panic, he's not about to make a run for it. Instead he looks at me in awe and holds my hand in both of his and says, 'It's a miracle! Two babies! Aren't we clever! Two for the price of one! Buy-one-get-one-free!' He is talking in clichés and exclamation marks again, which I've come to realise, is his way of dealing with shock or surprise.

I start to giggle, and it's contagious. He starts too, and the technician gives us a knowing glance as if to say, 'Yeah, parents of twins, seen it all before, the shock, the horror, the swearing, then the hysterical, uncontrollable laughter. You just have to laugh, being given news like that.'

'We'll have to move, buy a bigger car,' Tom is off on a roll, Mr Practicality kicking into action. 'Then there'll be the double buggy, two cots…' he goes on.

'Slow down, Tom, slow down,' I say, laughing at him again. 'Don't worry about all that, it's just a shopping list. I can do shopping, you know that!'

'We'll be an instant family, Grace, just imagine it! It's going to be brilliant. Four of us. Wow.'

'It is,' I say, and I know it will be. At this point in time I can't think of anything more wonderful. It IS a miracle.

In all the excitement however, both of us have completely bypassed asking the technician if the babies are OK. All my earlier worrying had been dissolved in the fizz of excitement. Whilst we were exclaiming and imagining and giggling though, our technician has been busy ferreting around on my stomach and with a pang of guilt at my own premature excitement, I dare to ask her. She reassures us that both babies are absolutely fine, as far as she can see, and for a moment I am convinced. But then she goes into all the scary stuff again about the twenty week scan being the big one, and that the babies will have a really thorough check then, when they're a bit bigger. Oh no, more worrying times ahead for me then. She sees the cloud of doubt pass over my face and does her best to reassure me.

'Of course, now that we know you're carrying twins, you'll have lots of scans, so you'll get constant reassurance that everything's fine,' she says. I'm relieved at that. I can cope with all the KY jelly and prodding about as long as I know my babies (MY BABIES!!!) are healthy. I'M HAVING BABIES. Not just A BABY!! WOOOO HOOOOO!! I whoop silently to myself.

'Let's phone your parents,' Tom says when we are back in the car, still reeling from the shock and excitement, still a bit awestruck and spaced out. 'Your Mum's going to be so excited!'

Mum answers the phone and with a trembling voice asks me if the baby is OK.

'Both babies are absolutely fine, Mum,' I say, very matter-of-factly, then there is a squeal and a thud as she drops the phone. It sounds like she's fainted, but when Dad comes on, I can hear her shrieking with excitement in the background, so I know she's OK. 'It's twins, it's twins!' She sounds like she's dancing round the room, doing the conga all by herself.

Dad, as ever, is much calmer. 'It's wonderful news Grace,' he says sincerely, and I can feel his hug coming at me down the phone line. 'Mum can speak to you now, she's got her wits back.'

Mum comes back on the phone with a whoop of sheer joy, and literally gushes at me. Tom can hear her from the driver's seat, so no need to pass her on to him for a word.

'I think they were pleased,' he says afterwards, pulling me to him in the car and brushing the hair away from my face as he looks at me. 'And how about you, are you pleased?' he asks.

'I couldn't be happier,' I reply, kissing him and nuzzling into his embrace. And really, I couldn't. I could never have imagined, during that horrendous week I spent at my parents' house after 'The Blonde' incident, that things would ever turn out as wonderful and perfect as this for us both. I'd been dredged up from the depths of despair to the height of absolute bliss by this wonderful man, who, it turns out, I need never have doubted.

We'd left Mum and Dad's straight away that day; we'd caught the train back together, rescued all my stuff from Evie's house, and moved me into his flat, all in the space of an afternoon. 'The Blonde' was still there, and she *is* his sister, and *is* gorgeous, but also a very lovely person and overjoyed that Tom had fixed the relationship that she'd inadvertently wrecked. And now utterly over the moon about becoming an auntie twice over.

I wake as I do every morning to find a cup of tea steaming by the side of the bed and Tom lying across me, his head on my thighs, stroking the ever-growing bump which used to be my lovely flat stomach and chatting away softly to the babies. He tells them what we're up to today, how much they are going to love it here, and what a great mum I'm going to be. And I am starting to believe it myself; I am going to be a great mother. All those months with Mark of resisting it, and not wanting it, and now it just seems so right. I can't wait.

Twenty-Six

'God, we had to put up a fight to get in here.' James' huge personality bursts into my room, closely followed by the rest of him, then Evie, who is barely visible behind the huge bunch of flowers she is practically wearing, complete with a couple of helium balloons, pronouncing 'It's a boy! It's a girl!' 'Well, they didn't have any that said 'It's twins!" she tells me later.

'Practically had to offer to build them a new maternity wing, before they'd let us in, the buggers,' James goes on, exaggerating, no doubt.

According to the medical staff, I'm not really supposed to have visitors other than family – infection control and all that health and safety stuff going crazy again. How do they know if my family are carrying fewer or more germs than my friends, for goodness sake? Do they do some sort of germ scan as they come into the ward – 'Only family germs will be allowed visiting rights, all other germs must wait outside'?

In any case, I'm glad my friends have managed to blag their way in, and I am grateful to James for whatever it was he had to promise. It probably helps that I'm in a side room on my own too; they won't be seen to be spreading their non-family germs to other mothers and babies on the ward, I suppose.

Evie comes over to me and gives me a huge hug, her eyes wandering instinctively to the two little cribs beside me, and she can't resist letting out a big coo when she sees little Pink and little Blue sleeping soundly, looking totally and utterly angelic.

'Oh, aren't they beautiful!' she exclaims. 'You're so clever, Grace,' she goes on, 'Oh and you of course, Tom,' she adds with a giggle, 'you did have some part to play in it after all!'

'No, it's all Grace's hard work and labour. My fiancée is the one who has put in all the effort, not me. I was just there to hold her hand and get shouted at!' He'd slipped in the reference to his 'fiancée' in the hope that someone would pick up on it. And they did.

Evie squeals 'No… you're not!' to which I shriek excitedly, 'Yes… we are!' And now they know, I remove my left hand from under the hospital sheet to show off my ring. Tom had come into the hospital this morning, bearing not just another tonne or two of clean baby clothes, but also a small box containing the most beautiful antique diamond ring. He'd sat on the side of my bed (there wouldn't have been much point kneeling, I wouldn't see him down there, plus I am too sore at the moment to lean over and reach out to him) taken my hand, and asked me if I would do him the honour of becoming his wife. I hadn't hesitated for even a second. Tom had primed the midwives at the nurses' station outside, and as soon as they heard my resounding 'Yes,' they were in the room with us, clapping and cheering and carrying the flowers that Tom had brought with him in anticipation of his offer being accepted. How could I possibly refuse?

And Tom *had* been very industrious that morning. On the assumption that I would say yes (there was never any doubt, was there?) he had been ringing round and booking up the church, the reception venue, and had even got as far as sorting out cars. Not bad for a man who'd been screamed at all night by a mad woman in labour and had had practically no sleep.

'Thought I'd leave flowers and the dress to you,' he giggles, as he explains all the plans he has made. 'Can't have you sitting around doing nothing, twiddling your thumbs with just the twins to look after, can we? I just wanted you to know how much I really want to do this,' he goes on, more seriously. 'I wanted to present it to you as a done deal, date set, church booked, and all that. I won't keep you hanging on, Grace,' and here his one reference to my previous, very long and unfruitful engagement doesn't go unnoticed. 'I want to marry you now. But now isn't available, so we'll give you a few months to get back on your feet, and then we are doing this! We'll have a fabulous summer wedding with all the trimmings. It's going to be perfect.' He sounds as excited as I am. This time I *am* getting married, there is no doubt about it. I am completely bowled over, not just by his proposal, but by the trouble he has gone to, to show me just how committed he really is. My wonderful Tom.

It would appear that James and Evie aren't the only ones to have secured special visiting rights. The first bout of excitement has barely subsided when there is another face round the door.

'Alex, hi, how are you!' I exclaim as she comes in and makes a beeline for me, arms outstretched, pink and blue gift bags dangling from one arm.

'I should be asking you that, you silly thing!' she exclaims. 'Although it looks like it was a piece of cake for you, popping out these two. You clever old thing. Ahhh, they're so beautiful, just look at them.'

'Hardly a walk in the park, but you forget very quickly, don't you?' I say. Amazingly, I have already joined that exclusive club of 'women who forget how much giving birth hurts.' Filing in the deep recesses of my brain all that pain and anguish and screaming (and swearing, I remember, embarrassed.)

'Mark's just parking the car,' she adds, 'he'll be in in a mo.'

Mark. Yes that's my Mark, or I should say, my ex-Mark. Alex and he got together properly towards the end of last year. It was inevitable really, I should have seen it coming when I look back on it. They'd had something of a special friendship right through the time when he and I were having problems; she'd been the one he seemed to want to turn to for help and advice. For a while it had rocked the balance of my friendship with her, but she was always lovely about it, insisting that she wasn't taking sides, that she was friends with both of us, and trying to remain impartial about it all. It had meant that I hadn't turned to her for support as much as I would have liked to, knowing that she was doing the same for Mark. It felt a bit traitorous, otherwise. I did think for a while that our friendship was floundering as a result of it, which broke my heart when I thought back to all Alex and I had been through together over the years. But at the same time I was glad for Mark that he had someone to turn to – he'd never bothered me again after that incident at my parents' – and aside from all the hassle of sorting out the house sale and dividing up our worldly goods, (and rescuing the rest of my wardrobe), I'd had very little to do with him since.

Actually the house sale and division of assets had all passed by surprisingly amicably. And Mark and I do get along pretty well when we see each other now; in a way I feel I have very little choice *but* to get along with him, as he's now Alex's partner, and if I value my friendship with her then I have to accept him as her chosen one. I no longer have any say in what he does, he's his own man now, and actually it's a bit of a relief for me that he is romantically linked with someone else, even if she is one of my best friends. It kind of eases the burden all round.

It is still a bit weird for me seeing Mark with someone else, though. I always have to rationalise it in my head before I know I'm going to see him, so I'm glad he didn't come in directly with Alex, and I have a few moments to get my head round it yet again. I'm just not used to seeing ex's once relationships are all over. I've never been one to keep in touch with men from my past, like some women do. The past is the past for me, but now I have to readjust that parameter slightly to be able to accommodate my dear friend, Alex.

I am happy for Alex that she has found love again, she so deserves it after all she went through with Peter. And Mark for his part acquired an instant family. The children adopted him as their 'new Dad' almost instantaneously; Archie finding it a little harder, of course, as he is the one with the most intact memories of his real father. But little Millie and Rosie are like his surrogate children, permanently attached to him and trailing him round everywhere he goes. Which he loves, of course. He wanted to be a Dad, and now he has that, three times over.

'Grace, Tom, congratulations.' Mark comes into the room, the large bouquet he is carrying threatening be the final straw when it comes to turning my little room into a florist's shop. There are so many flowers in here now, I just hope my babies don't develop hay fever before they let us go home.

Mark comes over to the bed and kisses me, and shakes hands with Tom, patting him amicably on the back and exchanging blokey congratulatory grunts. It must be a bit weird for him too, this whole scenario, just as it's weird for me to think of him as Alex's partner. There I am, his ex-fiancée, the one who didn't want to bear him children, with another man, who she left him for, and with whom she then went on to have twins. Life's twists and turns are so unpredictable. It's a crazy old mixed up situation but thankfully all the players in it now seem to have found their rightful places and have settled down happily.

'They're so beautiful, Grace. What are you going to call them?' Mark asks, smiling at me whilst cooing over the twins.

'We haven't decided yet, so for the moment, they are just Pink and Blue,' I reply. Pink opens one eye and looks at me with that newborn baby cute grimace which probably means she is hungry again, but for me it's her way of saying, 'Come on Mummy, think of a nice name for us, for goodness sake.'

'I'm hoping their names will just come to me,' I go on. 'That they will somehow let me know what they want to be called.' As I glance round the room at all the assembled bouquets, one flower in particular stands out, and I shiver with delight as the realisation hits me.

'Lily,' I say quickly. I grab Tom's hand. 'This is Lily,' I say to him, pointing to our daughter.

'And Jack,' Tom says. 'I've always loved that name. It's a good, strong name for my big strapping son,' he says, gazing at the tiny little boy snuffling in his crib.

'Thank you, Mark,' I say. 'Thanks for prompting us. There you are, we've named our children, just like that.'

'Talking of children, and babies, and all that,' Alex starts up nervously, and she reaches for Mark and pulls him to her side. 'Mark and I have some news of our own.' She gulps. 'We're having a baby.'

'You're not...!' Evie gasps, not for the first time today.

'We are!' Alex replies, as Evie throws herself across the room to wrap her arms around her.

'That's fantastic news, I'm so pleased for you both,' I say, beaming at her and Mark. And I genuinely mean it. I really am thrilled for them.

Visiting hours over, the dust has settled, or rather pollen, given all these flowers, and Tom and I are left alone with our little family.

'I'm so glad I found you,' he says, gazing at me intently and stroking my hand. 'Look at what we've got together. I can't wait to marry you.' And then he jokes: 'I can't promise to keep you in Manolos and Choos to the same standard, though, you know.'

'I know, and you know it doesn't matter to me. I have you, and we have Lily and Jack, what more could I need? Do you remember that day you called my meeting Mark story *'Head Over Heels?'* Well now it's *you* in the starring role. You're the Head, and I chose you over the heels. OK?'

Hand On Heart

… is the sequel to Head Over Heels.

Six years have elapsed and the friends are all older, though not necessarily wiser. James is going through a mid-life crisis which threatens to tear the family – and their business – apart. Teenage angst from their daughters only adds to Evie's dilemma.

Evie puts all her hopes into their upcoming holiday to France with Grace and Tom. But when a past love comes back to haunt Tom, with potentially life-changing consequences, he has his own choices to make.

Will the holiday bring Evie and James closer again? Or is two families under the roof of one chateau, for two whole weeks, simply a recipe for disaster?

Read on for the first chapter…

HAND ON HEART

One - Evie

July 2015

'This had better be good.'

Stony faced at her kitchen sink, Evie watched the taxi deposit her sixteen-year-old daughter on the gravel drive outside, before reversing into the turning space and speeding off. Imogen, dark bags under her eyes and wearing the same clothes she had left home in the night before, took a deep breath and braced herself to face the music. Or at least, her mother, whose music she fully expected to be less than harmonious this morning.

'So, young lady, you've decided to come home – finally.' Evie was unable to help the sarcastic edge to her voice.

'Sorry, Mum. Need a shower, can we chat later?' Imogen said dismissively, hoping to make light of her first wholly unauthorised absence. She attempted to bolt for the stairs, but Evie was having none of it, and grabbed her daughter by the arm, turning her around and forcing Imogen to make eye contact with her.

'Anything could have happened to you. Are you crazy, child? This is why we give you a mobile phone, not so that we can get a text from some girl we've never even heard of, at two in the morning, telling us you'll be back tomorrow. What the hell was all that about? I've been going mad with worry.'

'But I was only at Lucy's house, sorry Mum, my phone ran out of juice, you know how it is.' She shrugged, in that annoyingly nonchalant way only teenagers seem to be able to pull off with any aplomb.

'No, I don't know *how it is*,' Evie went on, folding her arms across her chest. 'There are still such things as landlines, you know. As far as I know they still work. That's what we used to do in the old, prehistoric days when I was your age. We'd phone. On a real phone with a cable. Sometimes it was still even attached to the wall.'

Evie couldn't stop herself from laying into her daughter; it was a defence mechanism for the blind fear she had felt only a few hours earlier. Part of her just wanted to hug her little girl tight and breathe a sigh of relief that she was home safely and nothing *had* happened to her, the other part was still steaming, furious that Immy could put her through so much anguish in the space of a few short hours. She'd barely slept a wink and she was teetering on the brink of losing the plot completely.

It was only the second week of the school holidays. If this was how the rest of the long summer break was going to be, then it would certainly be no picnic for Evie. She envisaged a living hell of six more weeks of teenage spats, confrontation, and endless attempts at pushing the boundaries from her eldest child. Thank heavens their younger daughter, Anastasia, hadn't yet reached the stage where she wanted to be out and about with her friends every night. Although it probably wouldn't be long, heaven forbid. Where had those innocent days of the sleepover gone, Evie wondered, when they'd been happy to have a few friends over, eat sweets, watch boy band DVDs and do each other's hair. If not at their own house, then at the home of another trusted friend, where Evie knew the mother and was comfortable that a similar standard of parental policing would most likely take place.

Now it wasn't just school friends they socialised with; there was a group Immy had fallen in with, kids from all over the town, none of which Evie had met, and although she realised they were going to come into contact with people from the big wide world outside their school at some point, she wished it didn't have to happen so soon. She felt she had lost control, and although she appreciated the fact that her daughter was growing up and becoming independent, she was only just sixteen, and still seemed so young, and in many ways, quite immature. Evie recognised the fact that Immy was legally old enough now to drink alcohol and – heaven forbid – have sex, but the consequences of all that filled her with horror. There were still many things that were off limits to her, but girls these days looked so much older than their years, so who knew what they got up to when out from under the parental eye? She felt sick, partly with worry and frustration and partly through lack of sleep, and she slumped down onto the bottom stair as Imogen finally escaped to the sanctuary of the bathroom.

The doorbell rang. Damn, Evie had forgotten Grace was coming round this morning. Perhaps her arrival was a good thing; it might prevent manslaughter taking place in the Brookes household.

'Grace, hi, how are you,' she said, welcoming her best friend into the hall, and pressing her hands to the frown lines on her forehead. 'Sorry, had a bit of a night with Immy. And morning. She's only just come home. I've had practically no sleep.' She rubbed her eyes wearily.

Grace kissed her friend on the cheek. 'What a nightmare, poor you, you look shattered. Shall I put the kettle on?'

Grace felt as comfortable in Evie's kitchen as she did in her own. The two friends never needed an excuse to get together, and they didn't have one for this morning either. Both of them were overwhelmingly excited about their impending holiday to France, and simply wanted to chat about it some more over coffee. As a teacher, Grace was already on leave, and occasionally at a loose end for something to do, particularly when Tom, her husband, had something Head-Teacherly to be doing, as was the case today.

'Where are the kids?' Evie asked, looking behind Grace for Lily and Jack.

'Sorry, they made a beeline straight for your garden,' Grace replied, moving over to the window to check on her five-year-old twins, who were already on the trampoline along with Jessie, Evie's gorgeous cocker spaniel/poodle cross, the hilariously named 'Cockapoo' breed. Jack never called the puppy by her real name; Cockapoo was what she was called as far as he was concerned. He had hit that age when scatological humour kicked in, and any word that contained 'poo' was far more exciting than calling the poor creature by her real name.

'Come here, Cockapoo,' she could hear him yelling. 'Poopy puppy poopachoo, bounce with me, come on poopy puppychoo.'

'Oh well, I suppose we should just be grateful you didn't get a Shih Tzu crossed with a poodle,' said Grace, laughing, and gazing fondly at her son, a die-cast 'mini-me' for his blond, curly-haired father. Evie laughed, her heavy heart lifting a little. Life had seemed so much simpler when her own children were that age. Oh, for the innocence of childhood, and that utter dependence on parents that small children had. Evie had found it a little stifling at the time, the constant need to keep an eye on them, the all-consuming fear for their lives every time they tried something new, even if it was just going down a slide, or trampolining for the first time. Now, though, she wished her girls needed her more than they did. Wished she still had some sort of control over what happened in their lives, and knew even just a little more about what went on in their world from day to day.

Poor Jessie was clearly feeling the strain of keeping up with a couple of energetic five-year-olds and was now sitting on the side of the trampoline, her head in Lily's lap. Lily was by far the quieter twin, although Grace knew that, from her position of calm and serenity, she well and truly ruled the roost, and had her brother utterly under her spell. He worshipped her, and would bow to her absolute wisdom and seniority (all twenty-seven minutes of it) if unsure of what to do in any given situation. Their characters were really starting to come out now, Grace thought to herself, they were proper little people, no longer babies. They had just completed their first year at Cropley School and she would never forget their little faces the first time they were allowed to go 'for real' to the big school where Mummy worked.

But Mummy wasn't their teacher, not just yet. Grace taught the Year Four children, and wasn't quite sure how things would pan out when the twins got to that stage. She and Tom had talked about moving them to his school before then. He was now Head Master at a larger, private school in Worcester. He and Grace had met whilst he worked at Cropley School, but it was always obvious that he was destined for higher things, and would need a greater challenge at some point. So it was no surprise that he was snapped up by the Cathedral Junior School when a vacancy for Head came up, a few years earlier. Grace missed him being at school with her, but bizarrely her career had flourished since he left – she supposed she was now out from under his shadow. Just recently she had been promoted to Deputy Head and, despite the additional paperwork involved, was loving every minute of it, working with Tom's replacement, a dynamic new female Head who had some great ideas for the school.

Evie and Grace sat down together to talk holidays, whilst the children entertained themselves, bouncing and tearing round the garden. Evie suspected that tired and stroppy Immy probably wouldn't put in an appearance this morning, but she had clocked Anastasia slinking quietly down from her room and into the garden to play with the twins, and smiled indulgently at her daughter. The girls adored the twins, and in the company of these two little monkeys, reverted to the children that they still were. Immy frequently babysat for Lily and Jack, and Ana was desperate to get her share of the action too, if only her big sister would let her get a look in on earning some money now and again.

The two families were all off to France together in less than two weeks' time. They were renting a chateau in the Dordogne, a huge place which would accommodate them all with room to spare, and had its own pool and acres of woodlands to stroll in of an evening. Grace couldn't wait. There was no way she and Tom could afford a holiday like that on their own, but James had been adamant that he and Evie take the lion's share of the cost, no protesting allowed. Whilst Tom didn't like the idea of handouts, it had been presented to him as a belated fortieth birthday gift from the Brookes, and he could get his head round that, sort of. Grace hoped he could relax about it and enjoy it without feeling like a charity case. It was still a very extravagant fortieth birthday present, they knew that, but the Brookes were good enough friends for it not to be an issue between them, even though they could never reciprocate to the same degree.

The planning was done; everything had been sorted out weeks ago. Both families were driving down to the chateau, with a stopover in northern France on the first night. All that was left to do was pack. At this late stage the two women reverted to a pair of excitable teenagers and were more interested in talking about what clothes they would take – Grace hadn't changed that much really, Evie mused. And of course they had to check out any good restaurants in the locality where they could dine out if they'd had enough of self-catering. Evie switched on her laptop and the two women settled down for some fun 'Googling'.

They giggled as they stumbled across 'Your 12 Point Plan for Holiday Packing Perfection'.

'Blimey, who sits about all day making lists like this?' Evie laughed. 'And who reads these things?'

'Um, er, well, looks like we're about to. Come on then, what do they suggest?' asked Grace, peering at the screen.

'Number 1, The Swimwear,' read Evie. 'Well, that goes without saying. Ooh, I must make sure that James packs his skimpiest pair of speedos. I know what a treat that'll give you guys by the pool.'

'Nooo! No budgie-smugglers allowed, absolutely not,' laughed Grace, safe in the knowledge that her friend's husband was much more of a Villebrequin shorts man than any attempt at looking like Daniel Craig in *that* Bond film. Thank heavens. No one could pull off a pair of light blue trunks quite like Daniel. Most men shouldn't even be allowed to try.

'Ooh, now look at this, Number 6, De-Fuzzing. I trust you've had your pre-holiday waxing session, Mrs Parry, and won't be subjecting us all to your overgrown nether regions. No one wants to see you knitting by the pool.' Grace almost fell off her stool with laughter.

'Yeah, I'll get Tom to get the heavy duty hedge-trimmers out before we go, don't worry.'

'Number 8, The Suitcase,' Grace read. 'Blimey, what do they think we are, morons or something?'

What a tonic her friend was, Evie thought to herself, the trauma of the morning beginning to fade. She couldn't wait to get going on this holiday. She just hoped James would behave like the loving, devoted husband she knew he really was, and they could all relax and enjoy it.

August 2009

'Eleven years,' Evie whispered to James as they lay on the sofa together. 'Eleven glorious years. Here's to the next eleven.' She raised her wine glass and clinked it against his.

It was a chilly summer's evening, so they had lit the fire in the sitting room. Their little girls had gone to their grandparents' for the night, and the two of them were alone to celebrate their anniversary together. They had eschewed a night out; James was just back from a business trip to New York, and the two of them craved some time together, alone. No waiters hovering around them, no fellow diners' conversations to distract from their own.

James had cooked dinner. Well, more accurately, he had heated up a Waitrose pre-cooked meal, but that was good enough. Evie had more romantic plans for their evening ahead than slaving over a hot stove for hours on end.

In the early days of their courtship, James had been something of a gourmet chef. He would spend hours in the kitchen, fiddling about and creating. He was one of those people who could pretty much conjure up a meal from whatever happened to be in the fridge. Evie had loved that. They hadn't waited long before moving in together and within a year of meeting they were married, with Immy coming along not long after, so nights like these, when they didn't have to worry about anything child-related, had been few and far between over the years. Now, when they had the time together, Evie would much rather that she were the centre of his attentions than the contents of the fridge.

'Yeah, I'd have got less than that for armed robbery, wouldn't I?' James joked, pulling Evie closer and squeezing her waist. She giggled. After eleven years of marriage the spark was still there between them. She still went weak at the knees when she saw him, still rippled with excitement when he came home from work of an evening. She knew it was the same for him too; they were very lucky to have such magic in their relationship. Right now James had that look in his eye, the one that said he'd like to have her for dessert. She'd made him wait long enough, and the rug by the fire was very soft and warm…

'Whatever did I do to deserve you?' James asked, pulling Evie down onto the rug, and tenderly stroking her hair.

'You don't deserve me,' she joked. 'I'm far too good for you, didn't my mother tell you that?'

James laughed. 'Oh, yes, on plenty of occasions. Even on the morning of our wedding, if I remember rightly. Bit late now, though, isn't it? Eleven years on and this wicked man has you trapped and is going to gobble you all up. I will never let you out of my clutches. I am going to make you scream, you gorgeous creature. Ha, ha, ha!' Evie giggled and succumbed to her husband's attentions.

July 2015

'Evie, I'm home.'

James looked shattered. The latest deal he was working on had him out of the house for upwards of fourteen hours a day, and he'd actually spent the previous night away from home. Evie wasn't happy about it; she could see what it was doing to his health, but in the current climate, he had to take business where he could get it. His financial advisory company had weathered the worst times of the economic storm fairly well, even after the issues of last summer, but both of them knew it would only take a couple of lean months to set them back again. They were responsible for a lot of employees, which in turn meant a lot of families, and she didn't want that level of guilt hanging over her. She wanted them all to stay gainfully employed somehow or other, until the tide turned fully and they were back on dry land again. Then they could start to think about good pay rises and substantial bonuses, and look after the staff who had been so loyal to them.

'Hi babe, welcome home. You look knackered.' Evie kissed his cheek and put a large glass of wine straight into his hand. He threw his laptop bag onto the kitchen worktop, loosened his tie and propped himself against the stove with a sigh.

'Not done yet, either, I'm afraid. Got some calls to make later, sorry. The girls in?'

'Yeah, both in their rooms. Immy's on Facebook again. Look in on her when you go up to change, will you?' She didn't have the energy to regale her husband with the events of this morning, and she was sure he wouldn't want to hear it, either. He had enough on his plate at the moment; Immy's adventures would keep. Their eldest could most definitely do with some fatherly intervention; James being away so much wasn't helping with the standard of behaviour, Evie knew that. In the past he had always been the one to get through to Imogen. She could run rings round Evie, but then defer to her father in a matter of minutes. It seemed so unfair, given that Evie was the one who put in the biggest share of child-rearing hours.

James cleared his throat, ran a finger around the inside of his collar and looked sideways. Evie had a feeling there was something coming that she wasn't necessarily going to like.

'Remind me again what date we go to France?' Uh-oh, here we go.

'Leave here on the eighth, stop over that night and arrive at the chateau Saturday the ninth. Why? You know all this, it's been in your diary for months. Don't tell me now there's a problem? We all need this holiday, James.'

She could feel her hackles rising but was wary of putting his back up practically the minute he walked through the door.

'No, nothing like that. Just that one of our potential clients is going to be out there at a similar time. I said we might meet up with them. Not for business, pleasure of course. We could get them over to the chateau for the day, maybe? Cook a nice lunch and get their kids together with ours? Everyone in the pool, barbie after, that sort of thing.'

Evie wasn't massively keen, but supposed it all sounded harmless enough. Sometimes she just wished holidays could be purely that, but appreciated that James needed to put in the work if there was a good potential deal coming their way. They couldn't afford to turn down new business; it was a competitive market.

It wasn't just on a professional level that this had been a hard year. They'd been through a lot emotionally and things were still quite awkward between them sometimes, but somehow they had ridden out the storm that had brewed up and threatened to destroy their relationship. She hadn't quite put what James had done behind her yet, but she was working on it. James *was* trying his best, but it was hard, with the hours he worked, for them to spend the time on their marriage that it warranted.

They needed this holiday badly. Some quality time together, away from all the distractions here. She just hoped those distractions weren't going to follow them across the Channel.

Head Over Heels

Saradowningwriter.co.uk

SaraDowningWriter

@sarawritesbooks

Printed in Poland
by Amazon Fulfillment
Poland Sp. z o.o., Wrocław